REVOLUTION

TJ Lee

979-8-9899988-2-1

DEDICATION

To anyone that has had to fight for their own rights.

ACKNOWLEDGMENTS

This Trilogy, I think, took me longer than any other book. Partly because I wanted the whole thing done at once, that way there would be a perfect flow from one book to the next (I hate plot holes). My friends, family, and Beta readers have had to put up with a lot from me. My poor children have already grown accustomed to mom being down the rabbit hole. But they seem to like talking to me about it. I think. My son, as always, is probably my biggest fan. No, he doesn't read them. Nor will I let him until he is grown, and I am not seeing him every day. But he does get very excited every time I finish a book.

I have made so many revisions, and my loved ones have had to read them over and over again. Even when this was not their favorite genre. I couldn't do it without any of them.

PROLOGUE

"Once upon a time, many years ago, all sorts of creatures lived free in the land. The shifters ruled over their own land. The Witches ruled theirs. But the Vampires had the most land for they ruled over the humans."

"How come the humans didn't have their own kingdom, mommy?" The small girl, with blonde pigtail braids, looked up at her mother curiously.

"Because vampires need to drink blood to stay strong. They kept all the humans in their kingdom so they could feed."

"So, the vampires were like Old McDonald on his farm, but instead of animals they raised humans?"

The mother laughed at her cheeky daughter. "Something like that. Now, are you going to let me finish the story or are you ready for bed?"

The girl zipped her lips with her fingers and threw the imaginary key over her head. As her mother started telling the story again, she tucked into her mother's side and closed her eyes, picturing the vampires and the witches.

"Each of the magical groups were gifted with what was called a fated mate, someone Mother Nature created to be their matching half. Like a soul mate. When the creatures met their mates for the first time, they felt a strong pull toward them. So strong, it was nearly impossible to ignore. Once they met, they would both start falling deeply in love with the other. As time moved on, the oddest thing happened. A few started finding their fated mates in other kingdoms. Some vampires even had a human for a mate. These mated pairings were difficult for many to accept. It was becoming common for one to reject the other. It was painful to the person rejected, but if it was early enough into their meeting, they could heal."

The mother paused, looking down to see if the girl was asleep. Her eyes opened again, wondering why her mother stopped. Seeing this, the mother smiled softly and started again.

"One day, a male vampire was roaming the edge of his land, checking their borders. There had been small skirmishes, fights, recently. It was his job to protect the kingdom. He paused, smelling something wonderful, something that took his breath away. He crept through the woods, following the enticing scent. He came upon a small lake, with water falling from the rocks behind it. And standing under that water, was the most beautiful woman he had ever laid eyes on. She was bathing in the water, enjoying the warm Spring day. She had beautiful black hair, and creamy skin. The vampire was entranced by her beauty. He came closer, wanting to get a better look at her. The woman sensed someone nearby and turned to look at him. When their eyes met, she felt it in her heart, that this man had been created just for her. She stayed where she was, worried he would reject her. For she was not a vampire, but a witch from the neighboring Kingdom. She need not have worried though, the vampire could not resist the pull to his mate. He moved quickly, dropping his clothes so he could swim out to her. As soon as he was close enough, he kissed her."

The little girl giggled and said "ew." Her mother stroked the side of her head softly, a silent reminder to settle down.

"I've searched high and low for you, my dear. The vampire told her. I've been right here, my love. Waiting for you to find me. Then bond with me that we may never be apart again. He begged her. The witch agreed and they sealed themselves to each other with both their magic. Now, they would both live and they would both die, for their magic had forever tied their souls together. They separated, promising to meet again the next day to decide where they should live. Only, the vampire did not show the next day. Or the next. The witch grew worried. She could feel him still in her heart. She knew he was safe, but she had not yet learned to read what the other feelings were. As that is something a mate learns over time. So, the witch snuck into the vampire kingdom and followed her heart to find her mate. She was relieved to find a small home near the castle, and to feel him inside it. Wanting to surprise him, thinking this was the home he found for them, she walked inside. She loved the small cottage and decided this must have been why he had not come, because he was getting their home ready for them. She walked through the house, looking through all the rooms. In the very last one, she found her mate. Only he wasn't alone. There was a female vampire lying with him in the bed. The witch screamed all sorts of things at her mate and ran out the door. He followed after, trying to explain. But there was no explanation for him betraying her like that. He had betrayed fate in the worst way possible."

"When she returned to her home, the witch pulled her coven together and told them what happened. Together, they put a curse on all the Vampire Borns. They would no longer be able to give birth to female vampires, they would only have sons. Each witch cut their hand and sealed the curse with their blood. Then they cast a spell on the vampires, causing a deep sleep to fall on them. The women snuck out of their homes that night, and crept into the vampire kingdom, and cut off the head of every female vampire. The betrayed witch stood over her sleeping mate, and killed the woman in his arms, the place she was meant to be. On the dresser, she left a note.

Because of your betrayal, your kingdom will wither and die. Your females are gone, and you will have no more. The curse will be broken when the hidden vampire prince accepts his witch mate and humbles himself to her.

The only females to survive the night of slaughter were two human mates. Both had been pregnant. Both had sons, and both died in childbirth. From then on, the humans of the kingdom gave daughters to the vampires, in exchange for rewards. Sadly, most never fell pregnant, and those who did rarely survived. And only sons were born. Hundreds of years passed, the vampire's numbers were getting lower, their kingdom getting weaker. They no longer had their mates to keep them strong. They began turning humans they deemed worthy into vampires, in order to grow their numbers again. They had hoped those females would be able to bear them a child, but they could not. Their bodies had been frozen in the state they were in before making the change."

"One day, the vampires had gone to a new village to collect the offerings from the people. They did this every few years and went to a different village each time. But this village did not want to give them their daughters. Many witches had found their mates inside this village and moved there to raise their families. One of the witches was even a descendant of the coven who cast the curse. The story had been passed down from generation to generation. Using their magic, the witches discovered that most of their daughters would die after the horrible treatment they would receive at the hands of the vampires. See, the vampires had told them that their daughters would be treated like royalty, spoiled, and pampered. The girls had all volunteered to go, some only because their families needed the money. But not this village, this village fought back. They killed many of the vampires. But they lost even more. Nearly the whole town had been killed. The king of the vampires was in the village that day, his guards got him out safely, but not before the king had grabbed one of the girls off the showing stage."

"The girl tried to kill herself many times, but then she fell pregnant. And she couldn't help but love her baby. She was sick the whole time. Her body had not been made to carry a vampire child. Still, she knew she would live through the birth. The girl had been raised on the story of the curse. She knew the vampires would continue to use her to have more babies, a life worse than death was paved before her, if she survived the birthing process. Which she did. She gave birth to a healthy baby boy, a prince. A few days later, she asked the king to walk with her in the mountains; she needed the fresh air. The king was so pleased that she survived, and that he finally had a son, that he agreed. The girl wanted to keep walking, in awe of the view below them. After the battle in the village, they had to go into hiding. All the human villages had started rising up against them, as well as all the other magical kingdoms. All this young girl had known for the last few years was the inside of a cave. The King let her walk for as long as she wanted. When they reached a tall peak, she spread her arms out at the edge and laughed. He laughed with her, happy that she was happy. And then she jumped. The King tried to grab her hand, but he had been too stunned to move in time to reach her."

"What happened to the vampires, mommy?" The girl asked sleepily.

"They are still out there, hiding, hunting, and waiting for their chance to take back the power. Which is why you must never walk in dark places. You must always stay in the light. Sleep now, my darling. You are safe with the blood of your ancestors running through you. You are doubly blessed as you have the pure blood from both your father and I."

CHAPTER 1

Carrie

I couldn't believe this. I rode in the back of a stinky bus for 7 hours to come see Bryce. We hadn't seen each other in almost three months because of his new job. He promised me that if he took this job, we would find a way to do the long-distance thing.

Just a year, he said.

That was all he needed to make a name for himself in the company, and then he could transfer back to Phoenix.

And I was the idiot that believed him.

I was the idiot that thought I should use one of my very few sick days and turn a three-day weekend into a four-day weekend, with the help of Labor Day, so I could come and see him. Not that he had made the effort to see me since he left. Even though he promised to drive down every other weekend.

I rode the hot, dirty, overfilled bus all night. The creepy old man next to me drooled all over my shoulder. I cleaned myself up in the bathroom at the station, trying to *not* look like I rode a hot, dirty, overfilled bus all night. My long hair had been braided all night, thankfully keeping it out of the path of drool. I relished in the feeling as I took it out. The blonde waves looked pretty good, in my opinion anyway. With that done, I caught an uber straight to Bryce's place.

I was there by seven. We could have at least had breakfast together before he headed off to work.

Bryce and I danced and flirted at a few parties together during college. It wasn't until our last year that I finally agreed to go out with him. He sure was a persistent sucker.

Every now and then he would try to push for more than I was willing to give, but he said it was because he loved me so much that he sometimes lost control. I knew that was a lie, but I was hoping it wasn't that *much* of a lie.

See, I have this weird gift, one that runs in my family, well, sort of. We all have our own unique talents. I always knew when someone was lying to me. When there was something not quite right about a person. When they were hiding something from me. I just didn't know what *it* was.

As much as I loved, or at least cared about Bryce, there was still something off. So, I wanted to wait. I hoped, in time, I would either get over it or find out what it was.

Guess I knew now.

I knocked on his apartment door, at seven freaking a.m., and some hoebag answered it.

She was dressed in nothing but one of his t-shirts. One I bought him actually. It was gray, with a green saguaro cactus on it. The words across the top and bottom said, "there is no place like the desert." I wanted him to remember where home was. Where he belonged.

Now this cheap floozie was wearing it.

"Can I help you?" She didn't seem very happy about me being there either, but probably assumed I just had the wrong door.

If it wasn't for that shirt, I would have been hoping for the same thing.

"Yes. You can tell me who the hell you are?" I was feeling more than a little irritable from the long night, I didn't handle it as well as I should have.

"Who's at the door, sweetheart?" A voice I recognized all too well, called from the back. Pretty sure steam came out of my ears.

I pushed her aside roughly, knocking her off balance. "I'll tell you who, *Sweetheart*." I answered him, my voice filled with the venom I wanted to spit at him.

Why couldn't my ancestors have passed down the power to spit acid? That would be awesome right about now.

Bryce stuttered to a stop, walking into his larger than I expected living room. It was certainly larger than what he had in Phoenix. He was wearing nothing but boxers, with a shocked and freaked out expression.

We then had our biggest, and final, fight of our relationship.

At first he tried to come up with excuses. His *Sweetheart* eventually moved to stand next to him. Confused but obviously planning on standing by her man.

When he realized that wasn't going to work, he went on the offensive. He got tired of waiting, of being celibate, which was a lie. I didn't need my extra senses for that. He had already tried the whole "nothing happened" and the "I swear this was the first time" crap on me.

Now, *those* I felt were flat out lies.

Sweetheart was a co-worker, the boss's daughter actually. They met during his first week there and she was basically living with him now. He even had the nerve to say if I had put out even once this may not have happened. I ripped the necklace he gave me for Christmas last year off, the one I wore every day, and threw it at him.

I called an uber, choosing to wait on the sidewalk, and went back to the bus station. Unfortunately, the buses between LA and Phoenix only ran at night. I couldn't say as I blamed them. People have been known to get sunburned while making that drive during the day. Through their windows. We didn't need a bus overheating from the drive and get stuck on the side of the road either.

I booked my ticket, and then tried to get comfortable in one of the worn-out cushioned chairs. Sleep was nowhere near an option in a large room filled with strangers, so I kept my eyes on the tv hanging in one corner.

A lot of people were doing that actually. The volume was off, so it took me a few minutes to catch up based on the captions on the bottom of the screen.

50 dead overnight, Sacramento. 100 dead overnight, San Diego. 52 dead overnight, Los Angeles. 27 dead overnight, Fresno.

I jumped when the volume turned on randomly. I turned, along with most of the other waiting passengers, to see the station manager standing behind us, remote in hand. His eyes were glued to the screen, not paying any of us any attention.

"As of 7:15 this morning, every freeway and highway leading into Northern California has been destroyed. Casualty numbers are not available for release at this time. Residents in the cities are claiming to have heard a jet followed by the explosions. Officials have so far refused to answer any questions or give an official report."

I gasped in complete shock.

“All over California, we are seeing a continued rise in what can only be assumed are gang related deaths. These attacks have been steadily growing over the last few weeks. From the beginning to now, one thing they all have in common are the two holes found in the neck of each body. Police are calling it a “calling card” by a new gang or terrorist group. This group seems to be attacking the entire state of California. Wait…hold on… reports are coming in now. Car bombs have recently been set off in front of the state capital and many other government buildings in Northern California. There is no word yet as to survivors.”

As the reporter began rehashing events I had heard nothing about - probably due to my preferring not to watch television and rarely listened to live radio - the other waiting passengers began talking amongst themselves.

I heard the word vampire thrown around multiple times.

My chest immediately tightened, and I started gasping for air. When was the last time I had a panic attack? Five years ago?

The sun was still up, making it safe, so I ran outside, bent over, and heaved.

Both my parents were strong believers in the supernatural. My mother had the talent of clairvoyance, my father could read people’s minds when he wanted too. I landed somewhere in the middle with my ability to sniff out a lie, so to speak.

I didn’t actually use my nose. That would just be ridiculous. What was I, a dog?

Five years ago, both my parents were killed in what the police called a random mugging. When I identified the bodies, I noted the two small holes on their thighs.

Yes, I know, the bodies were usually more covered than that, but the coroner was a friend of my dad's, and he knew my family wasn't exactly normal. He was nice enough to let me look for odd markings.

I didn't point them out to him. The cops didn't think anything of the little holes as someone had also shot them in the chest. Why? How the hell should I know? I wasn't the cop. Just the cop's daughter. My dad had put his talent to good use.

Once my breathing evened out, I sat on the ground outside, trying to figure out what to do. I rarely went out at night in general, something else that always irritated Bryce. I never felt comfortable telling him about my family ancestry.

Why was I with him for so long? I honestly didn't know the answer to that.

He was sweet most of the time and acted like he cared too. Maybe I was that sad desperate chick looking for a connection. Learned my lesson on that one. Will not be making that mistake again.

My stomach started grumbling, reminding me that I had not had anything to eat since dinner the night before. I had no interest in the bus station food, also known as two-year-old sandwiches in a vending machine. That probably wouldn't go over well with the remaining twist in my stomach.

Everything I packed and brought with me was in my backpack. For some stupid reason I thought I would finally cave to Bryce this weekend, so I hadn't brought much with me.

Maybe I was just naive.

I wasn't a virgin. At least I didn't think I was. When I was 17, my boyfriend at the time said he had gone all the way in. I felt gross, sticky, stuff all over me, but there had been no pain like my mom told me there would be.

She was never one to hold back details on anything she deemed important. You should hear the bedtime stories I got as a kid.

Anyway, there had been no pain, in fact, I hardly felt him at all. It took me a while to realize the moron had been a bit premature and then lied to save himself some face. My little gift was still growing at the time.

How far in did they need to go for it to count as taking your virginity?

Whatever, not important. At least, not right now.

That had also been the night my parents died. I was late meeting them for dinner at our favorite place, because I may or may not have been doing something else. Needless to say, I went through a self-hate/guilt phase for a while.

With my one and only bag securely strapped to my back, I looked down at the street the station was on, seeing if there were any close options. Down the right looked a little busier and had more colorful buildings. Down the left looked a bit shady.

I chose to go right.

I walked half a mile before I came to a Del Taco. Chicken tacos sounded good, so I went inside. I hung out there, munching on the yummy crinkle fries for a while.

The employees were all talking to each other and looking at videos on their phones. I didn't want to watch or hear any more of it. I just needed to kill time until my bus left at eleven tonight. I still had about twelve hours that needed to be murdered.

I walked down the street a little further, browsing various stores. I debated getting a souvenir, but I decided my broken heart (or was it my pride?) was enough for this trip. I would prefer to forget this whole thing had ever happened.

I thought about calling my friend Clarise and telling her what happened. But she would be busy teaching third grade right now. I picked up a new novel, something else I hadn't brought, thinking I was going to be in bed all weekend, and a sudoku book.

I made my way back to the bus station around three, giving myself plenty of time before the sun set. I looked at the tv once, the volume still on, more deaths were being verified. I tuned it out and opened my book.

It was supposed to be a happy story, something lighthearted. I hadn't realized it was a romance. I growled at myself for my stupidity.

I shoved the book in my bag, thinking one day I might actually want to read it, and pulled out the sudoku. This was better. Mind numbing even.

That got old after an hour though.

I plugged my phone into a wall and sat on the floor, opening my Netflix app. Nothing sounded good there. So, I switched to my Amazon Prime, realizing I probably could have saved money and read one of the hundreds of books on my TBR list, on my kindle unlimited app. Or one of the dozens that I have checked out on my Libby app (no night life leaves a lot of time for reading).

I blamed my overly tired brain.

I giggled, out loud, when my eyes fell onto the perfect movie I could watch. *Boyfriend Killer*. Turned out it wasn't exactly what I was hoping for, but it was better than a chick flick.

By the time the movie was over, the sun was showing the first signs of going down.

My heart rate picked up speed, and I frantically began looking for something else to watch. I had finally settled on the show *Psych* - those two idiots were always good for a laugh - when the floor shook, and my ears rang from a loud boom. People all around me screamed and ducked for cover.

Now, I had never been in an earthquake before, but somehow that didn't seem like what this was.

"Attention, viewers at home. Police officials are calling for an immediate curfew. Everyone needs to be in their homes ASAP. If you are not close to home, go somewhere with cover and get yourself off the streets. We've just received word that bombs were dropped minutes ago on the 10, 15, 14, 101, and 405 freeways, as well as some city buildings. Again, police are saying to get inside and take…" the tv screen turned to snow as we felt another shake.

Our power was still on. There wasn't so much as a blink in the lights.

Did they take out the news station?

I crawled around the wall I was leaning against and looked out the windows, with the other fifty people in the room, and watched fire and smoke reaching up to the sky. Many people screamed with shock when a few of the tall buildings started collapsing in on themselves.

Was this all vampires? Or were there really terrorists, or gangs attacking California?

All over the bus station people were screaming, yelling, and sobbing. It wasn't helping me try to keep my brain functioning like normal. The bus station manager stood on a chair and hollered until he had everyone's attention.

"All buses are canceled. With the roads being blown up, it's not safe to leave, nor can we really go anywhere. At least not in the dark. If you know someone nearby, I suggest heading there. If not, you are welcome to stay here until morning. Maybe we can get on the road then."

I started crying myself now. I was trapped here. Possibly in a city full of vampires. This was the *last* place I should be.

My parents weren't the first ones in our family to die from their bite. It had happened many times in the past. Mom always told me the magic in our blood called to them. She tried to explain why to me, I was sure it was in one of her stories somewhere, but by the time I hit puberty, I thought she was ridiculous.

And then I turned sixteen and started being able to tell some of my friends were using me. I had more than a few admirers on the football team. I may have gained a few trust issues after that. Especially when I realized how many of the guys weren't actually my friends either, they were just hoping to be the one to finally get me in their beds… or their back seats… or under the bleachers.

Was it any wonder I had trust issues? I kind of hated my gift sometimes. It carried a bit of a double-edged sword.

A good portion of the people ignored the stay indoors rule from the police and took off to try and find family and friends. Maybe half a dozen, give or take one or two, remained. I found a corner and tried to hide in there. As the world grew darker, with the exception of the fires, I had a harder time breathing. I needed air, and the dusty station was not helping.

I told myself I would stay near the door. That would be safe.

Yeah, I couldn't lie to myself either.

I crept out one of the back doors that led to the loading area and sat against the wall next to the door. The top half was glass, but the bottom half was brick. I took slow deep breaths, keeping my ears open for someone coming from down the street.

I wasn't listening in the right direction.

"Welcome, to Sunny Los Angeles everyone. Where the weather is a constant balmy seventy degrees and the sun always shines." A semi-deep voice shouted gleefully from behind me.

"Except for at night." Another voice added with a deeper giggle.

"Yes, and we rule the night. Actually, we rule it *all* now." They both started laughing at their stupidity.

I turned carefully, trying to keep my head down as much as I could and peaked over the brick portion. I saw two badly dressed men. They looked like they could have been any man really. Movies always got it wrong.

They weren't any paler than everyone else - unless they hadn't fed in a while. These ones had a slight tan. They also didn't have permanent red or gold eyes. And they certainly couldn't walk in the sun. Sparkly skin or not.

One of them licked his lips hungrily as he looked around the station. "We got us a buffet in here is what we got." The other just laughed along like the idiot he obviously was. "I'm so glad we got this detail tonight. Hmmm. Where to start, where to start. Ah. Yes. You, young man, look like you have just what I need to get me through the long night."

The vamp slowly started stalking over toward a muscular man, one who probably liked working out. The man took a few steps back, putting more distance between them. It didn't matter.

Movies did have the speed down.

They may not be as fast as Edward Cullen, but they were still faster than humans. The second the vampire's fangs sank into the man, the other vamp blocked the front doors.

And here I thought it was safer *in*side.

I sank back below the window, my legs frozen in fear. I could hear the people screaming from the other side of the glass. Men, women, and a few kids.

As the vampires made their way closer to the back door, I put my fist to my mouth to keep from screaming out loud. I was biting down so hard I started to break the skin. I had enough sense in me to pull back just a touch.

The last thing I needed was for them to smell my blood out there. I jumped slightly when I heard a voice up close.

“I don't know about you, but I’m feeling pretty full right now.” A dark chuckle sounded.

“Me too. But I smell something sweet that makes me want dessert.”

“I smell it too, but I don’t see anyone else in here. I bet they just didn’t taste as good as they smelled. We probably got them already. Besides, we need to get moving. Lucas’ orders were to clear out the main street tonight.”

“Eh. There isn’t much left. The other two teams should have cleaned up most of it by now.” The voices started fading away again. “If we hurry though, we can get to Deac’s bar before he closes up for the night.”

“I thought you said you were full?”

The dark chuckle sounded again. “Who said I was going to feed? He has some mighty fine donors who are up for more than just feeding. Besides, that smell has my sweet tooth foaming. All these guys were sour and salty from the fear.”

“Yum, that does sound good. Wanna split one? We each spend five minutes releasing, while the other feeds off the dopamine.”

"Sounds good to me. I don't think I could fit more than that in me right now anyway."

Their voices trailed off and soon I heard the sounds of the main door opening and closing in the silence.

I didn't know for sure how long I waited, sitting absolutely still, listening to any noises coming from inside. It wasn't until I heard movement down the road that I finally peaked inside the bus station again. It was a slaughterhouse in there. Dead bodies laid all over the room, some closer to the doors than others, as though they had tried to make a run for it.

When the noises grew closer, I opened the door and crawled inside.

I crawled along the wall, not trusting my legs to hold me, moving toward the ticket counter. I crept behind it, and nearly screamed at the same time as someone else. They were screaming so loud they would attract attention.

I hurried over, moving at more of a hunched run this time, before dropping again and covering her mouth with my hand.

"Sh, sh. It's ok. They're gone." The screams were lowering but the girl was crying loudly. "I know you're scared. But I really need you to stop making noise. I heard someone outside. We need to be as quiet as possible, so they keep going. Alright?"

The girl, who had to be in her teens, nodded and worked to stifle the tears. I moved my hand off her mouth and held her close, letting her use me for comfort. With her crying silenced, we could hear as the laughing approached. We waited with bated breath as they opened the door I came in through only moments before.

"Looks like Chris and Chris had some fun. They love to make a mess."

“Yeah, smells like they had quite a feast too. Do you smell that? Hmm. I wish we had made it here first. That smells divine.”

“You think there is any chance they left some behind? Look at my pants!” The vamp laughed. “It smells so good; it's making me hard. Which one of these humans do you think it was? Oh, it doesn’t matter.”

We heard the footsteps move further in. I lightly placed my hand over the girl’s mouth again as a reminder.

“This one looks pretty good. Still warm too. I’d say an hour, maybe two since they left.” I closed my eyes tight when I heard zippers.

“Yeah, I like this guy. He looks big and tough.”

A loud thunk sounded behind us and material was moved around. My eyes shot open as we heard something metal sliding across the tile floor, a belt buckle dragging on the hard floor. A large pair of pants slowed as it ran into the wall near us.

“Ah, yeah, there we go. Tell you what, freshly dead are some of my favorites. They are still warm enough to not freeze my balls off, but dead enough that their muscles don’t constrict. It’s nice and tight. Almost like a virgin.”

They both started making sounds that I never wanted to hear again but knew I would be hearing them in my dreams for a long time to come. When they finished, they didn’t bother dressing the used bodies back up again. Thankfully.

Because if they had, they would have seen us.

One cursed loudly, which made us jump after the somewhat quieter moments. “It’s nearly midnight. We need to move it. Lucas will be mad if we are late reporting back.”

"Yeah, alright." The one who preferred the freshly dead said disappointedly, as though he had been hoping to stick around for a while.

They had barely left when the girl started to speak, I pressed my hand harder to her mouth and shook my head. I made her wait at least ten minutes before I removed my hand.

"What did they do to the bodies?"

"Something very perverse." I didn't want to tell her. For all I knew, she knew those people. They could even be her parents. "My name is Carrie. What's yours?"

"Raya."

"Nice to meet you, Raya. Were you traveling somewhere with your family?"

She shook her head and pulled away from me, repositioning to sit shoulder to shoulder with me. "No. I work here. I was manning the booth when the bombs hit. Mr. Robertson said it wasn't safe for me to leave and said I should stay here until tomorrow. He offered to drive me home. He said he would have taken me tonight, but he didn't want to leave all the passengers here alone."

"Was Mr. Robertson the station manager?"

She sniffled and wiped her nose. "Yeah. Do you think he got away somehow? Like we did?"

"No, sweetheart. I saw him just before I saw you. Were you hiding back here the whole time?"

She nodded. "Yes. I had been out there, lying on one of the benches. But I heard my phone ringing. I figured it was my twin, Layla, worrying about me. My phone is under the counter. I was barely starting to answer it when the doors opened. What about you? Where did you hide?"

"I was having a panic attack and needed some fresh air. I figured if I stayed near the door I would be ok. They were right behind me talking, I thought they were going to find me for sure."

"Where were you taking the bus too?"

"Home. I'm from Phoenix."

"Why were you here?"

I didn't want to talk about it, but the actions and distraction seemed to be helping the girl calm down.

"I came to surprise my boyfriend. He just moved here for a new job. Turns out I was the one who got the surprise."

"What happened?"

I grimaced at the memory. "His other girlfriend opened his front door, wearing nothing but a shirt that I bought him before he left."

She gasped in dramatic shock. I talked to her for a little longer, until she started yawning. I promised her that I would keep an ear out, so she could sleep, her head on my shoulder. Eventually I fell asleep with her, my head falling on top of hers.

CHAPTER 2

Carrie

Raya and I jumped awake, startled, when we heard the bus station doors being ripped open and then slamming shut behind someone new. We both sat up and rubbed our eyes, blinking a few times. The sun was high up now.

"Holy…" A female voice echoed around the room. "Raya? Raya, I know you aren't dead!" The voice softened to a pleading sound. "Please say you aren't dead."

Raya jumped to her feet. "I'm not dead!"

I stood and stretched my arms over my head as she ran around the counter and fell against another girl. They were identical. Long straight black hair, mocha skin tone, and long legs. Which showed off in the short shorts they were both wearing.

"I heard the screaming before you hung back up last night. I wasn't sure if I should call back, I didn't want to be what gave your position away. But you never called me either. I was so worried. It took me nearly two hours to walk over here. Are you alright? What happened?"

Raya started crying again as she told her sister everything that happened. When they got to my part, the twins looked over at me. I gave a small, somewhat awkward, wave.

My stomach also chose that moment to let its presence be known. They were close enough by that point that they heard it. We all laughed.

"Any idea if there is anything open around here?" I asked Layla, the mirror version of her sister.

She grimaced. "Every place I passed on the way here had been broken into. I doubt anyone will be brave enough to go to work today." She tilted her head, thinking. "We could always just head down to the nearest place and see if we can get in and make something ourselves. We need to eat, right?"

"Sounds great." I gave them a tight smile, one that I didn't feel at all. I could always leave a little cash behind, not that I had much on me.

"Oh! Hold on, I have an idea." Raya ran from her sister and passed me as I was moving to go around the counter. She pushed a few buttons on the register, and it popped open. My jaw dropped as she cleaned out the till. She shrugged when she saw my face.

"Mr. Robertson is dead. The Greyhound bigwigs won't be coming anywhere near here."

Layla laughed as Raya divided up the money. She turned and handed me a small stack. "This is the refund for your bus ticket, both ways." She held up the one in her other hand. "And this is my last paycheck. See? Not stealing. Surviving."

I took the money from her hands, a soft sardonic chuckle on my lips. “Thank you for trying. I’m just desperate enough to choose and see it that way.”

I folded the money and stuck it in the small pocket of my backpack, then repositioned the bag on my back. This was all I had left in the world at the moment. My home in Phoenix no longer counted, seeing as I couldn’t get there.

“Shall we survive at a place with food next?”

The three of us walked the few blocks to the Del Taco, but the place had been nearly burned to the ground. The Jack and the Box next door went with it. I searched the skyline, noticing the buildings were smaller now, as well as the fires. The smoke was still plenty high though.

Another block away, we found a Carl’s Jr, looking at least halfway decent. One wall was completely gone, mainly because the windows had all been smashed in. Another wall still had bricks going through a crumbling phase. We stepped through the window carefully.

As we walked through the dining room, we were careful to step around and over the parts of the burned down roof. Outside of structural damage it was workable. Even the plumbing in the bathroom still worked.

Our first stop was in those bathrooms, where we cleaned up in the sinks as best we could. Nothing like a paper towel bath (using my packed body wash instead of the hand soap), followed up with finger brushing our teeth (with my toothpaste), to make a girl feel good about herself. We all took a turn with my deodorant, as well.

Feeling slightly better about our hygiene, we moved to the kitchen.

Inside the walk-in fridge, we found eggs, bread, bacon, and all sorts of things. Layla had worked fast food for a few months the summer before, so she knew how to turn their oven on. Thankfully.

We made a ton of food and ate most of it. The rest we wrapped up and put into any bags we had, not knowing where our next meals would be. Call me a snob, but I have never been a big fan of leftover fast food. Thanks to the last 24 hours, I didn't care anymore. Food was food by this point. Who knew where, or when, our next meal was coming from.

"Where's your parents?" I asked, as we walked down the street, not really having a destination in mind.

"Mom died last year, cancer. Dad didn't handle it so well. He's had one cheap floozie after the other spending the night. Sometimes he doesn't even come home for a few days at a time." Layla informed me like she was reading a schoolbook-report, not talking about her own father.

"He's a truck driver, Layla. He's out working all that time." Raya lightly scolded her sister.

Layla waved it away with a click of her tongue. "Tomaato, tomahto. He never used to work that much. Anyway, he probably won't be coming back now. Not with the freeways gone. That's if he wasn't on them when they blew up in the first place."

"Hey!" Raya stopped walking, we stopped and turned to her. "Where's that jerk boyfriend of yours, Carrie? Maybe we could hide out there for now."

Yuck. That did not sound like a good plan. I was going to tell them that too, but their faces looked so happy at the idea. I forced a smile.

"Sure. Let's go find, Bryce." I put all the fake enthusiasm I could into that.

Layla snorted as we started again. “Bryce? How did you not know he was a douche with a name like, Bryce?”

“Har, har.” I nudged her in the arm. “I always knew there was something off about him. I just couldn’t put my finger on it.”

Raya looped her arm through mine, effectively locking me in the middle of them. “Your next boyfriend needs to be cooler. Someone who is buff and goes all alpha male. That’s what you need.”

I laughed and shook my head as they both listed various attributes I should look for in a man. They had already informed me that they were *only* six months away from turning 17, and yet they wanted to give me boy advice.

Sadly, it sounded like they knew more than I did on the subject.

An hour later, we stopped in front of Bryce’s apartment building. The front door was hanging off.

We all shared a look. I motioned for them to get behind me, and I took the lead.

I gasped when I saw the doorman from the day before, slumped into a corner of the room. His neck was covered in dry blood. He had been semi-decent to me yesterday.

I vaguely heard the curse words flying behind me as I rushed toward the elevator. We didn’t bother stopping on other floors, I went straight to the 5th floor. We took soft steps as we approached Bryce’s door.

Which wasn’t closed all the way.

I pushed the door open, and slowly stepped through. It wasn’t long before we found them. Bryce was lying across the couch, and his new toy was lying on the floor. From the positions they were in, I had to wonder if it was the same set of vamps that rolled through after the others were dead.

I stood there, frozen in shock, as I looked down on the man I had dated for nearly two years.

“You know what? I think that hoochie saved your life.” Raya said in amazement.

“What are you talking about?” I asked her, tearing my gaze from Bryce’s vacant stare.

“Think about it. Where would you have been last night if she hadn’t been here?”

“Huh, you’re right. I would have been here with him.” I shook off the sadness and made my way to the room I thought was his.

In his nightstand drawer was his wallet, which I emptied without guilt. I then walked to his closet and searched for what I was looking for. I grinned like a maniac when I found it.

I used to tease Bryce for being so obsessed with security, to the point that he had a small safe. And I knew the combination. It was the day we went on our first date. I was only slightly worried that he would have changed it, but that had been fruitless. He hadn’t.

There wasn’t much inside, just a little more cash, a gold watch, important papers, and things like that. I was surprised when I found a small velvet box tucked into one corner. I opened it and found the diamond ring I had pointed out to him one day. It was simple, yet elegant. Something I could wear to work and not worry about getting broken.

“Oh. Who was that for?” Layla came around my side, looking at what I held.

“Me, I think. I pointed this very one out to him right before he left. He said he had to make a phone call for work and would meet me in the food court. I can’t believe he bought it.” I was shocked and amazed. I had no idea he was thinking about proposing.

What was with this other girl then? Or maybe he bought this before he ever came here. Before he met his boss's daughter.

A small tear fell out of my eye for the dead traitor. Layla snapped the box out of my hand.

"That's enough with that. He was an even bigger jerk than we knew. He was going to ask you to marry him, all the while having an affair. Odds are, he would have continued after the wedding. Screw him."

"Yeah, he was a grade A jerk, good riddance, I say. Now you are completely free to move on, no doubts about what happened." Raya backed up her twin. "You know what this calls for?" She gave us a big teasing grin.

I couldn't help but laugh. "What?" My voice was still a little shaky as I wiped my cheek.

The sisters looked at each other, then me, and shouted, with both arms in the air, "shopping!"

It was easy to forget they were both still teenagers. At least until they did that. I was really glad I met them when I did. They were great at keeping things light and helping me process all this. It was loads better than wallowing in my own fears and anxieties.

"Do you really think anything is open right now?" I asked incredulously.

Raya gave a nonchalant shrug. "Eh, who knows?" She grabbed my hand and pulled me to the door. "But we won't know for sure unless we try."

We made our way back out of the building full of dead people, thankfully the only other one we saw was the doorman in the corner.

By the time we hit the streets, things had picked up. More people were roaming around. Their faces pale, the sadness and grief shining in their eyes. Hardly anyone spoke to anyone else. It was like everyone was a ghost of their normal selves.

The twins led me down another street, and then another, back in the direction we came, just on another street. A few times we changed streets just to avoid the fires we saw still blazing along.

Raya whooped with joy when we got to an outdoor shopping center. It was short lived. We froze at the sound of a crash and a scream. It took a minute for our brains to catch up to our eyes.

The place was being raided.

Nearly every store had broken windows. People were running, screaming, fighting, and carrying things to their cars that they obviously did not pay for. Not that we should be judging others for stealing, but at least our contraband was on the necessity side of things.

I grabbed both of the girls' arms and pulled them to a small alleyway. "We need to get out of here. I did not survive a night with vamps to get killed by a bunch of random people who are taking advantage of a bad situation." I hissed at them.

They both nodded their agreement. Even still, we just stood there, around a building corner, unable to take our eyes off the insanity of what was now the world we lived in. No one said a word. We hardly even blinked.

We jumped when we heard a loud buzzing sound coming from somewhere near us. Almost like a helicopter, only smaller. All three of us spun around in circles, frantically searching for where the next horror was coming from.

Layla saw it first and pointed back the way we came. Sure enough, we saw a black drone headed down the street, toward us.

At least, I thought it was a drone. It was a lot bigger than any I had seen before. It looked like a small airplane, maybe one the military would use.

As it got closer, it got bigger, much bigger. Still too small to be a real plane, but big enough to mean business. The drone hovered in the air right in front of us. It had what looked to be a camera on the bottom of it, swiveling back and forth.

It had four wings, with propellers spinning on top of each of them. The camera rotated, taking in the madhouse in front of us, then turned to us.

We froze, our eyes on it. Nobody moved, not even the camera. I was so scared that all I could hear was the buzzing from the drone and the panicky breaths of my new friends. Until another large crash was heard.

All four of us turned to it. Then the drone took off. Not far from us, the drone began doing something new.

A long oval looking thing lowered from the bottom. Loud popping noises soon came from it, and people started screaming as they ran for cover. Many hit the ground, not moving again. The drone was shooting them.

With only one thought on my mind, I tightened the grip on the twins' arms and began running back the way we came.

When we heard the buzzing coming again, we ducked behind a dumpster, hoping to hide from it. I didn't release my breath until it had passed us by. We all fell into manic fits of panicky laughter, our eyes overflowing with tears.

"Maybe no shopping today." I said in between fits. They both started laughing harder, this time with more amusement.

Layla sank onto her butt, her breathing labored and her voice slightly lighter. "What do we do now? Where do we go?"

The way they both looked at me made me realize I was the adult here. Somehow I was in charge and responsible for them.

How in the hell did that happen?

“We need to get somewhere safe. Somewhere the other humans won’t go, nor the vamps.” I racked my brain on where that might be. I could only come up with two options, neither of which were sitting well. “We either go back to the bus station, or to Bryce’s place.”

They both grimaced. Yeah, I wasn’t thrilled with the idea of hanging out with dead people either.

“I vote for Bryce's. We can shower, and have real beds to sleep in. The vamps know they took it out last night. They have no reason to go back there. Same with the bus station, but it's farther and doesn’t have beds.” I crawled around the dumpster to get a better look at the street. Giving them a minute to think about it.

“Are you sure, Carrie?” Raya’s voice was shaky.

I looked around the area, noticing the sun getting dimmer. When I looked at the sky I realized why. Storm clouds were rolling in.

“Now more than ever. A storm is coming. That means the sun will be blocked. If we don’t get moving now, we’ll be overrun by vamps.” I stood up, ready to run.

They both just gaped at me. I clapped my hands together as hard as I could, making them jump.

“Think about it, they only come out at night. Right? Well, night is about to come a little early. Bryce’s apartment is the closest. And I know he has food there. Now!” I added the last in a shout, as both girls were still not moving.

They jumped up, their legs shaking in fear. All the bravado they had had was gone now. At least they followed me as I ran.

We ran quietly, no one talking, until we were getting close to our destination. The clouds nearly had the sun covered now. My eyes kept shooting up at them, and then around the street at all the new shadows.

I froze when I felt intent. This was one of the powers I wasn't all that good at yet.

Sensing the lie was one thing, that was easy. It had come first. Lately, I had been feeling intent. Was it their intent to deceive? Were they lying to protect someone? Or were they just uncomfortable talking about themselves?

This feeling was different. This was new. I could feel someone's intent to harm without seeing who, or where, they were.

I stopped running, putting my arms out to my sides to stop the girls. Then I put a finger to my lips. A strong feeling of darkness came into me, coming from the alley across the street.

It was aimed directly at me.

We were only half a block from Bryce's building, our safety zone for the night. It was waiting to see where I would go. It would follow.

Not for the first time, I wished my parents were here to help me with my growing powers. I closed my eyes, as they had taught me long ago, slowing my breath as though I were meditating.

Yes, the vamp would follow. It wanted me, but I had no doubts he would hurt these girls as well. No one else was around. It was me that was going to get them hurt. That left me with only one option.

Speaking through the side of my mouth, as quietly as I could, I told them what to do.

"There is a vampire hiding across the street. He wants me, not you. It's my smell, I think. He is watching me closely. You are going to walk back about half a block. I am going to get him to follow me. I will lose him and meet you back at the apartment when it is safe."

"No!" Layla whisper-yelled at me, her fingers wrapping around my wrist.

I turned to face them, placing one hand on each of their paled cheeks. "You will be safe. He only wants me. I can feel his intensity. Once we separate, he won't spare you a second glance." At least I didn't think he would.

Raya was silently crying, a plea in her eyes for me not to leave her. "How do you know? I can't even see him."

"It's a gift. I can tell when people lie, and I can feel their intent. This vamp's is so loud, it's practically shouting at me. Please. I can't stand the idea of you two getting hurt because of me. I will find you once I lose him. I promise." I tried to give them a reassuring smile. It was a little shaky.

We all knew what the odds of me getting away from him were. I kissed each of their foreheads, then with a deep breath, took off running, praying they would listen and be safe. The vamp stayed where he was until I turned down another street.

I sped up when I heard his steps behind me. He was barely jogging, enjoying the chase. He wanted me to feel like I had a chance.

I turned many times, listening, falling, running. My jeans ripped from falling and sliding against walls. He drew close enough that I could hear him, which I was sure was what he wanted.

"Hmmm, something smells good over here. Looks like I don't need to pay for a donor tonight. I can get myself a free snack, right here." I didn't need to see him. His voice was creepy enough.

I spun and started running again, turning down into another street. I screeched as the streetlights flickered out. I could hear a mixture of laughter and screaming somewhere in the distance. My heart stopped for a moment when I heard shoes scraping the pavement nearby. The vamp was getting closer now, he was about done playing.

My heart started pounding a mile a minute again.

I sped up, frantically searching for a place to hide. The steps, getting closer and closer. I turned down to another street. In my panic, and blindness in the early dark, I misread where I was going.

I hit the dead end of an alley.

Someone inhaled deeply from my only way out. "Hmmm, you smell divine. I bet you taste just as good too. Come my pretty, I promise to make it good for you."

I started screaming as he got closer, his glowing eyes shining in the dark. I reached for my bag, pulling it to one shoulder, desperate for anything that could be used as a weapon.

"Help! Help!" I started banging on doors, screaming, but no one was coming. I fled further into the corner of buildings, hitting everything I could.

Finally, a crack of light shone through.

"Help, please!" I desperately reached to pull the door open further.

I screeched when a hand wrapped around my arm and tried to pull me back. But instead of going backward, I flew forward, into the light. A man stepped between us, blocking me from the outside.

"I saw her first." The menace snarled. "She's mine."

"Not unless she is willing. You know my rules. You don't drink unless they are willing."

"Yeah, well, she wasn't in your bar. She was strolling around out here."

"She belongs to me. Everyone knows you can't touch a human that belongs to me without paying. You wanna pay, go around the front. I have rooms available and plenty of willing donors."

The menace grumbled something I couldn't understand and then left. My savior closed the door and turned to face me.

He had to have been the hottest guy I had ever seen, way hotter than Bryce. His black hair was pulled into a short pony on his neck, his skin had a touch of caramel, and his muscles had muscles.

What really caught my eye were his eyes. They were as black as the night, which should have scared me. Instead, I felt comforted, like they promised I would never be hurt again.

I felt like I could trust him, like he would protect me at all costs. And he would rather die than hurt me. Something I never felt with Bryce.

Something I had only ever felt with my parents.

Loyalty.

Devotion.

Home.

CHAPTER 3

Deacon

Colton and I were both working behind the bar when we heard it. No one else in the room even flinched. Not even the Nightwalkers behind the curtains could hear her over the music. We looked at each other as we heard it again.

Someone was yelling for help. A girl.

"I need to go upstairs for a minute. Watch the bar."

My old friend and bodyguard only nodded, but the look in his eyes said if I got hurt he would chain me up for a while. With pure silver.

I didn't run until I was out of sight, then used my own speed to get to the door. Even for the Nightwalkers my speed would raise eyebrows.

I opened the door just a crack and saw a young woman standing near my door. Her face showed terror beyond imagination. The light reflecting on the top of her blonde hair made it look as though there was a halo sitting on her head.

She reached for the door, trying to come in. “Help, please!” She begged. Her beautiful face was covered in tears. Then she screamed in terror, shooting a dagger through my heart that should have paralyzed me.

The Nightwalker behind her had grabbed her arm.

Reflexively, I reached out and threw her behind me. I recognized this Nightwalker. He’d been in my bar a time or two, he was always a bit rougher with my donors, a few people who knew about the vampires and were willing to trade blood for money. Typically, the desperate ones.

“I saw her first.” Victor snarled. “She’s mine.”

“Not unless she is willing. You know my rules. You don’t drink unless they are willing.”

“Yeah, well, she wasn’t in your bar. She was strolling around out here.”

“She belongs to me. Everyone knows you can’t touch a human that belongs to me without paying. You wanna pay, go around the front. I have rooms available and willing donors.” I didn’t know why I was claiming her as mine, but if it got him to leave her alone, then so be it.

He turned and stomped off, grumbling under his breath, not knowing my ears were better than his.

“You can keep her for now, but soon this city will fall, and I’ll be back.”

I sighed and closed the door.

I saw the news. I heard the rumors every night. Curtis was finally putting his plans into action. And this girl just unknowingly became a part of it. I turned and saw her balled up on my floor, at the foot of the stairs that lead up to mine and Colton's apartments.

When I bought the bar, sixty years ago, the top floor had been designed to be part of the bar. I closed it off and built two apartments. They weren't big by any means, but they were all we needed. At least they were better than the cave I grew up in.

I lowered down to be closer to her level, trying to look as less frightening as I could. "Are you alright, angel?"

"He... he…"

"Did he hurt you?"

She shook her head, her dirty hair flinging with it. She had dirt on her neck and her arms. Her clothes were torn, and not in the places people usually paid for them to be. She looked as though she was on the run.

"No. Was he… was he… uh…" She closed her eyes and laughed at herself. "Never mind. It'll just sound ridiculous."

"Try me, angel." She needed to accept what she already knew, or she would never be able to move on.

Her face fell as she realized she was right. "He was a vampire, wasn't he? All the attacks. Vampires?"

"Yeah, angel. The vampires are done hiding it seems."

Her lip quivered in fear for a short moment before she started full out sobbing. Colton peeked around the corner, silently appraising the situation. I looked at her and then the stairs. He nodded then went back to the bar.

I moved closer, my hands out in front of me. "I'm going to help you up and take you up the stairs. I won't hurt you, and there is a bar full of people that will hear you scream. Alright?"

The crying angel barely nodded her head. I slid a hand under her arm and pulled her to standing. She didn't seem all that steady, so I decided to just pick her up altogether. I felt a wave of possessiveness come over me, the undeniable need to protect this unknown female.

At the top of the stairs, I opened the door to Colton's apartment, and laid her on the couch. Her hands gripped my shirt and wouldn't let me move away. With an amused huff I sat down and let her cry on my shoulder.

I took a deep breath and caught a scent in the air. I sniffed again, trying to figure out what it was. This girl had a very sweet tint to her blood. It called to me in a way nothing ever had before.

No wonder Victor was so set on having her.

No wonder she looked like she had been through the wringer.

There was more to her scent though, it appealed to my tastebuds, but it appealed to other parts of me as well.

I had spent the better part of thirty years trying to find a human that could bear my child. As a Vampire Born, we were the only ones able to produce the seed needed. But thanks to the curse of a witch, we could only produce males.

We were left to use female humans to carry on our genes. Unfortunately, our seed was unable to attach to most of them. The few who did manage to get pregnant rarely survived long enough to deliver a live baby. Even fewer lived past the delivery.

The last baby to be born was nearly 450 years ago, my mother killed herself a few days later. I never had the chance to scent the birthing women. But something in the scent of this girl, no, woman, made me wonder if she would be able to at least last until the delivery. The scent smelled like… life.

When her sobs quieted, leaving a few hiccups in its wake, she placed a small hand on my chest and pushed off. I kind of liked how she felt in my arms. I wanted her to stay there, where I knew she was safe. In time, maybe she'd let me put her there again.

"Sorry, it has been one nightmare after another the last two days. I guess it all just caught up to me. I'm Carrie by the way."

"Deacon. You want to talk about it?"

She wiped her eyes and shook her head. "That might just make me start all over again."

"Is there someone I can call for you? Your parents perhaps? I'm sure they are worried sick about you." I wasn't sure how old she was, only that she was old enough for what I needed from her.

My mother was barely fifteen when she had been sacrificed to my father. A different time though, different culture. This angel was older than that at least. Her body was stronger and more developed. Very nicely developed.

Her plump bottom lip quivered. "No. There is no one left." She swallowed hard, trying valiantly to keep a lid on her emotions. Definitely not the time to talk about it, then.

"Do you have a place to stay? You shouldn't be out in the dark, especially now."

A bout of hysterical laughter fell from her lips. "Don't I know it. The first time I do anything spontaneous happens to be the same time California goes to hell and I come face to face with the very thing my mother warned me about!"

Her mother knew about us. Interesting. I wondered if she had been a donor at one time. Not many others would know we existed.

Well, that the vampire species existed at any rate. No one remembered my specific race. Thankfully.

"You can stay here for as long as you like."

"Oh, no. I couldn't impose like that. You don't even know me."

"You aren't imposing. This is a spare apartment above my bar. If it helps, you can work for your room and board." Colton has plenty of places he could stay, and plenty of money too. A thousand years walking the earth, you accrued a few assets. He missed wandering around anyway.

Carrie nibbled on her lip, thinking about my offer. "I can't work in a bar. I've never even been inside one." She snorted with amusement. "I'm a freaking Kindergarten teacher for crying out loud."

I couldn't help it, I put my thumb under her lip and pulled it out of her teeth. It was either that or nibble on it myself.

When was the last time I drank fresh blood? Or felt a warm body under me?

Hmm, if I was going to work her around to my side, I might have to satisfy some needs first.

"It's not that hard. Drunk men are no different from toddlers. I can teach you everything else you need to know."

"Are you sure you don't mind? I'm a fast learner. I'll carry my weight."

"I have no problem teaching you the ropes to everything." And I did mean everything. I sniffed again, this time looking for something specific.

Ah, yes. There it was. The scent of innocence. That made my chances of success even greater. And sweeter.

"Why don't you get comfortable? The bedroom is right through that door. I will bring you something to eat from the kitchen downstairs. A full stomach, and a good night's rest, and then you can start your new life."

Carrie enthusiastically jumped on me, practically landing on my lap as she threw her arms around my neck. Yes, I definitely needed to try this girl on for size.

"Thank you so much, Deacon! I promise you won't regret it."

I already knew I wouldn't.

Carrie took her bag to the bedroom, and I went downstairs. I stopped in the kitchen first and asked my cook to make up a bacon and cheese angus burger, with plenty of fries. I couldn't wait to smell her with the extra iron in her blood. I bet it would make her smell even better. If that were possible.

"So… what happened?" Colton asked as he closed out a tab for one of our human customers.

Things continue like they were, and I would have to expand my hours more into the daytime. I was lucky these guys were already here and drinking before the news of the curfew was sufficiently spread. The building the news station was in was taken out while they were in the middle of it. And that was yesterday. They never should have even come out today, but they probably needed a drink. A sense of normalcy.

I doubted some of these humans would even make it home. They shouldn't have doubted the rumors. Then again, night had come early today.

"Victor was hunting in my alley. She doesn't have much with her, and she claims not to have anyone left. Carrie is one of the many who are just starting to lose everything."

"Carrie?"

"That's her name. I gave her your apartment by the way. You can grab your things when she is asleep, she thinks it was empty. She is going to help out around here until she can get back on her feet. Permanently, if I can help it."

Colton laughed. "Going to try again?"

"Yes and protect her for now. There is a scent to her I don't recognize, but it calls to me on many levels. Victor was adamant about having her. I doubt I am the only one it calls too. When you go up, see if you recognize it. I also need you to run to the store for me tonight."

He lifted an eyebrow at me. I chuckled. "I need a uniform for my new waitress, and anything else you want to grab."

He shook his head at me. "Did you have anything in mind, my Lord?" His grin was teasing, but his words were annoying.

"Yes, actually." I told him what I wanted, and he barked out a laugh, drawing the attention of the patrons.

"I'll be back shortly. Let's just hope the humans haven't cleaned out every store in the city by now."

I silently agreed.

The raids started the day before, the greedy were always willing to get a jump on things, no matter the species.

"Do you want me to help you out back there, Deacon?" A syrupy voice called from the bar, a few minutes after he left. Alicia leaned on her elbows, pressing her money-making chest out. She was wearing a pair of short shorts and a bikini top.

The donors who were open to more than just donating blood dressed more provocatively, setting them apart from the others. I only had two or three donors on hand tonight. If the Nightwalkers made it out into the open, I was going to need more donors. Both kinds of them.

"Focus on the clients, Alicia. You are here for them, not me." We went over this every time she came in.

If she knew what I really was, she would probably back off, but there was no guarantee. Besides, nobody knew what I was. The Nightwalkers knew I was a vampire, they knew I smelled different, but they hadn't been around long enough to know why.

Many years ago, a few of them theorized that it was my age that made me smell different. I let the theory fly and ran with it. It was the safest option.

With a pout, she turned back around, facing the darker side of the bar, where the Nightwalkers tended to hide. I had a few curtained off areas, which I referred to as my VIP rooms.

When the cook told me my order was ready, I asked him to keep an eye on the bar while I took the food upstairs.

I knocked lightly on the door before entering Carrie's new apartment. I heard the shower running and stepped closer. A new smell wafted through the place. Lavender body wash. So, my little runner had packed soap.

She hadn't planned on living on the streets. The running may not have been planned then.

I set the food on the table and stalked toward the bathroom. I turned the knob slowly, pushing the door two inches open. Just enough to let me look through the mirror. The glass shower door emphasized her perfectly. Her wet hair was piled on her head, held tightly with a clip. I watched as she washed her body with a washcloth from the closet.

She didn't miss a single inch. And neither did I.

I snuck back out before she could catch me. I was antsy to close up the bar and get back upstairs. I couldn't shake this need to be near her. To smell her. To touch her.

An eternity passed before I was finally able to give the last call to the humans, the liquor portion of the bar and the kitchen would be closing in twenty minutes. I breathed a sigh of relief after the last one left.

"Last call on the donors. No curtains needed."

This was when I made a good chunk of money. The vamps that didn't like hiding would wait until two o'clock to buy their drinks.

Like clockwork, three more Nightwalkers walked in and took up a table. That made six I had in all. I waited until everyone was situated and waved my three donors over. Two women and one man.

"Alright, we have three for you tonight. Only one is open for playtime. What's your choice?"

The group of three signaled to share the man. He walked over and laid on their table, trying not to flinch. One female nightwalker sat by herself, signaling for Alicia to sit on the table in front of her. I was surprised, I expected her to go for the man. She was rather large herself, possibly a lumberjack or a wrestler when she was still human. I would have thought she would have gone for the testosterone filled donor. Guess she needed something sweeter tonight.

The last two Nightwalkers happily shared the other female donor.

I set a timer for ten minutes and began to clean up. My cook brought out a few more burgers and set them on the counter. The male donor especially would need the nourishment tonight. My cook wasn't new to this either, so he had prepared a double meat angus burger for him.

When the timer went off, the Nightwalkers released their prey, paid, and left. Alicia's customer paid more of course. The other female donor walked over to her and helped her clean up her thigh and fix her clothes.

They ate their food while I divided up their cuts for the night. It wasn't bad. I cleared my throat getting their attention while I began handing out the envelopes.

"I'm going to be honest. I don't like the way things are going in the city. If what I think is happening is happening," what I knew was happening, "the vamps are going to be out in the open soon. That means things are going to be tough all around here. Humans are not going to want to come out at night. I will stay open for vamp hour, from sundown to closing. If you are willing to risk it, you are welcome to come. I'm going to need more donors too, feel free to bring us help. I'm sure many of the bars will be getting on board soon, but I guarantee that I will be the more humane boss and give you more of the cut." Which was ironic since I wasn't human.

"Alright, that's it. Go home and rest. Remember, I won't let you back in this bar for at least three days. We don't want you dying on those tables."

"Will we still be able to choose what we are willing to do?"

I looked at the woman, who was still quite young. "Yes, at least in my bar. Be warned though. The curtains will disappear. Just like after closing time. Everything, and I do mean everything, will be in the open. Vamps don't care who is in the room. They will even take pleasure if you want to watch, bonus points if they embarrass you." She nodded and followed the other two out.

I cleaned off all the tables, turned the chairs over, setting them on top, and had just started on the floors when Colton came back.

"Darn, I was hoping you would be done before I got back."

"Har. Har. Were you able to find anything that would work?" I leaned the broom against a table and walked toward the bar, where he was setting down his contraband.

"Yes. I grabbed a few different kinds, that way she can wear clean clothes every day and have backups for spills. We have two of the pencil skirt kind, nice, tight, and will barely cover her butt. Black and Green. We have the catholic schoolgirl style, in both red and black and blue and black. Again, they will barely cover her butt. Finally, two jean skirts, that will ...."

"Barely cover her butt, yes. Thank you for making me feel like a dirty old man." I cut him off.

Colton barked. "Well, you kind of are."

"Oh, please. You are literally twice my age. Now, what about the tops?"

Colton pulled out a few shirts and laid them on the counter, they looked like strips of material and nothing more. Two were literally just that, one red, and one dark green. They had no sleeves, not even a single strap. The next two would wrap around her back, then cover her perfect specimens, while crossing in front of her neck. The valley wouldn't even be covered. She'd be just as covered with nothing but her fingers. Or mine. These two came in white and black. Another was black leather and zipped up in the front. The last was a set of three sports bras that dipped low in the front. Pink, black, and dark blue.

I held the last up. "Really?"

He shrugged. "Options were limited, and you have to admit, they cover more than some of the other tops. With her walking around in these, you are going to have an increase in clients and patrons."

"No one is allowed to touch her." I growled menacingly at him.

He put up both hands and took a step back, shock written all over his face. I shook my head, a bit confused, myself.

“Woah. I was just saying. If you don’t want anyone to touch her though, you know what you have to do. It won’t work with the humans, but it will cut down on the battles with the Nightwalkers, and maybe help cover up whatever that scent was you got off her.”

I frowned. I hadn’t planned on doing anything of the sort, but he had a point.

Colton started re-bagging the clothes. as I went to continue sweeping. I did notice a few more items in one of the bags, of a small lacey nature. And he had two shoe boxes.

A scream ripped through the bar, causing us both to freeze in confusion and look around. It took less than a second before I dropped the broom and ran through the bar as fast as I could up the stairs, my friend right behind me.

Colton placed a hand on my chest at the door to his apartment. If there was a threat, he would be going first. I may not want to accept my royal duties, but he would never shirk them. He sniffed the air and placed an ear to the door.

“No one is in there but her.” He stepped back and I shoved my way through.

Carrie was in the bed, sleeping, but thrashing around. A nightmare, she was having a nightmare. Not sure what to do with that, we both went back out to the small living room. At least she had eaten the food.

“Do you recognize the scent?”

I waited as he stood in the doorway to the bedroom, starting to look, and sound, more like a Doberman than a vampire. He gave up after a few minutes.

"There is something familiar about it, ancient in a way. But it has been too long to place it. If you do decide to keep her and try her for breeding, we can take her to your father and the others. Surely one of them would remember. I was never part of the breeders."

"No. I won't take her there unless I have no other choice. If they think it's possible, she will be passed around like my mother was meant to be after me. We both know what happened next."

"Your choice. In the meantime, I am heading out. You have extra help now, and I want to look into what Curtis is up to."

I took his hand and pulled him into a hug. "Be careful, my friend. Keep in touch."

"You as well, your highness." Carrie whimpered in the other room again. "She must be having one hell of a nightmare. If you want to spare yourself some fights over her, you know what to do. Those who understand the purpose of it will back off. And those who don't, need the lesson."

"I'll think about it." I kept my eyes on her door as he left.

Quietly, I joined her in the room and sat on the edge of the bed. A few strands of her hair had fallen from the loose braid she had created and fell into her face. I gently moved it away, my fingers grazing along her forehead. At my touch, her breathing slowed and her face relaxed.

Interesting.

I sniffed again, the fear and panic were receding. Contentment was taking over. That special scent of my angel's was getting stronger. My instincts pulled me closer to her neck, bare of all except a thin strap of material. I sighed happily with the stronger scent.

Yes, she would have been driving every Nightwalker in the city crazy. What must her life have been like?

Unable to resist, I kissed the spot softly, and then licked it. A small taste of what she had hidden deep inside her.

The sleeping angel's breath caught, her chest rising higher. A sweeter scent began to permeate in the air.

Colton was right, I needed to make it so the others would know to stay away from what belonged to me. Princes did not share what belonged to them. Whether they be donors, lovers, or pets. Whether they be willing or not.

I did not share.

I moved to lay by her side, the smallest pout forming on her lips from the temporary distance between us. I chuckled softly to myself. I could take her right now. Her fight wouldn't last long.

But I wanted her to come willingly. The blood tasted so much better that way.

Some may prefer the fear being strong in the blood, but not me. It always tasted too bitter and sour to me. It would spoil her sweetness.

Once I was in position, I lifted Carrie's head, resting it on my right upper arm. I bit into my wrist, puncturing the skin with my teeth. With my left, I traced under her bottom lip, and then on top. Her mouth opened just enough, with the slightest moan on her lips.

I lowered my right wrist down and let my thick blood drip into her mouth. Soon, my wrist was resting on her soft, warm lips, making sure every drop reached its destination.

Her eyes moved quickly behind her closed eyelids, and the scent of panic began to rise in her blood again. I cursed at myself. I should have waited longer to do this. Her fear of Victor was probably freaking her out right now.

I leaned toward her ear, not wanting to wake her, and kept my voice soft enough to be a whisper in the wind.

"Sh, now angel. You are safe here. I will protect you." Her eyes slowed and her breathing began to calm. My blood was already beginning to slow, as vampires did not bleed easily. "I need you to suck the drink up, angel. It will help you to feel better. It will heal you of your fears and nightmares. It will give you peace."

Her tongue licked me tentatively, causing me to press my own lips together to keep any sounds out that might wake her completely. She licked again, this time with more pressure, followed by her lips locking around my skin. The suction was pure bliss.

I never shared my blood with another before. I never wanted to risk it. Both vampires and humans were easily addicted to our blood. It could cause an incredible increase of dopamine, which led to a hunger for more intimate acts.

From the sounds of things, my little angel was feeling the effects as strongly as I was. I lowered the blanket to her stomach, feeling slightly disappointed at the thin material covering her. But the more she drank, the more the shirt tented up. I was having a similar issue, only more pronounced.

I lightly passed my free hand over the tents, enjoying the feel of them. I froze when my angel's hand landed on top of mine. I looked up quickly, but she was still out cold. Her hand was squeezing mine tight, so I squeezed her. Her hand released and moved away.

Someone was deep into dreamland, and this dream was starting off better than the one before.

I massaged her through that shirt, both her hands gripped onto the blanket, while her suction on me increased.

The spoiled prince in me needed more.

I slid my thumb under the rim, and over the tent stakes. The angel whimpered against me, her tongue sputtering. I moved the shirt all the way up, soaking in the sight before me, and continued without the shirt in my way.

I was putting myself in a right mess, but I didn't want to let go until she was done. Besides, it would help move my blood through hers faster, forcing the marking into place.

Soon a new scent bled through the air, along with her sigh, and her hands releasing their grip of the sheets. Her tongue did one last tired swipe and she released me, her mind and body falling into a much deeper sleep.

My tongue was salivating. She wasn't ready for my bite though, not yet. Not after what she had been through lately.

But the sleeping angel was deep enough now, that I should be able to get a small taste. And since she was so kind as to invite me to the area, I might as well enjoy it while I could.

Very carefully, I placed her head back on the pillows. I crawled to be partly over her and lowered my own tongue to her. The urge to bite was stronger than I anticipated. I was shaking with the battle against my inner demons.

Quickly, I unzipped my jeans and found another way to satisfy the demon inside. While I worked, her breathing increased, her hands flying up to hold my head. Her back arched as my teeth sank in, not quite breaking skin but deep enough to leave a mark on her. A mark even the humans would recognize the point of.

I pulled away, chuckling at the small whimper she made in her sleep. I laid by her side, enjoying the view until the sun started peeking through the curtains. I carefully, and regretfully, covered her again. Not caring about my own state of dress, I snuck out her door and back to my own apartment to catch a short nap.

I could go days without sleeping, but it was uncomfortable. And if trouble arose, I needed to have all my strength and wits about me.

And this woman was going to be trouble, lots, and lots of trouble.

CHAPTER 4

Carrie

I rolled over and stretched, pushing my butt into the air like a cat. I must have been exhausted last night. I couldn't remember the last time I slept that deeply. It was probably because I hadn't exactly slept much the night before. Or the one before that, on the bus.

The hot shower had been just what the doctor ordered. I almost didn't pack my own soaps, thinking maybe I would just shower with Bryce. I had never been a big fan of that Axe crap he used though.

My lavender and vanilla body wash did wonders for me. And I felt smooth.

I nearly slipped in the shower when I heard someone moving around in the apartment. I hurried up to get out, but he was already gone. I was pretty sure it was Deacon anyway, seeing as there was the biggest burger I had ever seen in my life, sitting on the table.

I ate every bite and refused to feel guilty about it.

My night had started out rough. I fell asleep nearly as soon as my head hit the pillow, and I landed right back in that bus station. Only this time I hadn't been outside when they came in. The dream got so real, I even tasted blood.

Obviously it was only a by-product of my dream. Unless I bit my tongue… and it healed already.

My mouth tasted normal, sort of. My throat didn't feel dry and scratchy after a long night of sleep. And it held a sweet aftertaste. Huh.

Oddly, the blood created a shift in my dreams. Deacon was there. He stepped between me and the vampires, and they just sort of disappeared. Almost like he commanded them to leave me alone. Then he was holding me. And… well, yeah.

Even if my high school boyfriend actually had done the deed, he must have been really bad at it. It was technically his first time too, obviously. But last night, dream Deacon made me feel things that the other idiot never had.

Even Bryce couldn't do so much with so little. I caved after a while and started taking my shirt off for him. Maybe if he had made me feel so good with just that, I would have caved to a little more. I would have loved for things to move further last night, in my dream.

I didn't know Deacon well enough for it to happen for real. Or, like, at all.

That thought made me pause as I rolled over to turn my phone on from where I had plugged it in the night before. I didn't know Deacon well, but in my own way, I knew he was a good man. There was something… more to him. I couldn't figure it out.

Last night he told that vampire in the alley that I belonged to him. I was pretty messed up at the time, but I didn't get the sense that he was lying. Or when he said that I was safe here. I believed him. Which was why I agreed to stay.

My phone started dinging like mad as soon as it was fully on. Clarise had blown up my phone with calls and messages. I laughed at myself for wondering if Bryce tried to call and check on me. He didn't. He was probably more worried about himself and his new little girlfriend. Well, up until they were killed anyway.

I really hoped the twins made it back to his apartment okay. I wanted to go check on them, but I worried I would run into that vampire out there again and lead him right to them. They were probably better off without me anyway.

I called my best friend, knowing she was more than likely climbing the walls.

"It's about dang time! Where the hell have you been?" She answered with a demand, telling me I was right, she was freaking.

"Girl, don't even get me started." I sighed and scooted back under the soft covers. Why did my chest feel sore?

"Uh, no. You have got to do better than that. I have been watching the news nearly nonstop since I got home on Friday. Please tell me you are alright. That you and Bryce are safe somewhere."

I huffed. "I'm fine, he's definitely not though."

Clarise gasped. "What happened?"

I groaned. "The douche has been cheating on me. For months. His boss's daughter was practically living with him. She even answered the door wearing the shirt *I* bought him."

"No! What did you do?"

"The same thing I should have done months ago. Seriously, why was I still with him? We both know I never fully trusted him."

She sighed. “I don’t know. I wondered that myself, from time to time. Maybe he was just something familiar. So, where are you now? Where have you been? Did you at least get out of California before all hell broke loose?”

I chuckled sardonically. “I spent the entire day sitting at the bus station. I was there when everything started blowing up, literally. The other night I started having one of my panic attacks, so I sat outside the back door.” I heard her gasp shockingly through the phone. “Girl, I know it was not the safest idea to do, but it saved my life. Not long after, these two guys came in, talking all sorts of crap. Then one bit someone on the neck.” Clarise gasped again. “Thankfully they never saw me. I waited hours until I decided it was safer inside then out. Even found a teenager hiding behind the counter. We spent the night and all day yesterday together. We got split up though when another vamp showed up. I insisted her and her sister hide while I led him away. They’re just kids. I had to protect them; ya know?”

“Of course.” She repeated.

“Anyway, I ended up in this dead-end alley screaming my lungs out for help, and this guy opened the back of his bar and let me in. I slept in one of the apartments above the bar last night.”

There was nothing but dead air, to the point I had to check my phone to see if I lost signal. “Clarise? Are you there?”

“I’m here.” Her voice sounded squeaky. “So, are you saying there really are vampires attacking Cali?”

I sighed. “No doubt about that, unfortunately.”

“What are you going to do? Where are you going to stay? How are you going to get home?” That last question came out a touch on the high-pitched side.

"Honestly, I don't know when I'll even be able to try and get home, not with all the freeways blown. Deacon has an empty apartment. He says I can work for room and board."

"Ooo, who's Deacon?" Seriously, all this end of the world drama, and Clarise still cooed over a new guy in the picture?

I rolled over and buried my head in the pillow. "He's the bar owner. The one that saved me last night."

"Is he cute? How old is he? Is he single?"

"Oh, my gosh, girl. You have got to chill out. I'm surrounded by bombs and vampires. Who has time for gorgeous men?"

She giggled. "So, he's gorgeous, huh?"

I groaned. "Fine, he's drop dead, change my underwear gorgeous. Happy?"

Like, seriously. I never cared for guys with long hair before, but Deacon really made it work for him. His long black hair was tied back the whole time, but still. It looked way hot.

"Good. you might as well have some fun while you are trying to survive. Have a rebound with him, get Bryce out of your system."

"Clarise, until further notice, he's my boss."

"So?"

I rolled my eyes. "Would you sleep with Mr. Sorenson?"

"Ew, no. But he's old and fat."

I couldn't help but laugh. I heard the front door open and close, so I figured that meant Deacon was back. It should bother me that he technically barged into my new apartment, but it didn't.

"Listen. I gotta go. Will you let the school know they are going to have to cover me for… I have no idea how long?"

I could hear her little pout. We met at orientation just two months ago and hit it off. She was like my best friend-soul mate. We were heads and tales different, but we balanced each other out.

"Fine. Promise to take care of yourself, and keep in touch with me, okay? I'd say send me your address so I can have the kids make you cards, but I don't see mail getting there anytime soon."

I sighed and sat up. "I don't either. As long as the phone lines stay up, I don't see a problem. But don't worry. I feel really safe here. Like, my kind of feeling, feeling. Ya know?"

It was weird how easy it had been to confide my weirdness to her. She was a big believer in tarot readings and astrological signs. I probably could have told her all the specifics about that vamp chasing me, I just didn't feel like getting into it right now.

"Good. That makes me feel a little better at least. Love ya, Car!"

"Love you too, Clare!" I teared up a little as I said goodbye to my friend.

I could hear movement in the kitchen, so I wiped my face and got out of bed. Deacon was in the small kitchen, cracking an egg over a frying pan when I walked out. In the light of day, I could see just how well he filled out his jeans and the black t-shirt he was wearing.

"Good morning." I announced myself, feeling a little shy. What do I say to this guy? Thanks for the awesome dreams?

"Morning, angel. How did you sleep?"

Angel? Was he one of those guys who forgets names easily, so he uses pet names to cover up for it? Or was he one of those guys that called all the women he knew pet names?

I walked over to the small table next to the kitchen and sat down. "Really good, actually. I knew I was tired, just not *that* tired. Guess that happens when you don't sleep for two days."

He gave me a curious look, his eyes lingering on my old ratty tank top and biker shorts. I get claustrophobic when I sleep, so I wear as little as possible. If I had been at home, I probably would have ignored clothes altogether. Odds were, once I adjusted to being here, they would disappear again.

"Why didn't you sleep for two days? Have you been scared with all the stuff going on?"

I laughed softly, tapping my fingers on the table. I might as well tell him, seeing as we were going to be spending a good deal of time together. I never thought it was fair to keep secrets when no one else could do it around me. This wasn't even that big of a deal.

"I didn't even know about most of this until the other day. I live in Phoenix. I took a bus up to visit my now ex-boyfriend, as a surprise, on Thursday night. I do not recommend it. It was disgusting and gross."

"What happened with him that made him an ex?"

I rolled my eyes to the ceiling, wishing I could smack myself. "He has only been living here for a few months, and he was already shacking up with someone else. I'm not even sure they made it a week. Whatever. I should have dumped his annoying butt a long time ago. I always felt there was something off. Now I know what it was."

Deacon poured the eggs on to a plate that already held toast and brought it over to me with one hand. His other hand carried a glass of orange juice.

"Thank you, you didn't have to do this, ya know." He just shrugged like it wasn't a big deal. "Aren't you going to eat something?"

Maybe it was a trick of the light, or a remnant of my nightmare, but I swear the whites of his eyes glowed and flashed to my neck.

He shook his head, his eyes closing for a short moment. "No. I'm not much of a breakfast person. I'll have someone pick up groceries for you today, that way you are covered. Unless you feel up to venturing outside to go shopping?"

Just the idea of it sent shivers down my spine. Vampires, raiders, and drones that shot people. Hell to the no.

"No. Thank you. You don't have to buy me groceries, I can pay for them myself."

He waved my comment away nonchalantly.

I ate in silence, not feeling as uncomfortable as I normally would have when I was the only one eating. It was hard not to feel comfortable around Deacon. Which was weird, but again, felt totally normal.

"I probably should make time to go shopping soon though. I only packed for the weekend. I don't have a lot with me."

Deacon stood up, a look of both amusement and bashfulness on his face. "I, uh, sent a friend of mine out to the store last night. He helps out at the bar when he is in town. I had him pick up a few things for you. Most of them are things for you to wear while we work. It didn't look like you had much with you. I hope you don't mind."

Deacon carried over a few bags, a large rectangular shoe box, and a smaller square one. My jaw dropped.

"You didn't need to buy me so much. The agreement was room and board, Deacon."

He tskd and shook his head, like it was the most ridiculous thing he'd ever heard. "Consider this a bonus. My bar isn't exactly normal."

I raised an eyebrow at this and carefully opened the bags. "Um. Are you sure this is the right bag? This looks more like a bag of spare material." I lifted up a piece of checkered material and spread it out in my hands, my eyes widening. Probably more than the skirt was capable of.

"I've already been through most of it. It's the right bag. He did throw in a few extras, like the shoes, and I think, um…" he cleared his throat awkwardly, sticking his hands in his front pockets. I was not naive enough to miss the growing problem he was trying to hide. "Underwear, I believe. Why don't you go get dressed? That way I have time to show you the ropes and such before we open for the lunch crowd."

Apprehensively, I carried the items to the bedroom. My nerves were having a party, making the boxes a bit harder to juggle with the bags, so Deacon helped. He set them on the bed and then quietly left the room. I opened the bags and dumped them on the bed.

This was scary. And maybe a little bit of fun.

Maybe I could live differently here. I wasn't the cop's daughter. I wasn't the kindergarten teacher. I wasn't Bryce's shadow of a girlfriend.

Here, I was a waitress in a bar. I worked for a man who could be a model. And he seemed to like me, I think.

I felt no vibes from him that said I couldn't trust him. The opposite in fact. Every vibe in the air said I was home. And it made me feel braver. More confident than I ever had before. Almost like I was finally finding me, the real me.

I pulled on one of the lace thongs, something new for me, and a strapless bra. Next, I pulled on a simple black mini skirt, it kind of reminded me of some of the skirts I wore to job interviews. Only a foot shorter, and a whole lot tighter. I topped that with the dark green top. It was like the baby sister to my new skirt. If it had been an inch wider and half an inch longer, it would have been the same size too.

I walked into the bathroom and checked out the new outfit. Not bad, even if I did say so myself. Just for kicks and giggles, I lifted my arms up. Sure enough, the top lifted to the very edge, my black bra showing just a bit. I then bent down and giggled again as I pulled the shirt back up.

Definitely going to have to act like a lady in this outfit.

I went back to the bedroom and opened the shoe boxes. The large one held a pair of tall black boots, the kind that zipped up to your knees. The smaller box held a pair of black strapless heels.

Not quite ready for a full day in three-inch heels, I pulled the boots on. They had a small heel to them, so in time, I would be used to it. I always wore my tennis shoes to work before. They were easier for chasing five-year-olds around a classroom, or a playground.

I didn't pack any makeup, I never cared much for that stuff. To me it was like lying to both you and everyone else. Bryce always said I didn't need it anyway. I brushed out my long blonde hair and redid the braid I slept in.

Taking a slow, deep breath, I returned to the living room.

Deacon was sitting at the table, looking at his phone. His eyes shot up when I opened the door, and his jaw dropped. Just for funsies, I turned a bit, and bent over, pretending to fix a zipper on one of the boots.

Out of the corner of my eye, I saw him shift in his seat, trying to fix his pants, again.

Score one for the new me.

CHAPTER 5

Deacon

Best decision I ever made. And possibly the worst. This angel looked hot as hell in that outfit.

"Well, how do I look?" Carrie raised her arms to the side and spun, presenting herself to me.

I wanted to unwrap that present and take it for a ride. Or have her take me for one. Either way would work for me.

She was giving me a knowing, and somewhat amused look. Right, I was supposed to say something. I probably looked like a teenage boy, seeing a real woman for the first time.

I didn't care. It almost felt like I was.

"You look…wow. Angel, you look…" Screw it. "You look sexy as hell."

She tipped her head back as she laughed, opening that luscious neck to me. It was a good thing there was still a table between us. Not that it was much of a hindrance to me, but still.

Her whole face was flamed in a blush when she looked at me again. I could feel the fire in my blood begin to boil from the need to taste the blood running through her veins. I stood and turned to push the chair back in, keeping her from seeing my burning eyes.

I didn't need to see them to know. I could feel the fire burning that ran through my own veins, which would ensure they were glowing. I barely caught it earlier before she noticed.

"We should head down, I'll be opening earlier than normal from now on, since most people will need to be home before dark."

She followed me to the door and took the arm I lifted. It wasn't something I had done in many years, or decades, but it felt natural to escort her like a princess. Even though she looked like a goddess.

"I have to be honest. This isn't what I was thinking of when you said uniform." She admitted to me softly as we made our way down the staircase, which was just wide enough for us to walk side by side.

"What did you have in mind?"

She shrugged self-consciously. "I don't know. Jeans and some kind of shirt."

If she was anyone else, it would have been just that. But I wanted to be able to see as much of her as possible, all the time.

"And it might be for some bars. We are going into hard times. People, men in particular, are going to come to try and escape. You, looking like this, might just keep my bar open. Sex sells, angel."

"I am not a hooker." She stated it so matter of factly that I had to laugh.

"No. And no one will be allowed to touch you either. They may try to flirt, but if they get too obnoxious with their comments, there will be consequences." I bit back on the possessive growl wanting to come through me.

It wasn't the first time this morning I felt that way. I listened in on her phone conversation earlier, not that I had to really work for it. As soon as I heard her mention her ex, I nearly lost it. Then when she explained that she dumped him for cheating on her, I wanted to kill him for hurting her.

She seemed over it already, but I was sure it had hurt when she found out. Mates weren't supposed to betray you. And they weren't even mates yet.

I led the angel on my arm toward the serving bar and sat her on a stool. "I don't expect too many people in this afternoon. Not after yesterday. Some will come, needing to get drunk and escape the world for a few hours, most will be at home, trying to make sense of their lives now. For the most part, I will have you waiting tables. This isn't a fancy restaurant, just ask what they want, write it down, and bring it to me. As the orders come in, I'll show you what to do. Times when we aren't busy, I will show you how to make their drinks. This crowd isn't all that creative. A beer, a shot of whiskey, bourbon, or scotch, and they are good. The cook mostly does burgers, wings, fries, and sometimes sandwiches. I will have to make changes based on what supplies are available to me in the near future."

I watched her, as she watched the bar warily. My angel was so far out of her comfort zone right now. It made me sad.

"Come here." I waved her behind the bar, and she slowly followed. I pulled down a shot glass and poured her a small amount of scotch. "Drink this."

"Oh, I don't really drink very often. A glass of champagne at parties, or a glass of wine with dinner. That's about it."

I took her hand and set the glass in it. "You need it to help steady your nerves. Especially when I get to the next part."

Her eyes widened as she realized there was still more, and she wasn't sure she could handle it. I could smell the panic rising in her again. I nudged her hand, hinting for her to drink. For someone who wasn't a drinker, she downed it like a pro. I set a bottle of water next to her. That one shot was stronger than what she was used to.

"Alright, hit me." She set the glass down roughly and I held back a laugh.

How to put this…

"For as long as I've been open, I have had a certain *type* of clientele at night."

Apparently that was enough. Carrie started stepping backward, her heart racing so fast I could practically feel the movement in the air. I grabbed her arm and pulled her closer.

"Let me finish. They used to stay hidden in the corner, but we both know they won't be wanting that anymore. I fully expect them to start piling in now. And they won't want to hide behind curtains." I started talking faster, seeing as this woman was on the verge of a panic attack. "I won't say they are on their best behavior while they are here, but they do behave better. You are safer in this bar, with me, than you are anywhere else in the state, possibly the world."

"Why?" The vulnerability in that one word nearly knocked my knees out from under me. Her fear was more dangerous to me than a silver dagger to the heart.

"Because, I have created a reputation for myself. So, to speak. I've been around for a while." The look in her eyes told me she knew I was skirting the truth. "I have a few humans who come in and work as donors. They get paid well for it. One of your jobs will be to make sure they have plenty of water and that they eat something while they are here. Every vamp knows they do not harm my donors. They belong to me."

"That's what you told the vamp last night." Her body tensed. I could feel Carrie wanting to pull her wrist out of my hand, but she wasn't. That was something.

"Yes. I claimed you. And before you freak out and run, you will *not* be donating or anything of the sort." Not to them anyway.

Her air turned to confusion, her body relaxing at the conviction in my voice. "How will they know I belong to you then?"

"That's easy, you will be here. With me." I stepped a little closer, bringing her next to me. "I will need to make it look like you are more than just my employee though. It will help keep you safe."

I struggled to fight back the grin when her eyes flashed to my lips. Naughty little angel. How did she make it this long while being so innocent?

"How will you do that?" Her voice was still soft, but the shake wasn't from fear, this time. The panic and fear in her blood was fading, something much sweeter overriding it.

"Just a few small touches in public. I'll keep them decent. I promise." For now.

One day, she will let me do more. I had no doubts about that. I put my hand on her lower back, her skin as smooth as it had been the night before.

"Things like this, or…"

I stepped around her, my hand sliding to her stomach as I went behind her. I leaned down and kissed her neck. I let the grin fly this time, since she couldn't see me, when her breathing stuttered.

"Little things that hint at something more."

Carrie cleared her throat and stepped away from me. I hated the feeling of her sudden absence, but I also didn't want to push it too much on her first day.

"Is that it then? Vamps will be coming in to feed from the donors. Do they drink or eat food?"

I placed an elbow on the counter and leaned on it, trying to not look like touching her affected me so much. Why the hell did it? She was far from the first woman that I have held in my arms, but she was the first that I missed.

"Some do. Some buy it for their donors. I told my donors last night to spread the word that I will need more. What you really need to prepare yourself for is the show."

Her head tilted slightly to the side, confused again. "Show? Like a band or something?"

I laughed and shook my head. "No, angel. The show is what *you* are about to get. Vampires don't care about privacy. They get a thrill from voyeurism." The angel grimaced. "Many prefer to play with their food while they feed, it helps the donor's body create chemicals in their blood. It changes the taste. It also helps the vampire get what they need. Their bodies don't create enough blood, or enough of the chemicals. That's why they feed. Of course, some are just gluttons, and are addicted to the taste of human blood."

Previously, I had always looked at them with distaste when they got addicted, but looking at this angel, I had a feeling I was about to experience that need firsthand.

"And your donors are willing to do that?" Her tone said she was only partially horrified by it. The rest was curiosity. She folded her left arm across that sexy stomach and braced her right arm on top. She began to chew on her thumb nail nervously.

"Only if they are willing. And they are paid extra for it." I waited while she processed everything.

I decided she needed something else to think about. And I needed that finger out of her mouth. I reached up and grabbed it, folding my fingers around hers.

I hadn't thought about it. I just did it. It felt right. Natural.

Carrie froze, then it was like her body sighed with relief. Not in a way that could be heard, and you could only see it if you were watching, which I was. I pulled her out of the room, not wanting to give these odd feelings any more thought.

I led her down a hall and opened a door. "This is the cellar. The storage room, I guess you could say." I led her down the stairs, into the basement I used. "Pretty much everything is down here. If we run out of anything this is where you get it." She pulled her hand out of mine and started walking around the room, looking at everything.

Just like earlier, my body felt her absence.

I cleared my throat, feeling uncomfortable with all these new and raw feelings, and pushed my hand through my hair, hoping to wipe away that disconcerting feeling, then tightened the band holding my hair back. When I left home, I stopped cutting my hair and trying to look the part of a royal. My father had been a stickler about appearances in front of our people. If we acted like all was right in the world, while bunking in caves, they would feel all was right. When everything was most definitely *not* all right.

"I'm going to head back up and get the place ready to open. Feel free to look around and familiarize yourself with all of it."

The human shift was barely half of what it would normally have been. Many humans were trying to find a way out of the city, maybe out of the state. So far, it was mostly the larger cities that were getting hit. The freeways were being bombed, as well as taking fire from drones, near the state lines.

Someone was trying to cut California off from the rest of the country. Curtis was sloppy, but effective.

We had enough customers that I was able to help Carrie practice behind the bar, and turn food orders into Mike, my cook. My favorite was teaching her to pour a shot. She wasn’t a complete ditz. I knew that she could have probably just poured it on her own. Even still, I insisted on standing behind her and helping her pour it.

And then kissed that aromatic neck again.

When she gave me a questioning look I just winked and told her the humans needed a warning too.

CHAPTER 6

Grace

"Where do you think they went?" Todd asked, kicking the knocked over kitchen chair.

I huffed, leaning against the wall, with my right leg bent to brace against it for extra balance. "Who knows? They are probably trying to get out of Cali like everyone else. Didn't you hear them last night? They believe the vamp rumors. I don't know how they think they are getting out though. All the freeways have been destroyed. They weren't exactly in the right shape to climb the mountains either."

I played with a shoulder length strand of my black hair and the awesome purple tips I gave myself last week.

We were all released early from school the day before, nobody wanted to stay when bombs were dropping around us. As soon as we got home, our foster parents forbade us from coming out of our rooms for the rest of the night.

I hardly slept last night because of the noise. They fought all the time, and not just with their words. Dick never laid a hand on Karen. He just threw things. Although sometimes I wondered if she might have been the one to throw things. They each had a temper on them.

From the looks of things this morning, they ran off in the middle of the night, leaving us to fend for ourselves.

"What are we going to do?"

I looked up at his odd question. Todd was your typical Cali boy; tall, skinny, blonde hair and blue eyes. And an idiot who thought the world revolved around him.

"We? Since when did it become a *we*? I've always been a *me*," I pointed one finger at my chest and then pointed at him, "and you've always been a *you*. Don't act like it's ever been anything different."

Todd grinned at me and stepped closer. "Awe, come on now, Gracey. We've had a little fun together now and then." He placed one hand on the wall next to my head, the other on my waist.

Sometimes I forgot how much taller he was than me. Thanks to my mom's side, I was barely five and half feet.

I snorted. "We've burned steam off, nothing more. Don't start acting like you've ever cared about me. I had an itch, and you had the only scratcher around."

Todd and I went to the same school for years. A school that looked down on foster kids. I was far from thrilled when I got put into this house with him, just a month or two shy of a year ago. He was kind to me one day, after a really awful day at school. I needed a break from reality for a few minutes. One thing led to another, and there you have it. After that, if I needed a break, or a release, I just knocked on his door.

Todd was a man-whore. Not that I was much better. Hell, my mother was a paid one.

As soon as I hit puberty she had one of those birth control implants shoved in me. She had dreams of us working together, going after father and son duos. Her favorite movie was *Heartbreakers*, where the mother and daughter were a con team. Unfortunately for her, her next client was her last, and I was in foster care by the end of the week. Cops never really told me what, or who, killed my mother. I may not be a genius, but I also wasn't stupid. I was sure it was one of her marks.

I wasn't going to get all therapisty and say Todd and I were the way we were because neither of us felt loved in our short lives, so we acted out in order to try and feel it. But it was logical.

"Doesn't mean it wasn't fun, Gracey." He deepened his voice, which sounded stupid.

Todd was okay looking, I guess. His confidence made up for what he was lacking, most of the time. His intelligence lacked too much for it to do any good there.

I just glared at him until he finally got the message. He lifted both hands in surrender and took two steps back.

"Look, we both know this place is going to hell in a handbasket right now. I think it's better if we stick together. Two heads are better than one and all that."

As he spoke, flashes went through my mind. This had happened to me enough times that I had mastered the art of keeping a blank face through it all. If my mother knew I had one, then she would try and use it to her advantage. It only took me a few times to realize that.

The first flash was of Todd and I, together. A lot. A lot, a lot. But it showed signs of being further down the road. The second was still of us both, only dead. In the clothes we were wearing now.

Only two options laid before us. Either we stuck together, or we both died. I wasn't sure where the specifics of what we were doing and why came into play. The important message was clear, if we wanted to live, we had to be together.

I sighed and leaned the back of my head against the wall. "Fine, we stick together. We can watch each other's backs."

He grinned and stepped toward me again. I raised my hand to stop him, not saying a word, just glaring at him again. Once again, he laughed as he moved away.

Just because the vision said it was going to happen, didn't mean we had to start the other part now.

I rolled my eyes at him, then dropped my foot and turned to walk to the living room. "I'm putting the news on. I want to know what's going on out there."

Todd quietly came and sat on the small couch next to me. I turned the old tv on, then pulled my feet up next to me, putting them between us. The only news channel that still worked was one of the major broadcasting networks that were stationed outside of our sunny, hellish, state.

We sat there for hours, watching the news cover different cities and towns all over California.

Occasionally, they showed clips of soldiers gearing up to come to our aid, firefighters and cops trying to put out fires (figuratively and literally), and even government officials debating how to respond.

At some point, Todd made us sandwiches. The only time I moved from the couch was to use the bathroom. It was all too surreal. I just couldn't take my eyes off the screen.

"We can see thousands of cars trying to take the smaller roads through the mountains, trying to escape from Sacramento. This same scene can be seen in all the major cities throughout California. Bombings have wiped out the freeways, major highways, and government buildings." The perfectly put together blonde reporter was saying.

"Look at them, are they even moving?" The man wearing a very bad toupee asked her.

The blonde's eyes scrunched as she looked at the video in front of her. "It doesn't look like it, does it?"

We watched with them, waiting to see any movement.

The sudden flash of light blinded us both, causing us to flinch back and cover our eyes. The small camera screen in the upper corner went black. A moment later, the reporters pulled themselves together, visibly shaking, and holding a finger to their ears.

"We are hearing from our chopper in the sky that what we just witnessed was in fact an explosion coming from the road. We are getting reports of similar explosions happening all over California."

The blonde didn't look so put together now. Nope, she looked like she was trying not to pee her pants. Even her makeup couldn't hide the paling of her skin.

Mr. Toupee broke in. "This just in, many of the bodies found in Northern California, from attacks over the last week, have been autopsied. What had once been thought to be the calling card of whatever gang is responsible looks to actually be the cause of death. As each body studied so far has been completely drained of blood. While no one wants to make it official, it seems like California is in fact being attacked by a horde of vampires."

The blonde began laughing hysterically, like she was about to lose it.

Todd and I both jumped when an explosion was heard not far off, the windows shook from the pressure, and all power in the house blinked off. In less than a second, it felt like we were thrown back into the stone age.

“Was that just the breaker? Or did Pinky and the Brain forget to pay the power bill again?” Todd asked, using the nickname he sometimes used for the loving and responsible foster parents we had the privilege to live with. The wife was short, fat, and cranky. Her husband was tall and skinny, and a complete airhead. It was obvious to see who wore the pants in that marriage.

I pushed off the couch and walked toward the front door. The sun was beginning to set, but the streetlights were not on. Todd came up behind me, putting one hand on my back, something I actually appreciated now. I was scared spitless.

Neighbors were on their front steps hollering to each other about losing their power. We could see smoke and flames riding in the sky from somewhere in the distance. Coming from a few different places. How much more could our poor city take?

Todd pulled me inside. “We need to lock all the doors and windows. Now.” Even though he was trying to sound firm, I could still hear a small shake in his voice.

We were both high school seniors, nearing the end of our incarceration in the foster system. Neither of us should have to be the ones calling the shots right now.

We split up and ran around the house to make sure everything was closed up tight. Afterwards, Todd grabbed my hand and dragged me into the master bedroom. It wasn’t much bigger than ours, but the bed sure was. We both had beds that were barely bigger than a cot.

“Why are we in here? This room has the biggest window.”

"Yes, but this window faces the backyard. Both of ours face the sides of the house. And I don't know about you, but I really don't want to be alone tonight." He put a hand up to stave off any remarks I would make. "I'm not saying we are going to be messing around, I'm just saying the comfort of someone else would be nice, that's all."

He made a good point. I nodded and sat on the bed. Todd climbed into the middle, leaning against the headboard. He put a hand up for me, inviting me to come closer. The stubborn part of me wanted to argue. The scared stiff and on the verge of a mental breakdown part took his hand and let him hold me.

Neither of us spoke for over an hour. I didn't know about him, but I had silent tears leaking out of me.

Todd put a hand over my mouth, smothering my scream, when we heard a window crashing in the house next door.

We listened as the family screamed, until they weren't anymore. The sound of deep laughter was growing closer, and another flash flew through my mind.

In the first one, Todd and I both became vampire food.

In the second, we didn't. The difference between the two was odd. But I didn't give it a second thought, as I was in no hurry to die tonight. I spun in my seat, straddling Todd, slamming my lips against his.

As a teenage boy, he reacted immediately. He was already ripping my shirt over my head.

Todd stalled as we heard someone jumping the fence to our yard. I grabbed his face and held it firmly, forcing him to look at me.

"Todd." I whispered. "Follow my lead, ignore them, just go with whatever happens. This is the only way we will survive." He opened his mouth to argue, I cut him off instead. "No! Just listen to me, I will explain how I know this later. But right now, you need to follow my lead." I kissed him again and forced out a smile. "Scratch the itch, Todd. Focus on that and nothing else. No arguing."

He nodded numbly, the voices becoming clearer as Todd rolled us to my back, making quick work of my jean shorts.

"Think we'll find any goodies here? Those last two left a sour taste in my mouth."

"I hope so. I don't mind a little fear once in a while, sour can be fun. But that's all we've had for days."

Todd started to pause as their shadows appeared in front of the window. I gripped him hard and pulled him, helping him where he was sadly failing. Understandably. I needed him to be sharp though. It didn't take much before he caught up to me.

"Hmm, smell that, Rick? I think we just hit pay dirt." One of the deep voices chuckled. "Think they'll let us join?"

Rick laughed. "Think we'll give them a choice?" The other laughed as his fist went through the window.

I held Todd against my lips, keeping both of us from screaming.

"Ooo, Rick. It's puppies. I've always wanted a pet. And look, they don't care about anything else going on." The other man whimpered like a begging child.

We heard the sound of broken glass being moved, and what sounded like someone climbing through a window. Todd and I both kept our focus on each other, not sparing the vampires a glance, trying to pretend they weren't there.

One of them ran a hand down the back of Todd's head slowly, moving down his back until he landed on his butt. Then he smacked him hard. I bit back the hysterical laugh when Todd rocked into me harder. The hand then came between us, moving along both of us, inspecting us.

"Ryley, we don't have time to play. We need to keep moving." Rick said, his voice not as sure as his words were. He wanted to play too, but someone had to stay on task.

We heard a zipper moving in the dark. "Just give me a few minutes, Rick. This won't take long. I can't tell you how much I love puppies. It's not fair that we aren't allowed to have a harem like Curtis and the others."

Todd barely held back the grunt of pain at what was going on behind him. It didn't take long before he was moving faster into me, all thoughts of the men in the room gone.

Either that or someone else was behind him moving him along.

"They have a higher rank, of course they get harems. Hurry it up. We don't want to get in trouble for being late." Rick sighed as Ryley was obviously not in any hurry. "Fine. I'll wait outside. Leave them alive and you can make them your little pets another day. No feeding though, you've already wasted enough time."

By the time Rick had gone through the bedroom door, checking out the rest of the house, Ryley was grunting and both boys slowed.

"Such a good puppy." Ryley cooed, petting Todd's head. He knelt down at our side, his pants still around his ankles. "You two stay right here, and I'll be back tomorrow. Maybe I'll be nice and bring you food. We won't tell anyone else. You can be my *secret* harem. It's not like I have any important information that you could overhear like the others." He rubbed his hand down my chest again, and then went lower. To where Todd and I were still connected. "Such a pretty pussy cat. Hmm. Yes. I'll be back. And I will take care of you." He leaned in and licked my chest, and then Todd's.

He was smacking his lips and humming happily as he walked out the door, finally putting his pants back on.

Todd started to move away, but I wrapped my legs around his thighs, rocking my hips. It wasn't time yet. They could still come back. We waited long enough to finish what we were doing, something that only biology could have been to blame for.

When we were sure they were long gone, Todd collapsed next to me.

"My butt hurts." He complained, making us both break into a short burst of laughter.

He pulled me into his arms, and I cried. I was pretty sure I felt tears falling on my head too. Soon enough, we both fell asleep.

I woke up the next morning, the sun brighter than it normally would be as it shone through the broken window, the curtains still moved to the side. Todd was already awake, he looked like he hadn't gotten much sleep. I pushed away, sitting up.

"Care to explain what happened last night?"

"Not really, no." I stood, stretching my stiff limbs.

"You said, if I followed along and didn't say anything, you would tell me." His voice was accusatory. Probably thinking of what happened to him the night before because he followed my insane plan.

I pulled my t-shirt over my head and turned to face him, my hands on my hips. "Look. As crazy as it sounds, what we did, saved our lives. You heard them talking last night. What that vampire did to you was better than draining our blood until we were dead."

While I was talking he turned his body to face me, all his teenage glory out in the open. "You think they were vamps?"

I pinched the bridge of my nose before looking at him again. "I don't know what to think. For now, I'm going with that."

"How did you know that would save us though? Have you dealt with vampires before?"

I sighed and sat back down on the bed, might as well get this over with since we were going to be together for a while. At least according to my vision.

"I get these flashes, kind of like visions of the future. Only, they come in like twos or threes. Like they are potential futures or something. The future isn't set in stone, our decisions change it every day, every minute. Last night, when we heard them coming, I got two flashes, one where they bled us dry and the other where they didn't. I chose door number two, obviously."

When he didn't say anything back, I headed into the master bathroom. One look at the huge tub - well it was bigger than ours at any rate - and I knew what I was doing that morning.

I had only been soaking for a few minutes when the bathroom door opened. I sprang forward, holding my knees to my chest.

"Knock much? What the hell are you doing in here?" I yelled at him.

Todd didn't even close the door behind him, he just strolled forward, still not dressed. He didn't answer me until he was stepping into the tub.

"Move up a little. I need this more than you do. I earned it after last night."

I started with a small laugh at first, and then broke into full laughter. Todd said it with such a straight face, and he was right. As soon as he was down, he pulled my chest to lean me against him.

"I don't know what you are trying to hide. I've already seen it all, a few times now."

"Shut up." I elbowed him in the ribs and let myself relax against him.

We let the hot water melt away some of our fears and stress in silence. The water was nearly cool when he spoke up.

"What do we do now, Gracey? Are we staying and waiting for him to come back, so we can become his little pets?"

"I don't really know. I've been thinking about that all morning." Well, the half hour or so that I'd been awake anyway.

"Well, what do your visions say?"

"Wow, you're accepting that pretty good." I had never told anyone before. I was already labeled a freak because of my foster status. I didn't need another one.

"Well, the way I figure it. Your little psychic thingy probably saved our butts…no, saved our lives. My butt was not saved, my butt was sacrificed." I worked to stifle the giggle at his indignation. "If vampires are real, then I figure your little psychic visions are too." I felt his shoulders shrug behind me.

"They don't really work like that. They mostly come on their own. I'm working on calling them, but I'm not very good yet. I've mostly been practicing during exams, like when I didn't know an answer."

"Ok, well. What do you do that brings them up then?"

I thought about it carefully, wanting to make sure I did this right. "I think about the path laid before me, and my options."

"Alright, so let's start with that. Option one, stay here and become vampire pets. Which probably means he is going to be drinking from us once in a while. Unless once is all they can do and then we are dead."

"He did say he'd bring us food, too. That means we won't starve."

"True. He also called us his own personal harem. What was that all about anyway?"

"Um. A harem is a group of like concubines or something. So, I think the boss vampires have their own harems. People they probably feed off and do other things too. They are always there. I imagine it's like a status thing with them. Only the higher up ones have their own. Ryley said we wouldn't be hearing anything important. I wonder if that means harems are chosen like a job thing, humans they know won't tattle on them to other people."

"Alright. So, option one is to become this guy's pets, his secret harem, and have food, and stay off the streets. Option two, is… to what?"

"Option two is to leave here, find somewhere else to stay, and pray we don't get killed by someone else."

"Yes, but now we know what will keep them from killing us." I smacked his wandering hand that he tried to demonstrate with. "Hey, get used to it babe, it's you and me against the world. We ain't got no one else." He leaned down into my ear, continuing softly. "Besides, you know you like it."

"Shut up." I grumbled, trying to hide the smile at his playfulness.

I didn't stop his hand from moving up the next time, he only held onto me. A bit possessively too if you ask me.

"Do we have any other options? Cause, neither of those sound good to me."

I closed my eyes and steadied my breathing, as close to meditating as I could get in a shared bathtub, focusing on one option or the other.

If we stayed, we'd be turned into Ryley's personal feeding trough. He would get all the benefits along with it. I also saw him failing at his promise to bring us food, at least not bringing enough for us to live off.

The other option bubbled up in my mind, a shelter, groups of people. I could sense a path that led from there. A third option we hadn't yet considered. One that led to a large house, with an evil looking man, and groups of humans. I saw myself with a purpose. I saw war. A large one.

"The first option does not look good. Ryley will not provide us with enough food. The next leads us down a long path. We find shelter, and food. We will find more friends and take them on this journey with us. We travel somewhere with them. To a larger house. And there will be a war. What we decide will affect the way the war turns. I can't see all the details, there are too many decisions that need to be made first."

"Option two, for now, it is then. Until we figure out option three."

"I think option three is going to be us creating our own harem. I think we can use it to spy on the big bad. Yes, I see it more clearly now." I closed my eyes tight, focusing. I saw a cell phone in my hand, one I hid under a mattress. "We can get close to the vamps in charge. We can spy, we can send information back to the good guys." I didn't have a cell phone, so I had no idea how that was going to come about.

Todd held tighter, not in a search of pleasure, it was his reaction to the unknown, and him trying to stay strong for me.

"We don't know who they are though. We don't even know who the big bad is."

I sighed and rotated to my side, laying my head on him. Forcing visions was tiring. “That part of the path will reveal itself as we go along.” I yawned and felt his other hand move up and down my arm. Todd really wasn’t so bad. I was kind of glad he was on my side.

“So, what you’re saying is that my butt better get used to being sore before all this is over?”

I giggled tiredly at him.

“Yes.” I patted his chest softly. “And accept the fact that you may be the one hurting someone else’s too. And doing a whole lot of things you never dreamed of… unless you did. No judgment.”

He pinched my butt and I yelped, jumping away, splashing water out of the tub. After laughing at me, he sighed.

“I guess someone has to do all the dirty work to clean this mess up. Might as well be us.”

I barely hummed in agreement as I fell asleep on him. I woke up an hour later, back in the big bed. Todd was in the kitchen, packing up whatever he could find.

CHAPTER 7

Carrie

I stood quietly behind the serving bar, staring out the window along the front wall, not far from the main entrance, watching the sun go down. It had been nearly an hour since Deacon suggested all the human customers go home. Even Mike said he was out.

Deacon mumbled something about needing to hire a Vampire cook now.

My focus was so intense, that I jumped when a warm hand touched my bare back.

Over the last few hours, I adjusted to wearing the outfit. It had been the common opinion that I looked hot - among the afternoon customers anyway. My confidence was doing better than ever, not one of them had lied or been trying to get anything from me. They were just stating a fact. They were all surprisingly easy to read. My powers seemed more solid today than they had the day before.

“Hey.” Deacon said softly. “It’s going to be alright. I promise.”

"You don't know that. You don't know how many of them have killed my family members over the years."

Deacon's hand, which had been moving up and down, trying to soothe me, stalled at my comment. "How long have you known of… their existence?"

There it was again, the tingling that he was skipping information. I still felt safe with him though. It didn't feel like deceit when he was lying or walking the line between honesty and truth. I wasn't exactly telling him everything about me either, so I was going to have to trust that what he was hiding was for his own protection and trust issues.

If anyone could understand trust issues, it was me.

I shrugged. "My family has always believed in the supernatural. I stopped listening to the stories when I was younger. The deaths were always ruled as unsolvable, or unexplainable. It's tradition for my family to look for the bite marks when we identify bodies. My dad was a cop, the coroner was a friend. He let us."

Deacon hugged me from the side, placing a soft kiss on the side of my head. I swear he was sniffing me again. He must really like the smell of lavender and vanilla. Although they had to be wearing off by now.

Booms went off rapidly outside. The windows shook and the bar was suddenly cast into pure darkness. The power went out. I let out a very unlady-like screech and turned to Deacon, letting him hold me completely.

"Sh, now angel. You're safe with me. Deep breaths. I have a generator, a couple actually. Just give it a minute and one will switch on."

I nodded and whimpered into his chest, my hands next to my head, his arms wrapped tightly around me.

We both waited in the quiet darkness.

I had to blink a few times when the lights did come back on. It was a bar, it wasn't like we had a ton of lights on in the first place but compared to the pitch black of the room the moment before, the sun might as well have come back up.

"See? All good." I just nodded again. I didn't move away. I was too busy shaking in my boots. "Tell you what. Why don't you stay behind the bar tonight? I can take care of the tables until you get used to them being here."

I finally turned my head to look at him. I tipped my chin up, placing it on his chest. The top of my head came to his shoulders, so this move put him awfully close to my lips. He looked down, his eyes glancing between my lips and my eyes.

"You sure you don't mind?" I didn't think I needed to mention that I was shaking… badly. He could probably feel it.

He licked his lips as they moved again. "Yeah. Anything you need, angel."

"Why do you keep calling me that?" I hadn't meant to ask that, but it had been nagging me on and off all day.

He laughed. His right hand lifted and began tracing a line under my bottom my lip. "Because when I first saw you last night, the light from the bar, and your beautiful hair made the most exquisite little halo over your head. You looked like an angel."

I only heard about half that, my eyes were slowly closing as his thumb worked its way back and forth. I couldn't see him, but I could feel his breath as he got closer to me. It was warm, just like the rest of him.

I felt something wet and hot softly gliding over my lips.

A low moan escaped me, and shivers ran through my body. These were much better than the scared ones I had a moment before. No sooner had the moan left me, then his lips met mine with force, like that little sound had cut the net holding him back.

I let my arms slide up and wrap around his neck, his arms tightening around my back and shoulders. One of his hands gripped my butt and held it tight. I was more focused on the heat of the tongue melting me from the inside, then I was to his warm hands. Bryce always had cold hands. I had never kissed a guy who was literally hotter than the rest.

Everything else in the world faded away except for him and me.

Deacon lifted my thigh, and I wrapped it around his leg as he spun us, putting my back to the counter. With my leg up, I felt even more of him. My body was screaming to feel it without the barriers, something I had never done with anyone since that first night, when my parents died.

I didn't know if I would have let him, my ability to think clearly was long gone. Enough so that I jumped when I heard a loud voice.

"Well, well, look who finally got a girl of his own." It was a loud deep voice, followed by a few chuckles and giggles.

Deacon pulled away laughing, maybe at them, maybe at the blush on my cheeks and how I buried my face in his shirt.

"Yes, and no one is allowed to touch her. If anyone asks tonight, make sure you tell them she is not on the menu."

"You got it, boss. Hey, how do you have lights? Half the city lost power half an hour ago."

The footsteps all moved closer, and I moved my leg back down, mentally telling myself to get it together.

"Generators. You know me, I'm prepared for anything." Deacon shrugged. He looked down at me and winked. "Guys, this is Carrie. She is going to be helping out. If you need anything, let her know."

I turned slowly, still feeling the blush heating my cheeks. There were about half a dozen people standing there. I gave a small wave, my voice not quite working yet. Deacon seemed to find it funny. He wrapped his arms around me from behind again, as though it was something he had been doing for years and not hours.

"Angel, these are tonight's donors. Carl, Chelsea, Katelyn, Ethan, Mona, and Lucy. As I'm sure you all already know, the humans won't be coming out at night anymore. Which means, no curtains. The vamps are free, they don't want to hide what they are or who they are. For them that includes living in the moment. No privacy. We're going to be more open about things too. If you are open to more than just blood, lose the shirt. Or tie it up for you girls if you want."

Lucy and Mona left their shirts on and tucked in. Everyone else's shirts were either taken off or manipulated to be barely there.

"When you are done, just let me or Carrie know. We will be keeping your money divided up all night, so it will be easy for you to go. We are going to be outnumbered, so make sure you pay attention to how many vamps used you, and for how long."

He let go of me with one hand, reaching under the counter, and pulled out a small box. He opened it and handed the items out to each donor.

"These are stopwatches. I won't be able to use just one timer anymore, and I'd rather not run the risk of you getting hurt. Set it for how long they paid for. When it beeps, tell them time is up. If they refuse, call me, or wave a hand, or do something to get my attention. I don't expect tonight to be too full, but in time, it will be. If your friends talk about needing work, tell them to come. We are going to need more donors, a lot more donors. If it helps them sleep at night, remind them that the more the vamps use donors, the less they are out hunting. If they are hunting, the demon inside takes control. Hunters rarely leave someone alive."

He spoke to them for a few more minutes, but stopped as a few men trickled in. They looked tired and haggard.

"Deacon!" One yelled.

The donors split to take their seats along the bar as I saw a man who kept his hair shaved close to the scalp, making it hard to discern the color. He was rough looking. He approached Deacon from across the bar and shook hands with him.

"Carter! It's been a long time. How are you doing?" Deacon was smiling as he greeted him. Maybe he wasn't a vamp but an old friend. Maybe even an old donor. "Last I heard you were in New York."

Carter laughed. "I'm good, man. I was. Man, the nightlife there was always *popping*. I heard the word about Curtis moving on Cali, I had to come and see for myself." He lifted both arms and spun in a circle, taking a deep breath. "Freedom smells lovely, doesn't it?"

Definitely a vamp then.

He sniffed again, checking for something he almost missed, and then his eyes landed on me. His grin grew. "Lovely indeed."

I squeaked, as his eyes began glowing, and jumped behind Deacon.

Deacon put a hand up to stop Carter, a warning. "Not on the menu, Carter. She's mine." A low growl sounded from Deacon, and just like before, I felt the truth of his statement. I belonged to him.

Well, he believed I belonged to him anyway. And I was kind of beginning to be okay with that.

I looked around Deacon's side, curiosity getting the better of me. Carter's eyes were wide with shock. Probably not used to a human standing up to him. Even though Deacon didn't feel like a human, he didn't feel like a vampire either.

"Are you claiming someone, Deac?" Carter sniffed again. This time his grin was more like the kind you got when you were happy for someone. "Look at that, you are. Well, good for you. I'm a little jealous, though, she smells divine." His voice went deep again, and his eyes, which had faded, sparked back up.

"No! Carter, you know what will happen if you do it. I won't hesitate, you know I won't. Doesn't matter how long we've been friends."

Carter shook his head, clearing it. His eyes were actually a pretty dark blue. When they weren't creepy headlights.

"Sorry, man. We've been working a lot. Curtis has had us collecting rubble from the buildings and all those abandoned cars on the roads. The only blood I've had in the last week has been sour. It was fine the first few times, but I need something more."

Deacon's stance relaxed, one of his hands sliding to mine, supporting me. "Take your pick. Might I suggest a testosterone boost?" Deacon pointed at Ethan and Carl.

Carter walked in front of them, eyeing and sniffing them carefully. "Prices same as before?"

Deacon nodded his head. "40 for every ten. Unless you want more than just blood. Then it's 100 for every ten."

Carter nodded and pulled out a hundred-dollar bill. He handed it to Deacon, then tapped Carl's arm before pointing at a table.

A few more vampires walked in, and I listened as Deacon talked prices and donors like he was selling cars. I looked up at Carter and Carl once, then decided I should not look at the tables anymore.

Carl was sitting on the table, facing out, while Carter stood in front of him. His fangs in Carl's neck, and his hand was working Carl out where everyone could see everything. At least that was something I could say I had seen before, sort of.

Bryce tried to tempt me a few times by walking around naked, touching himself. It always annoyed me. It also convinced me to stop sleeping over at his place.

Again, why was I with him for so long?

Deacon always found it funny when my eyes accidentally strayed. I didn't know if it was the kiss, or because he was making a statement, but he was never near me and not touching me.

A few others asked about me, each time getting a low growl from Deacon. He must have learned how to deal with them after all these years of working with them. It was working too.

I stayed behind the bar, only having to pour drinks every now and then. I gave water to the donors every time they came back. Over time, they trickled out.

We didn't have too many vampires, but Deacon said it was still more than normal. We maybe had a dozen, they hung out and talked with friends before or after they fed. If it wasn't for the donors, they would have seemed like humans.

Well, mostly. I did feel like I was going to go blind when I caught a few "handling business" either on their own or together. No donor needed.

Deacon came up behind me and kissed my cheek after walking the last donor out, locking the door behind them.

"How are you feeling?"

I smiled. I could feel his sincerity all the way to my bones. The same way I felt with his touch all night. He wasn't faking anything. He wanted to touch me. He wanted to kiss my neck or hold me against him. It still felt right having him there, so I didn't mind in the least bit.

I knew he wasn't telling me the whole truth when he talked about making a claim in their eyes. I just had to hope his desire to be near me was all he was trying to hide.

"Better than I thought I would be, actually. Besides drink preferences, and their manners, they aren't much different than the humans were. In here at least. Out there…" I trailed off as I remembered the bus station from a few nights before.

Deacon was still standing to my right side, so I laid my head on his chest, and he put a hand on my shoulder.

"Yes, they have it in them to be somewhat civilized. Humans have done quite a few violent acts in the name of war and whatever other reasons they had as well."

I frowned. I didn't like him defending the vampires. I also couldn't argue. Humans could be just as evil.

"What's their reason then?" I snapped at him, lifting my head to look in his eyes.

He put a hand to my cheek, trying to soften his words. "They are tired of hiding. For centuries they have had to live in the shadows, not free to be who they are. Not free to live. I'm not saying they are going about it the right way, or that I agree with them. But this is no different than any other revolution."

I wasn't sure how I felt about this. Technically, he wasn't wrong. I was sure there were many people in other countries who had lived like this for years. Raids, fighting, war. I could also feel he wasn't trying to placate me by acting like he didn't agree. He didn't agree but he understood.

I also found it incredibly difficult to be mad at him when he was so close to me. Why did his presence, his touch, soothe me like this?

"Let's get upstairs and get you to bed. We can clean all this up in the morning."

As if on cue, I yawned, and then laughed.

I let him lead me up to my apartment. I turned at the door to say goodnight, but the words never made it out of my mouth. He swiftly pressed me against the door, attacking my lips.

I was severely tempted to take him inside with me, but that wasn't me. I had already stepped way out of my comfort zone enough for one day. I pulled away, trying to catch my breath. Deacon started kissing down my jaw line, making it hard to stick to my guns. His fingers were barely under the bottom of my shirt, playing with the rim of the bra.

I whimpered and pushed him back. "Goodnight, Deacon."

He was disappointed, that much was obvious. But he didn't complain, he didn't push. He gave me one more soft kiss and said goodnight before stepping away. I closed the door behind me, then leaned against it.

Ho. Ly crap! That was hot.

I didn't fight the grin. No one was here to see it. I didn't fight back the teenage squeal building up inside of me either. A long hot shower was definitely needed to help me calm down.

Which also happened to be when I found a strange bruise on my chest. Obviously, I knew it was a hickey. Bryce had been quite fond of leaving those.

But how in the hell did I get a hickey on my chest? The only action this part of my body had seen in months was in my dreams last night.

Did that have something to do with this new power I was experiencing?

Completely ridiculous idea, but nothing else made sense right now.

I really missed my mom.

It took me forever to fall asleep, I couldn't stop thinking about Deacon, and how easily he backed off. Or how much I knew he was already growing to care about me.

There were definitely perks to my little gifts.

CHAPTER 8

Deacon

I underestimated the strength of her blood. My angel's blood was like a siren to vampires. It sang to them, calling them closer. My mark on her barely made a dent. If I hadn't made it physically obvious, there would have been more of an issue tonight.

Not that I was complaining. I would never dream of complaining about touching her. Holding her. Kissing her.

That last one had not been part of the plan, not yet at least. I hadn't expected her to respond so easily to me. Or for it to feel so… I didn't know what.

Would I sound like a human female if I said it felt right? Would I care?

I showered and then paced in my room. I let my mind replay the night as I waited for her to fall asleep.

Carter said they were collecting rubbish. I talked to a few of the others. They were doing shifts. Some worked in shadows during the day, collecting what they could. Some worked nights. They all piled everything into large trucks that were being taken to the state line.

Carter was building a wall out of things from the city. It seemed as though Curtis planned to keep California. Which meant he would start backing off on killing the humans. He had too. If he didn't, he would be killing off their food supply.

We more than doubled our usual clientele tonight. My donors pushed it. I forbade any of them to come in for the next week. They promised to start sending more help. Many people lost their jobs, lost the breadwinners in their homes. The people in the city, at least, would need to find a way to make money.

If I knew Curtis as well as I thought I did, and I did, he would have left the more rural towns alone so they could keep growing the food that the humans would need. He effectively turned back the hands of time. He was taking us back to the time period he was created in.

A time when vampires ran their own kingdom.

I wasn't born until it had all been destroyed because of one male betraying his mate. A witch.

Never betray a witch.

Especially when they were your mate.

I sighed with relief when I heard my angel's breathing deepen and slow through the wall. It had been nearly two hours since I left her at her door. It wasn't easy backing away like I did, I was ready to lift her up and carry her to bed. But she wasn't ready for that.

This was why she was still so pure. She knew how to say no. I couldn't push her. I needed her to be willing. I needed her body to not fight my seed. I needed her to be equal in what I wanted to do to her. Part of me screamed for her willingness for a different reason. One I did not understand.

I quietly slipped into her bedroom, and stood at the side of the bed, watching her sleep. Even in her sleep, she still looked like an angel. Even without the light.

I couldn't wait any longer to be near her, so I stripped off all of my clothing this time, knowing I was going to have to do more. She needed to be completely covered in my scent. We needed to make it stronger. It couldn't just be running through her veins. It needed to be more obvious, less subtle. I was glad she had already showered. It would last longer that way.

I lifted the blanket just enough, as I didn't want the cool night air to wake her. I had turned the generator off when I locked up. I wanted to save the battery for as long as possible. I had a separate generator just for the fridge and freezer in the bar kitchen and the apartment kitchen. With only those things on it, it should last a while.

As for heat, the fire running through my veins would help to keep her warm at night.

This also meant I had a deadline for bringing her around to my side. She was going to need my heat during the long winter nights. With the power lines destroyed - which I believed was one of Curtis' ways of cutting the humans off from the rest of the world - we would have no heat.

I carefully raised her head again, sliding my arm under her neck. She purred like the good little kitty she was and curled into me. My reaction was immediate. With her as drawn to me as I was to her, I would be meeting that deadline very soon.

Carrie had a stubborn streak though, so I shouldn't get my hopes up too soon.

I bit into my left wrist again and held it over her mouth. She flinched away when the first drop hit.

“Drink, my little angel. Drink it so I can protect you. Drink it so you can become one with me. Drink it so you can be *mine*.” I really needed to get control of the growling thing. I just couldn't help it. The idea of anyone trying to take her away turned me into an animal, making me act more like the Nightwalkers, than my own people.

At the sound of my voice, her lips spread, and she locked onto me. With every swallow she became more and more greedy. I was trying too hard to keep my laughter quiet - loving that she craved my blood - so much so that I was shaking the bed.

Just like the night before, my blood pushed her into a coma-like sleep.

I hadn’t spoken to many who had marked a human before, so this was new to me. All I did know about the effect our blood had on them was that it increased whatever they were feeling at the moment. In moments of pleasure, it made them hungry for more.

Maybe, when she was tired, it helped her sleep better.

If she felt peace in my presence, a calming one like she did to me, maybe it would give her a more restful sleep. Or maybe I was just a prideful SOB.

All equally likely scenarios.

Even in her deep sleep, she still pouted when I removed my hand from those angelic pillows on her chest. I slowly slid my body over her soft skin. Her legs moved of their own accord, making room for me. It was a good thing she was wearing those tiny shorts again. They would serve as a reminder of where I could not go. Yet.

I let my natural instincts take over just enough, my nose lowering to her chin, bringing in her sweet aroma. It blended so perfectly with her body wash. I licked her neck softly, then pulled a small piece of skin in, sucking on it.

Her fingers found my hair, and she began to move under me.

Perfect. She was helping me prepare her blood just the way I liked it.

My hands coasted over her again, building her up higher. I gave a little too much to my instincts, as my hand went lower than I planned. The dopamine in her blood spiked to all new levels, giving me a high just from sniffing it.

I left two perfect marks on her neck before I finally let my fangs sink in. She even tasted like heaven.

My angel made all the right sounds, she moved in all the right ways, pushing against my fingers just right. I barely caught myself from tearing her shorts away and finishing this the way we both desperately needed.

I released her neck and licked it, healing the wounds. This was one of the few blessings we gave to humans. It also helped hide who we were. I was shocked when she said her family always had the marks left behind. That was usually only done as a warning. A sign. Or the vampire had just been careless, possibly in a crazed state.

Her family had always been hunted for some reason. If they shared her blood, I could understand why.

I lifted her butt and pulled her shorts down enough for me to see the last bit of her. Just as perfect as the rest. A little red, but I hadn't exactly taken it easy on her. I teased us both, causing her to whimper in her sleep. Then picked up where I had left off until I was able to physically cover her in my scent. I rubbed it all over her waist and below, nearly setting myself off again.

With my mission completed, I laid next to her again, pulling her against me. I slept lightly, making sure I would awake before her. When I felt her breathing begin to change, I kissed her neck one more time, and then left.

I was already back in her kitchen, making sure she heard me like the day before, when she came out. She was still in her night clothes, which were a bit off center, thanks to me. And her hair was messy.

“Good morning.” She yawned, her arms stretching above her, lifting her shirt to show me the stomach that would one day carry my son. “So, is this going to become a regular thing? You sneaking in and cooking breakfast?”

I laughed. “Yes. Why? Is that a problem?”

I leaned against the entryway to the kitchen and folded my arms. I was challenging her to say something. It was my job to take care of her, I could feel it deep in my soul. Well, the part I was born with anyway.

She shook her head with a small laugh. “Fine, but you have to eat with me. I don’t like eating in front of people, especially when I am the only one.” She blushed.

My angel had some self-confidence issues, as well as trust. I wondered if it was only because of the idiot she had recently been dating or if it had been accrued over time.

I played along, like it was such a hardship. “Fine. Twist my arm.”

She laughed again and walked closer. My arms just opened of their own accord, and she snuggled into me, like we did this every day. Like she had been with me for decades, not days. I brushed my thumb on her cheek, and she purred again.

“Did you sleep well last night?” I asked her. I knew she had, at least from my point of view.

I felt her cheeks heating against my skin.

"Yes. That bed must be magic or something. I've slept better here than I have in years."

My vote was for the or something. She always slept more peacefully after I marked her. I kissed the top of her head, inhaling as much as I could of her. My scent was stronger today.

"Good. I would hate for you to be scared in here all alone." I looked down and grinned at her. "Although, if you ever do get scared or lonely, I'd be happy to join you."

She gave me a playful scowl and poked me in the ribs. That wasn't a no. I laughed at her and kissed her lips softly. Just once. I was finding it easier to behave myself this morning. I wasn't sure why I felt calmer.

"Are you hungry? I just finished making French toast. Mike went shopping yesterday for the bar, so I had him pick up a few things, for up here."

It wasn't so much shopping as scavenging he said. He told me all about the drones monitoring humans. As long as they behaved, they were safe. Anyone not behaving was shot automatically.

Curtis didn't want them killing each other off.

My angel smiled wide, very happy. "French toast is my absolute favorite food in the whole world!" She even started bouncing in my arms from excitement.

I couldn't resist and kissed her again.

"Then I will have to make sure I make it for you often." I pulled away and swatted her butt. "Sit. I'll bring it to you." She yelped when I hit her and walked quickly to the table.

"You said the other night that you were a Kindergarten teacher?" I carried two plates to the table, having made extra for me in case she asked again. Never eating in front of her was bound to set off alarms in her head. While my body didn't dispose of things the way humans did, my fire would burn it away within a few hours.

Her grin at my question was obvious, she must have enjoyed that job.

"Yes. It was all I ever wanted to be. I always liked helping with the little kids and babysitting as I got older. Since my parents wouldn't let me work part time jobs after school, people usually brought their kids to me. Most of the time they were family friends anyway."

"How long have you been teaching?"

We hadn't broached the age subject yet, something I was loath to do. I would have to lie flat out if she asked. No human reached the age I had, especially looking as young.

Her smile slipped. "This was my first year. I just finished my credential in the Spring. The school I did my student teaching at hired me to take over for a teacher who was retiring."

Still very young then. I had assumed as much. At least she wasn't a teenager anymore, she was a full-grown adult. I waited until she finished with the bite before asking my next question.

"Have you always lived in Phoenix?"

She nodded as she answered, sipping the milk I gave her today. One way or another, I would make sure her body stayed healthy. Especially if I was going to have to feed from her every now and then.

"Yes. When my parents got married, they bought a piece of land just outside of Phoenix. No trees, not even a cactus came near our house. "

I smirked. "No shade for anyone to hide in. The sun was your protection."

Carrie pointed her fork at me. "Exactly. They left it to me when they died. Up until a few days ago, I still lived there. Just because I stopped listening to their stories didn't mean I pushed all their teachings away."

They had protected her well, I wanted to ask what happened to them, but I sensed it was still a sensitive subject.

"Have you always wanted to own a bar?"

I kept my grimace internal. I knew she would turn some of these back on me.

"Yes and no. I roamed for a while with a friend of mine. When we came to Los Angeles, I worked here with the old owner for a year. When he decided to retire, I made him an offer and he took it. He flew off soon after to Florida, where his grandkids were. I haven't regretted it since. Colton, my friend, still comes around from time to time, helping out."

She gave me a playful grin. "Is he the one I have to thank for my lovely uniform?"

I barked out a laugh. "Yes. I will admit, I told him what to buy, he just had fun while on the errand." Before she could ask anymore, I cleared our empty plates. "Why don't you go get ready, while I clean up." It was more of a command, then a suggestion. But I did it nicely enough.

"Alright." She stood and kissed my cheek. "Thank you for breakfast. It was wonderful."

"Anything for you, angel."

She blushed and disappeared into the room.

I listened carefully, crossing my fingers she didn't shower again. My scent was still on her skin, which not only heightened the warning to the others but seemed to calm me at the same time.

We had very few laws that everybody held. The one to keep our secret obviously meant nothing to some. But the other two were non-negotiables. They held heavy consequences. The first was the protection of a human we marked and claimed as our own. This extended to my employees, just not on the same level. If another vampire were to lay harm to someone I claimed, it was my right to kill them. Only once did I have to act on this.

In the mid 80's, a female nightwalker attacked one of my donors after hours. She bled my donor dry. She never got to taste another drop of blood again. Colton and I tied her up and left her in the middle of the desert.

If anyone were to so much as touch my angel, I would kill them with my bare hands.

The second, and held at the highest, was in regard to mates. Be they witches, shifters, humans, or another vampire. The punishment would be a long-drawn-out death. I would also have the choice of body part to remove and display as a warning.

If they only touched, it would be their hands. If they forced themselves on her, I would cut something else off and shove it in their mouths. With the vampires in the open, I could now leave their corpse in the middle of the road to burn into a large chunk of charcoal, as well. I would place it right in front of my bar, where everyone would see and know, you did not touch what belonged to me.

These laws dated back to a time when Vampire Borns were higher in number. Before the curse, before we lost our power. Tradition kept them going. Vampire Borns were innately possessive and territorial. We shared, but only with those that we choose, and only on our terms.

The Nightwalkers held no such honor, they lost most of their humanity when they were turned.

I had a few I would call friends, but I still did not trust them. Carter was one of those. We became friends because we had both been around a while, even though I had a few centuries on him. He may be maturing, gaining better control over his instincts, but it would always be work for him. Last night was an example. An example of many things.

I turned and faced the bedroom door when I heard my angel emerging from the room.

Today, she had chosen the red and black checkered mini skirt with pleats. I could tell she was feeling more comfortable today, as she had chosen to pair it with the black top that wrapped around her back and twisted over her neck. The only part it covered on her front were two of the best things I had ever seen in this world. The tall black boots were the icing on the cake.

I didn't bother holding back my response today. Her eyes widened as I stalked closer to her, she started to step back but stopped herself. I crashed my lips into hers, bringing her against me. I lost control for a moment and slid my hand inside the covering. Her fingers gripped my hair harder. It took everything I had to pull back.

I kissed down her jaw but forced myself to stop at her neck. I laid one last soft kiss on the marks I left, which were showing proudly. I wondered if she even noticed them yet. Or how she explained them away.

"Sorry. You look so good. I couldn't help myself." I could have cleared my throat to sound more normal. I didn't want too though. The roughness was affecting her. Or it could be the fact that I hadn't removed my hand yet.

"Don't apologize. You never need to apologize for kissing me." Her eyes kept rolling back and her breath stuttered.

Well, that was an invitation if I ever heard one. I had her back up against the wall a moment later, her leg around me again. I lifted her up, and she wrapped both legs around me. I pushed the cloth off altogether and lowered my head.

Her sounds were much better when she was awake. Her skirt was up, I could see the tiny pink thing underneath. The underwear, not the part I wanted to see.

I lowered her down a few minutes later, helping her fix her clothes. "Should I be apologizing for that?"

"No." She whispered. "But I'm…I'm not…"

"You're not ready for more. I know. It's okay. We're going to go at your pace, even if it doesn't feel like it." I held her to me again. "Never be afraid to tell me to stop. You have no idea the effect you have on me."

"I think I might have the same problem. I'm having a hard time saying no myself."

I loved the sound of that. I led her out the door before I had her in that bed and ended the debate for both of us.

CHAPTER 9

Grace

"Hey. What are you doing?" I asked Todd, as I leaned against the door frame to the kitchen.

"I found this duffle bag in their closet. I figured I would pack up any food I could find. We don't know what all is out there. I'd rather have too much than not enough. Plus, you did say that we were going to meet others, and they would join us on our mission. We all will need to eat."

I was astonished. I'd only ever seen the selfish side of him before. I didn't know he had it in him. Well, except for in bed. He was never selfish in that aspect. I'd been around enough to know the difference. There were a couple jocks in school that I spent time with, once upon a time. They never lasted long and left once they were satisfied. Hence why our time together never lasted long either.

"That's a good idea. Did you find any other bags?"

"No, just this one. And our backpacks of course. They probably took all the rest." He paused and turned to me. "Do you think they made it out?"

"No. I think everything is happening the same in each city. They were all given one plan and are doing it repeatedly. We should pack our clothes in our backpacks. We won't need much, but it would be nice to clean up once in a while."

He nodded and I turned to pack what I had.

I only made it a few minutes before I crumpled on my bed crying, the fear and the reality of our situation setting in.

When I was first put into the foster system, I ran away as often as I could. I purposely caused problems. I just wanted my freedom. Now I was getting ready to sacrifice my freedom to help others get theirs. I had no idea if I would even survive all this. I wasn't ready to be a grown up. For the first time in my life, I wanted to be the kid that got to hide behind strong parents, someone to protect them from the evil that was headed our way. But that wasn't my lot in life. Ever.

I wasn't aware Todd had come into the room until he was kneeling in front of me, holding me while I cried. I pulled away a few minutes later, embarrassed. I wiped my eyes and tried to clear my throat.

"Sorry. It just got to me for a minute."

"You're allowed to be human, Gracey. We all are. And what we're doing isn't easy. If it makes you feel any better, I already had my breakdown while you were sleeping. That's why I started packing, I needed to move. I needed to do something. What we're doing may be wrong on *so* many levels, but I'd rather be trying to help end this, then hiding in a corner hoping someone else was brave enough to do it."

I nodded and lowered my forehead to his shoulder, using him as my crutch. He kissed the side of my head softly.

"We got this. As long as we have each other, we got this. That guy last night talked like we were a prize together. So, we stick with that. We work together. We find the group meant to help us and we all work together. But it's you and me, babe. All the way until the end."

I sniffed. "You and me." That's what the first vision showed. Me and Todd. "Partners." I leaned back and stared at him.

He winked, the cocky side coming back.

"Partners in every way. Now, I don't know about you. But if we are going to be successful, we need practice." I giggled as he pushed me backwards, kissing wherever he could reach. "Lots and lots of practice."

"You do know that means you will also need to practice the guy stuff too, right? When we find our people, we will all need to practice together. We have to know what we are doing if we want to make it to Curtis. If we want him to accept us. We have to be able to distract them, so they don't realize we are listening."

Todd was moving fast, already having both our pants moved. "Don't care. I'll get used to it. We need to, or it will be the death of us all." My eyes rolled back. He did have an efficient scratcher. "When this is over, I will take you somewhere far away. Just you and me."

"What makes you think I want to go anywhere with you after this? Maybe I'll be tired of you by then." I yelled out as his hand hit the side of my butt.

"You will never get tired of this, Gracey. You are already getting attached to me." He didn't let me retort, which I totally would have.

By the time we had both relieved the stress, I had let the topic go. Having a plan for the future might just help me stay focused. A goal. And who else would ever understand what I was about to do, or why, better than the one man who chose to walk the path with me?

We stood at the front door an hour later, staring back at the inside of the house. It wasn't home, it had never felt like a place we wanted to be. But it was safer than what we were about to do. We both had our backpacks on, and Todd had the duffle in his left hand. He held his right up for me and I took it.

Together we walked out of the house and into the unknown.

The street we lived on was quiet. Eerily quiet. We stopped at a few houses, checking them out, the doors and windows broken.

Everyone had been slaughtered. Parents, grandparents, kids… babies. I ran out of the first house and lost what little breakfast I had had in a bush. I dropped onto the porch steps of our neighbor's house, the ones we had heard screaming the night before. The swing on the playset in the front yard was moving in the soft breeze, the screeching of the rusty metal was the only sound that could be heard.

Todd left me after a minute, then went to their kitchen and grabbed more supplies. After four houses, we stopped going inside.

We turned off our street, headed for the main road. A few blocks later, we found a house that had not been broken into yet. Todd looked at me and I nodded, I was mostly sure it was safe. We knocked on the door and waited. No one came.

"The sun is up. The vampires are gone. We are looking for anyone else alive. You can join us if you want. Safety in numbers." I called through the door.

We heard small movements and waited. A curtain moved in the window, and then the door opened.

The little girl was no more than ten. Her long black braids were pulled into a ponytail, the pink beads laid quietly on her back. I got down on my knees and smiled softly. "Hi, sweetie. Are your mom and dad home?"

A tear came down her eyes as she stepped back and pointed to the floor in front of the couch. Where her dad laid, two holes in his neck.

"Mommy made me hide under the bed. She's in her room. She screamed a lot and then she didn't anymore."

My heart broke for this little girl. Todd knelt next to me and picked up her hand. "Do you have a bag you can pack some clothes in? You can come with us. We don't have parents anymore either."

We followed her inside and to her room. It was covered in unicorns and ponies. I helped her pack some of her warmer clothes, just in case. I knew there was no way this was going to be ending any time soon.

We were back on the road ten minutes later. The little girl insisted on bringing her stuffed pink unicorn with her. If it made her feel better, then so be it.

We picked up a few more strays as we walked; one elderly woman, two pre-teens, a toddler, a middle-aged couple, and a baby. I had no idea why some of them were left alive, while others weren't. But all of them, even the adults, followed us.

We spotted cop cars near our high school and headed that way. An officer was standing outside as we approached.

"You folks looking for shelter?"

"No, we're looking for somewhere safe. We all had shelter. But it wasn't safe." I snapped.

I was tired already. On a normal day, this walk would have taken ten or fifteen minutes. It took nearly two hours this time.

"Well, we are turning this school into a shelter. You all are welcome to stay. We have officers being assigned to live in each one, and they will do their best to protect you. Are you all family?" He seemed a little confused, and stupid apparently. We had all races in this group. Obviously we weren't related.

"No. My girlfriend and I gathered anyone we could find while we walked." Todd answered.

I opened my mouth to argue the girlfriend part, but he squeezed my hand to shut me up. I decided to let it go for now, but he was going to get a piece of my mind later.

"I'm glad you did. We haven't made it to every neighborhood yet. Yours seems to have gotten the worst of it for last night." He stepped out of the way and pointed toward the gym. "Go on in that way. There are people in there who will help you get settled. The local Red Cross has been dropping off supplies to each of the shelters. We only have what our city has stored, so take it easy. We don't know when supplies will come again."

We nodded our thanks and passed him.

The gym looked the same as it always did. The only difference was a table blocking the entrance to the room. We were greeted by a perky woman and a man who looked like he would rather be anywhere else. She gave us the rundown, telling us we could pick a spot anywhere in the gym, and they would bring us blankets, and such. Cots were already laid out throughout the room. They were still folded, but semi-organized.

Todd and I walked to the farthest corner, tucked into the right. The bleachers were pulled against the wall, locked in tight to give more room. We grabbed a few of the closest cots and pulled them over.

Where we chose would give us just a touch of privacy. Which was good. We would need space to plan.

A few minutes later, the man came and dropped, literally, the supplies on the floor. The woman was right behind him. The only time he didn't glare was when his eyes were roaming over me. Something I should probably get used to.

For now, we decided to keep our stash of food a secret, making it our emergency stash. Todd set up our two cots next to each other in the corner. He spread out the blankets like we were sharing a bed. I was too tired to argue. The other cots he left folded near us.

The middle-aged couple we found kept the baby, and the toddler with them. The elderly woman took the others. Both groups were grateful we helped them, but neither wanted the surly teenagers close by. Not that we invited them to join us either.

As the day wore on, more people trickled in. Some came on their own, looking for help, and were ushered in this way. Just like we had. Some were found by the cops as they searched for survivors. Part of me wanted to ask what would happen to all those that had been killed. The bigger part of me didn't want to know.

The bigger part won.

A couple of teenagers came in without any parentals and we subtly waved them over. Whether they became part of our plan or not was yet to be decided. If anyone was going to be near us though, I would rather it be people our own age.

By the end of the day, we were joined by sixteen-year-old Native American twin sisters, an eighteen-year-old boy, who was a mix of probably white and black, and two fifteen-year-olds, a boy and a girl. The boy was similar in coloring as Todd, but the girl was dark as night. That made seven of us altogether, three boys and four girls. We had just enough cots for all of us.

We all talked a little on and off, whether we all started out the same or not, we were all homeless orphans now. None of us had anything left to lose, except our lives.

The next two days dragged on. We were bored. More people came in, no more teenagers alone. We were the only ones who could disappear and not be missed.

The second night, when the lights were turned down low, Todd decided he wanted to play. The others were still awake and talking, but all in their own beds. They had set them up in a semi-circle, somewhat facing ours. It closed our group off, making our own little area separate from the rest of the room. Todd's hand slid to my pants and started pushing them down.

"What do you think you are doing?" I hissed at him, grabbing his hand to keep it from going further.

"What do you think I am doing?" He laughed softly, going in to start kissing my neck as he spoke. "This place is sucking the life out of us already. You said we would need to practice, so why not break the ice this way? Tomorrow we can start talking… planning…" his hand slid out of mine, "and practicing. If we aren't willing to do it in a room full of strangers, why should they be?" He made a good point, so I let him get on with it.

By the time we finished, more than one of our new friends was watching. Todd just winked at them. I covered my mouth to hold the laugh in. Such a cocky idiot.

The next morning, the guys were high fiving Todd. I noticed the twins - Raya and Layla - eyeing the oldest boy, Scott.

After we had all gone to collect our breakfast from the cafeteria, Todd led us to the outdoor basketball courts.

"We have gathered you all here today for a reason." Todd started out, trying to sound like a judge or a preacher. I hit him in the gut with the back of my hand and he laughed. "No, seriously. We did.

And before you all flip and start freaking out on us, hear us out. And please. Never tell this to anyone, whether you decide to join us or not."

"Join you with what?" Rachel, one of the fifteen-year-olds, asked warily.

"Join our mission to get close to the head vamps." Todd just laid it right out there.

"Say what, now?" Justin, the other fifteen-year-old, asked incredulously.

I rolled my eyes at the idiot next to me. "Look, the adults have no idea what they are doing, they just react and clean up. No one knows what to expect. We want this nightmare over sooner, rather than later, and we are in the prime spot to do something about it."

I told them what happened the other night, all but my visions. I wasn't ready for that. I just made it sound like Todd and I were already getting busy when we heard them.

"So, you see, this Curtis guy and his little puppets, all have harems. They hear the big stuff, the stuff that could help us end this." Todd added.

"What does this have to do with us?" Scott asked cautiously. I think he knew where we were headed.

"We are going to start our own harem and find a vamp to take us on. Eventually we will move up until we find the head vamp himself."

"But how will we know if the vamp we chose will actually have access to higher up ones?" I loved that the twins were already talking like this was a done deal.

Todd tilted his head to me and shrugged. He said from the beginning that I would probably have to tell them. I sighed and gave up.

“Because I get visions. They give me the path each choice will take me. That’s how I knew to basically jump Todd the other night. That’s why we came here instead of staying where Ryley could find us. He would have been a very bad pet owner. My vision also said we would find a group that would go with us. This is going to be a long war. We can all see this shelter thing is not going to last for long. Many of the men already argue. How long before more breakout?”

“Um... I’m just going to be blunt here. I’m still a virgin. I have no idea what to even do.” Rachel didn’t even blush as she said it. I had a feeling I was going to like this girl.

“Yeah, I’m not so sure how I feel about the guy-on-guy thing.” Scott was wary.

“I’ll be honest. It hurts like hell at first and is completely uncomfortable after that.” Todd made the others laugh with the face he made. He picked up my hand and held it, giving me a soft look. “I probably would have caved and let him kill me if Grace hadn’t been part of it.” He turned back to the others. “We are going to teach you. Grace and I were both little hoebags.” I pulled my hand away and slapped him on the back of the head. He just laughed and took my hand back. “We are all going to get to know each other *really* well. And when the time is right, Grace will let us know.”

“Where exactly are we going to do this?” Layla, I think, asked, looking at Todd with a hungry look. “We can’t all fit in your cot at night.” We all laughed with her.

“We can sneak into classrooms for now. As you get comfortable with it, we should start doing some in the gym, just hand things mostly. We got the feeling the other night that vamps prefer for people to watch, or at least they don't care if they do." Todd checked her out, but not in the same way she was doing to him.

His hand held mine tighter when he noticed the way the other two boys were looking at me. I had a feeling someone was getting a little jealous. Sweet, but very bad for business.

Scott licked his lips, his eyes on me. "When are we starting? It's been a little longer than I would like. And that vision could come in any day now."

It really said a lot about our situation that everyone was willing to help and accept my visions like it was just another day. Rachel looked the most concerned, but she wasn't going to let that stop her.

"You believe me about the visions, then?" I had to be positive. We couldn't risk someone doubting me later, it could get dangerous.

"A few days ago, I," Raya looked at her sister, "we probably wouldn't have believed you. But we had someone with us before we came here. She had an extra sense too. It saved our lives, but it cost hers." Raya wiped a tear from her eye. "So, yeah. We believe you."

"All the unbelievable crap is real now anyway, why not psychics too?" Justin added, the rest nodded along.

"Well, then." I said as I looked around the grounds, thinking about where we could go from here. To get to a classroom, we would have to steal keys from the office.

Todd reached into his pocket and pulled a set of keys out. I just laughed and shook my head. We cleaned up our mess, not wanting to leave a trace of where we had all been. Or run the risk of them banning us from eating outside again.

Todd led us to the nearest classroom and opened the door. We spent the next two hours locked in that room together. By the end of it, nobody could claim innocence anymore. We broke up for lunch and gave Raya and Rachel a chance to work out the soreness they were both new to.

Then we went back in and, to the boy's dismay, went over different things. Todd was the only one who was able to sit when we got back to the gym.

The next week went by in a similar fashion. We spent most of our time in that classroom. Todd had been smart enough when we were raiding some houses and pocketed a boat load of condoms and birth control pills. The other girls started on the pills. We saved the wrap for emergencies.

During the down times, the boys started working out in the weight room. The lock just mysteriously came unlocked one night. Nobody complained. People needed to do more than just sit on their cots.

By the end of the week, we were already practicing the hand stuff in the gym. We were far enough away that no one seemed to notice. Or at least didn't care. I noticed a few of the younger couples slipping into the bathrooms in the middle of the night, or just trying to be really quiet under their blankets.

I hoped they were being careful, or they would be adding another body to the shelter soon.

No matter who we were with throughout the day, or what we did, Todd still insisted we sleep together. And he didn't always want to sleep. I was starting to believe that I was his security blanket.

CHAPTER 10

Carrie

A week went by, and then two weeks. Before I knew it, nearly a month had passed. I managed to charge my phone while we were using the generator during the day, when needed. I sent Clarise messages every few days, and then shut my phone off. I just wanted to let her know that I was alive.

Every night since I got to the bar, I slept deeply and peacefully. And vividly.

So vividly in fact, that I woke up with those same bruises every morning. Oddly, they were where I dreamt Deacon was giving me hickeys. I was pretty freaked out the second morning, when I found new ones. More so that he would be mad than anything else. He was very possessive and insistent that nobody touch me, period.

I waited and waited. But nothing came.

Every morning, Deacon fixed me breakfast. Every morning, he greeted me with a kiss, and then stepped back. Same with every night. He kissed me good night at the door, and then backed off. Not once did he push for more.

At first I thought maybe he didn't see them, then he started kissing them. I even caught him grinning at them in the bar, lightly stroking them with his finger. Like he was proud of his handy work. Which made me wonder if my dreams were not actually dreams, but real.

I didn't see how I would sleep through something like that though. Those dreams were fairly intense. No one could sleep through that if it were actually happening to them.

I'd gotten the hang of things down at the bar. Deacon didn't do mixed drinks in his bar, thankfully. So far, Deacon was the only person to touch me, although a few have come close. Carter just liked to push Deacon's buttons.

I knew this, he knew this, Deacon knew this. But it didn't stop Deacon from hitting the roof every time. The nights Carter comes, the dreams increase in intensity, and I wake with more hickeys than the other mornings.

We both were listening to the vamps talk at night. Many of them have been helping build the wall. Deacon didn't seem all that concerned about it, even though our supplies were beginning to run low. Mike was having a harder time finding what we needed lately.

I heard the movement one Friday morning, 28 days after the freeways were blown up, signaling that Deacon was already here. I swallowed the giggle as I climbed out of bed. I loved how he liked to take care of me all the time.

That and I was a really crappy cook. My mom wasn't. Sometimes, I would sneak out of my room at night, and would see her helping a few other women learn to cook something in giant pots. It was always on nights they had their "book club" meetings. They read some pretty big books.

I ran into the bathroom and cleaned up, checking for new marks. It was routine by now. Sure enough, there were two new ones. A few inches below the collarbone. One day I was going to catch him or figure out how he was doing this.

I walked out of the bedroom, took two steps, and then froze.

Deacon was not alone.

For one awkward second, I thought about going back and getting dressed first. Then I remembered that my pajamas covered more of me than my work clothes did.

"Um. Hi?" I said to the new man, who sat at my table, staring at me.

"Good morning, angel." Deacon gave me his usual greeting as he walked around the still unknown stranger and kissed me. It never failed to ease my anxiety and fears.

"Morning. Who's your friend?" Hint, hint.

Deacon turned, like he was noticing him for the first time. "Oh! That's right, you two haven't officially met yet. Carrie, this is my friend Colton. Colton, Carrie."

I just gave him a small wave as he said "hello." I sank into my usual chair at the table, feeling awkward under the new man's intense gaze.

Colton was similar in height to Deacon, but stockier. His hair was dark brown, and his eyes two shades lighter than his hair. He was pretty good looking himself. If we survived all this, I might just introduce him to Clarise so we could double.

A light bulb went off in my head, later than it probably should have. "You bought my clothes. Well, what little there is of them anyway."

Both of them started laughing. And kept laughing until Deacon carried our plates of homemade waffles over.

“Are you joining us, Colton?” I asked as I began to pour a generous amount of syrup on my waffles, only to be stopped by Deacon.

“Angel, you are sweet enough. Besides, we don’t know what the stores still have.”

I pouted as I let him take the syrup back. “But I like syrup.”

He just laughed and shook his head. I scowled at him and turned to Colton. Still waiting for an answer.

“I have already eaten but thank you. Deacon, have you talked to Eric?”

“We’ve messaged a few times. He says he can meet me at the gate in Mojave in a couple weeks. I have that long to come up with a supply list. I want to see what they have in the stores around here first. After that we will need to set up a regular meeting time.”

My first bite didn’t even make it to my mouth before I set it back down. “You’re leaving?” I didn’t like that idea. Not at all.

“Just for a few hours, a day at the most. Normally that trip would only take half a day, but I don’t know what kind of shape the freeways, roads, and smaller towns are in. Or how long it will take me to get through the gate.”

“You will be gone at night, and the vamps are guarding those gates. There aren’t very many of them for a reason. That’s too dangerous, Deacon. Can’t we get supplies another way?” I was in pure panic mode now.

Deacon slid off his chair next to mine and sank to his knees in front of me, holding both my hands. “I will be just fine, trust me. I don't have everything worked out yet, plans may change. But, angel, you have to believe I know what I am doing."

I believed that he believed that much was clear to me.

"And what about the bar while you are gone? I can't do it all by myself. What about vamp hour? Those buggers push the limits as it is."

Deacon stood back up and kissed my forehead, before sitting back down. "Anytime I am gone, Colton will be here with you. How long are you staying this time?"

"I can stay for a week or so. Just let me know when you need to leave, and I'll come back each time." Colton's eyes drifted to me and then back. "I thought you took care of the problem with the vampires? Are they not following the rules?" He was skirting around something, it was obvious, both verbally and powerly to me.

Deacon handed me my fork again. He was always so pushy about me eating enough.

"They are, but many of them like to walk the line. I worry about them crossing it altogether when I leave."

Colton cleared his throat awkwardly. "Have you thought about double teaming?"

I had no idea what he meant, and I didn't care. It was taking all my willpower to force a few bites down. It didn't matter what Deacon said, I still thought the supply trip was a bad idea. Deacon set his fork down slowly, his eyes on his best friend as he leaned back and crossed his arms. He looked at me, and then back at Colton.

"I hadn't. We're talking about you, right? Because there is no way in hell I would trust anyone else to do it."

Colton shrugged. “Who else would I be talking about? We can keep it surface level. Just enough to let them think she has double the protection.”

I didn’t like the sound of that. I picked up both our plates, mine still half full, and carried them to the kitchen. Deacon was right behind me.

“You didn’t finish.”

“I’m not hungry. I’m a big girl, Deacon. If I want to stop eating, then I will.”

He sighed and pulled me in for a hug. “I’m sorry. I’m being pushy. You’re right.” He pinched my jaw and tipped my head up. “Everything will be fine, I promise. And Colton’s plan should work, to make sure you are protected.” He turned to look at his friend again. “You want to start today, let it build so they know you aren’t trying to sneak around behind my back?”

Colton stood up too. “Yeah, that should be fine.”

“What are you two talking about?” I had zero patience for this today. All I could read from them was that they had good intentions and believed in whatever plan they were hatching. Besides the desire I read off both of them. Deacon’s was spiking pretty high too.

“Do you remember how I was going to claim you in front of everyone, making sure they knew you were mine?” Deacon asked carefully.

I blushed. I remembered that morning very well. It had been after my first dream, or not dream, of him. It had left me very sensitive to his touch.

“Yes, I remember. Why?”

“Colton is going to do the same thing.”

"I'm sorry, say that again. It sounds like you just said your best friend is going to be touching me while I work. Something you don't let anybody do."

Deacon shrugged and nodded toward Colton. I didn't look to see what he was giving him permission for because my eyes were on Deacon.

"Colton is different. I trust him not to hurt you or try to cross any boundaries we set."

"Deacon… woah, hello!" I jumped when I felt two hands coming from behind me, wrapping around my waist.

The jerks thought it was all very funny.

Colton bent down and kissed my neck, right on top of a fading hickey. "We wanted you to get the shock out of your system now."

I barely gave out a few forced laughs, verging on hysteria. Deacon gripped my sides tighter and laughed.

"Relax, angel. This is for your protection. You know vampires have a thing for groups and sharing partners. They will see Colton with us, and they will know your protection just doubled. They wouldn't dare go against the two of us."

See, comments like that were what confused me. Deacon fully believed what he was saying, but that wasn't possible. Vampires were stronger and faster than humans. One of them alone would be more than enough to take down both Colton and Deacon. At the same time.

Still, as usual, the assurance in his eyes had a calming effect on me. When he kissed me, the anxiety melted away completely. Even though his friend was still kissing along the back of my neck and sliding his hands under my shirt. At least he stayed on my stomach. I did feel a small tingle of desire for him to move up, but I was putting that to the way Deacon was kissing me.

Yeah, this was getting beyond weird.

I pushed Deacon back and started swatting Colton's hands. "Aright, that's enough. I got the point. Thank you. Can I go get ready for work now?"

"Actually, I was thinking of going to a few stores this morning. And maybe swing by a shelter or two. Do you want to come with me? Get out of the bar for a bit?"

I squealed and jumped on him, my arms and legs wrapping around him when he caught me. He chuckled and held me tight, sniffing me again.

"I take it that's a yes?"

I pulled away enough to look at him. "Yes, please. Why are we going to the shelters?"

A few of the human customers told us about them. What was left of the police force and the local red cross had set up shelters in schools and churches for those who had lost homes and family members. Those who needed help the most.

"As far as they are concerned, I am seeing if there is anything they need most that I can order with my supplies. But my real reason is because we need more donors."

"You're going hunting for donors? Is that something you would normally do?"

"No. I usually went off word of mouth, or if I found someone on the streets that needed to make a little money. Some of them preferred to earn it rather than accept charity. The people in the shelters are strapped tight, they don't have any other options right now."

“That sounds horrible, like you're going to prey on their vulnerability. I know that’s not what you are doing, at least not completely. But still.”

He sighed sadly. “Does that mean you don’t want to come?”

“Oh, no. I’m totally coming. I need to go out for a while. And I’m a little curious as to what it looks like out there.”

The bombings and attacks stopped after the third night. The vampires still roamed the streets freely at night, but they weren’t actively hunting and slaughtering. The humans stuck to their curfew unless they had extra protection to be out after sundown. Deacon had even taken to writing his name on his donors before they left, that way the vampires would know they were his.

Deacon kissed me again and set me down, smacking my butt as I turned to go get dressed.

“You’ll watch the bar?” I heard him ask Colton before I closed the door.

I went to the bottom drawer of the dresser I was using and pulled out the clothes I had packed to bring with me. My jeans felt a little weird, as did the full V-neck shirt I pulled on. I had a small moment of claustrophobia from all the extra clothes, thankfully it passed after a minute or two. I just needed to get used to them again.

The two men were talking quietly when I came back out, their faces and the vibe from them told me it was something serious and private. Deacon stood up from the couch and walked over to me with his hand up.

“Are you ready?”

"Yep." Colton stood and walked over too. "Am I supposed to hug you? I don't know you that well, or at all. Yet you just felt me up in the kitchen and plan on doing it again later."

Colton stepped over, both of them laughing at me again, and didn't give me a choice on the hug.

"The sooner you get used to me, the better it will all be. And feel." He kissed my cheek, then winked at me as he turned to open the door for us.

I just blushed and ducked my head.

Deacon and I went through a few grocery stores close by, they had little to nothing left. The manager told us that he was informed by the vampires that his shelves would be getting stocked soon from other cities in California. Everything California farms produced would be divided out to the various cities. And things that were made in the factories would do the same.

Unfortunately, harvest was long over, and a good portion of those things had already been sent to whoever the farmers had deals with. It could be months before the shelves got restocked.

I kept one eye out as we walked the streets and outside stores, looking for the drones. I thought I saw one sitting in a tree, after the second store, but I wasn't sure.

Deacon insisted on going into a clothing store and buying me a jacket. It was getting chilly. I refused to let him buy me anything else. I was glad too, our stop at the shelter made me feel bad for even having that much. They only had blankets and even those were thin. The school had a generator, but they saved it for the nights so they could use the heater and not burn out the generator as quickly. The opposite of how we did it.

Despite not having a heater at night, I never got cold. One more reason for me to think that Deacon was somehow in my bed every night, he was always warm when he held me.

The first shelter we stopped at was in a high school. I talked to the red cross manager while Deacon walked around the gym. He spent a good deal of time talking to a group of teenagers in the corner. I wasn't thrilled with that, but I was reserving judgment for now.

The manager was a bit creepy, so I ended up waiting for Deacon outside. The fresh air and sunshine felt nice, even if it was chilly.

CHAPTER 11

Grace

It was another lively Friday morning(ish). The seven of us were just sitting around, trying to decide what we could do for fun. Such a hard choice with the limitless possibilities at our feet. The flash took over my eyes unexpectedly, causing me to gasp.

“Gracey? What’s wrong?” Todd asked, worried about me.

I lifted my hand up, needing a moment to concentrate.

The first flash was of us just lying around, day after day. Nothing changing.

The next flash was of a new man walking around the gym. We were still lying around, but not sitting still. A few had hands moving. This one subtle difference changed everything. A path was laid out from there, one with numerous other people, or rather, vampires.

“The time has come. Finally.” I was about to say more when we heard the doors to the gym open.

A man and a woman walked in, stopping by the front table, talking to the others. The man's head looked slowly around the room.

"Layla, Scott. Get your hands moving. No, don't ask questions, just do it. I don't care what." I cut them off and they swiftly jumped into action.

Layla was sitting near Justin against the wall. She slid her hand up his knee, until she was unzipping his pants and reaching in. I was just leaning against Todd, my back to his chest. Scott was sitting in front of us, the two had been talking about sports, speculating on what was going on everywhere else in the world.

Scott lifted my legs and placed them on his lap.

Despite the cold, I was wearing shorts. I didn't exactly have many other options. When I packed, I only thought about them being small enough to fit a few pairs in my bag, not about the weather. He began gliding his fingers up and down my thigh, getting higher and higher. I gave a small shiver as the goosebumps started.

Todd decided to play along too, his fingers traced the lining of my V-neck t-shirt, pushing it lower and lower.

The man walked toward the center of the room, his eyes scanning around, assessing. When his eyes landed on us, he gave a small grin and walked over. I watched him intently, trying to figure out who this man was and how he would be helping us.

He wore basic jeans with a black t-shirt. He had long black hair pulled back on his neck. He was still too far for me to see the color of his eyes. All I could tell was that they were a dark color. He was strong and carried himself like he knew how to fight.

As he approached, his eyes took in the various things going on in our corner, and he smiled wider.

"Can we help you with something?" I let the teenage attitude fly.

He squatted down and sat on the back of his heels, putting himself on our level. “Oh, I’m sure we can all help each other.”

“How so?”

He kept his grin as he pulled a business card out of his back pocket, holding it between two fingers. “My name is Deacon and I run a bar. It just so happens that I am in the need of more employees. My side business has… grown. Immensely.”

I scoffed and rolled my eyes. “We are not old enough to work in a bar, sorry.” I must have misunderstood the flash, surely there was nothing he could do for us.

He waved my comment away like it was just a fly in his face. “Your age doesn’t matter. In fact, my clients enjoy youth once in a while.” I didn’t say anything, just stared at him, so he continued. “Once the sun goes down, the vamps come out. Humans who work for me as donors make a lot of money.”

His eyes stared pointedly at Layla, she grew a bit self-conscious and pulled her hand out of Justin’s pants. She didn’t realize he was fully out and locked into place. The man, Deacon, winked at her.

“Those willing to donate more than blood make even more money.”

Deacon’s eyes came back to me, somehow pegging me as the leader. “I can help you and your little group relocate closer, get out of this paradise of a place. Those who work for me get a decent cut, they work once or twice a week, depending on how popular they are, and they get two full meals while they are in my bar.”

I knew when Todd realized what he was talking about, when he realized why this was important. His hand staggered for a split second before continuing again.

“How much?” He asked the older man.

"My donors pocket anywhere from 200 to 800 in a given night. The higher the money, the longer I expect you to rest in between shifts."

"Deacon?" A female voice called from across the room.

The man turned to look at her, she signaled that she would be outside.

"Is she a donor too?" I asked, just because I wanted to keep my rep for being a brat.

Deacon's head spun back around, and a small growl came out. His eyes even sparked, like they were going to light on fire. It was probably just the reflection of the light coming through the windows.

"Sorry." He shook it off. "No. She runs the bar with me, but she is not to be touched without *my* permission." He stood back up, one eye on us, one eye on the door. "Weekends are always the busiest for the… extra services side of things."

"What makes you think we'd be interested?"

He glanced at my thigh, and then at Layla's hand, which had slid back in to finish the job. "Call it a hunch. What you have here is very similar to vampire culture. You will fit right in. If you decide to join us, just show up. I pay cash, every night, and there is no paperwork." He turned and walked back out to where the woman waiting for him was. I was pretty sure she was at least his girlfriend.

"Was that what we have been waiting for, Gracey?" Todd asked, his voice rough.

I could feel him poking into my back. He was excited. He also had a thing for doing things in the open, something he recently discovered. He liked the way the man had watched his hand and not cared.

"I believe so, yes. If we hadn't been doing anything, he would have passed us by. Our actions are why he came to us. This could be how we can finally get started, finally get a foot in the door to the vampire world."

I shifted enough that I could reach in and grab a hold of Todd from behind me. Scott decided to do the same to me.

Justin put a hand to Layla's head and pushed her down, ready for her to end his slow agony.

"When are we going?" he grunted.

I closed my eyes, the sign I was searching the future. I thought about tonight, but saw that Mr. Ryan, the shelter manager, would be watching closely. We couldn't risk being kicked out until we had a for sure thing set.

I thought about tomorrow and saw that Todd and I would run into an old vampire friend if we did that. Ryley was still not happy we had disappeared on him. It would cause a big commotion. And this guy, Deacon, would intervene somehow. The path from there was fuzzy but I got the feeling it wasn't good.

I thought about Sunday, and I saw a vamp who took a special interest in us. One who did not look as poor and pathetic as the rest.

I opened my eyes and smiled at my group. "We go on Sunday. I say, tomorrow we go for a little walk and visit some of the empty houses in the neighborhood. We need to find the right clothes, at least us girls do."

They all nodded, agreeing with me.

It felt good to have a plan, to have the next part of our path open in front of us. Good enough that I turned over in Todd's lap and gave him the same treatment Justin had just finished receiving. Scott didn't miss a beat, his fingers egged me on.

I sighed happily, lying my head on Todd's thigh after, his hand rubbing up and down my back.

The next day, we left Layla and Justin behind to keep an eye on our things while we were gone. Anytime the whole group was out of the room for an extended period of time, we got the feeling someone had been going through our things.

We always left at least two behind now, just in case.

It took a few tries until we found what we were looking for. The fifth house had had a younger woman in it at one point in time. Someone had gotten around to cleaning out the bodies, not sure who. I found a few long sleeve shirts and sweaters, deciding to take those with us as well. We also found a closet full of clothes that had been worn clubbing or planned to be at any rate.

Rachel found a purple and black plaid outfit and handed it to me. It matched my hair perfectly.

The top was a spaghetti strap bikini style top that tied in the front. The bottom was of the same material, and was a short, hemmed frill skirt. I found a black leather jacket that was more of a short jacket, not even making it to my belly button.

Rachel picked out a pair of white jeans, and a black long-sleeve top that ended above her midriff. That morning, we decided that only four of us would go for the first night. Rachel and Scott, Todd, and me. The twins and Justin would stay behind.

We had all broken up into these pairings anyway. Layla was more like a floater, she floated from one couple to the next. Her preferences were beginning to lean more towards the female side than the male's.

Late Sunday afternoon, Scott and Todd stole a car from one of the empty houses and took us to the bar. When we entered, the first thing I saw was Deacon's girlfriend, and some other guy. He was holding her from behind as they danced behind the bar. It could have been innocent. But it didn't seem like it.

"Hey, you guys made it!"

I turned to the right and saw Deacon coming out a side door, carrying a box that jingled from glasses bouncing together.

"Head on up to the bar. We are waiting for a few more people and then we can get started."

As we walked toward the bar I couldn't help but watch as Deacon set his load down and walked over to the couple. The other man didn't remove his hands as Deacon slid a hand to the girl's back and then slowly kissed her, his hand grabbing her butt. I was fairly certain he was rubbing the man with the back of his hand at the same time as well.

Whether on purpose or not, I had no idea. I didn't care much either. Not like I could really talk about sharing partners.

Over the next ten minutes, more people walked in, coming to sit at the bar. All but two older men acted as though they had been here before. Deacon sized us all up and walked around in front of us.

"Good evening." He rubbed his hands together greedily. "I can't tell you how happy I am that so many of you showed up." I looked down at the row of stools near bar, there were nearly two dozen of us. "For those of you that are new. Sundays can be a bit… crazy."

"More like psychotic, bordering on completely insane and disgusting."

Deacon laughed at the interruption from his girlfriend. She walked over to stand next to him and I noticed what she was wearing for the first time. A green mini skirt and a black leather top that zipped up in the front. With black three-inch heels.

"Yes. Sundays have become the busiest, and not just for blood. Vamps are reveling in the freedom they haven't felt in a long time, and they are taking advantage of it. The rules are simple." He nodded to his friend, who started handing out watches. "Every time you go to a client, make sure you start your timer for the time they paid for. It's typically in increments of 10 minutes. If I cut you off, you are done for the night and expected to eat and rest. I will not risk your lives for a few extra bucks. Many vamps like to play and not just eat. Men, if you are open for that, take your shirts off and hand them to Carrie. Women, you can either take them off, or tie them up somehow. Showing skin helps them to see a clear line between their different options. If you need water, wave Carrie down. If the vamp refuses to stop when the timer goes off, wave Colton or myself down. Do not let them get carried away with trying for extra anything. If you want it, fine, just wait until after we close. Any questions?" Nobody said anything. "Good. Food will be right out. Eat up, the more iron you have in your system, the more appealing you are to the vamps."

Deacon lifted Carrie with one arm, making her squeal and laugh. He carried her toward the kitchen with him.

CHAPTER 12

Deacon

As soon as I had Carrie in the kitchen, I attacked her. Watching her dance with Colton so freely, laughing and having fun, got my blood pumping. When I pressed her into me, needing to feel her, I felt my friend too. He had been enjoying dancing with her as much as I had watching her.

I messed with him a little bit. It added to my need for my angel. The desire I smelled off both of them fueled the fire in my veins. I barely made it through the intro speech to all the donors.

I lifted her onto the counter, her legs moving to let me get as close as I could. Her skirt split right up, letting us rub some very frustrated parts together. I knew that was still a no-fly zone, so I put my focus on what she would let me have.

I unzipped her shirt and let it fall. She held my hair and head, keeping me there while she bucked against me. She needed me as much as I needed her.

One day. Soon.

"Deacon. The donors need to eat." She reminded me - much too soon in my opinion - trying to bring us both back down to reality.

I groaned and released her, moving to lay my forehead against hers.

"What brought this on?"

I chuckled and stroked her side with my thumb. "Watching you dance with Colton. You were so free in those few minutes, having fun."

"Are you sure you are okay with him touching me all the time? I wasn't expecting him to start dancing just now." I kissed her softly, knowing she felt guilty for some reason.

As time went on, it was getting easier and easier to read her. It had only been two days since Colton started double teaming with me, her walls with him have dropped more and more since.

"I told you before. I trust Colton. He would never hurt you. And he would never betray me. There is nothing wrong with having a little fun now and again. Maybe next time I will dance with you both, with you right in the middle."

And maybe one day, it wouldn't just be dancing. That thought wasn't new. It had slowly been creeping in over the last few days. My desire for it to happen was creeping up with it.

I stepped back and let her put her shirt back on. I'd never watched her trying to put this one on before. She wore a strapless bra under it, needing the extra support for what she had been blessed with.

She reminded me of someone working to close an overstuffed suitcase. Once she succeeded, we loaded up trays with burgers, fully loaded, and carried them out. Mike did all the heavy work for us before he left for the day, thankfully making extra.

I kept an eye on the newbies as the vamps started trickling in. Sundays were our most… interesting crowd. They had their fetishes and things they liked.

William was the first to arrive. He sat down at his usual corner booth and waved over his two usual donors. His whip laid around his neck like a necklace. By the time they were sitting on the table, back-to-back, William's friend showed up. They would run a tab and pay at the end of the night. This had been going on for years.

Both vamps were more than pleased to see the curtains down the first time.

Besides the teenagers, I also found two men on the larger side in a church that was being used for a shelter. Both were married, and both had seemed stressed when I found them whispering off to the side. I hadn't expected them to take their shirts off, but I guess if you need the money badly enough, you'll do just about anything. They would be good for the vamps who wanted the testosterone boost.

That was one of the reasons I approached the teenagers, the boys were in the process of bulking up. The other reason had been obvious, they were bored and were open to being open. I had also noticed a familiar smell coming from the girl, not as strong as my angel's but it was still there.

They were standing altogether, watching everyone. The girl with the black and purple hair looked like she was looking for someone in particular.

It was about an hour in, they each had already been chosen for a ten-minute play time round already, when I could see her attention be drawn to the door. I didn't know why she was looking for him, but he didn't keep pets, so whatever she wanted wasn't going to happen.

Carter met me at the bar, dropping onto a stool. "Hey, Deac."

"Hey, Carter. What's going on? You look tired."

"I am, so very, very, tired. We've been working nonstop on trying to get that wall up. Our end finally met up where the next section began. I can't tell you how glad I am to be done with it."

"You need another boost? I have fresh meat. Young, too."

I might as well let her have her fun while she could. I lifted my hand toward where her and the boy were standing. I gave a small wave and they both came skirting over.

The girl placed a hand on Carter's shoulder and slowly slid it down, moving his arm so she could step closer. Carter's smile grew. She had balls. I'd give her that. Carter looked her up and down, licking his lips. Then sighed as he turned back to me.

"She's not exactly filled with what I need for an energy boost, Deacon."

"No, but he is." The boy leaned against the counter on Carter's other side, his hand brushing against Carter's thighs.

"Hmm. He is, isn't he?" Carter's arm wrapped possessively around the girl. He was having difficulty choosing.

"Time and half, old friend?" I asked him, referring to a special order, in which he got two but only fed from one.

His eyes widened, obviously he had forgotten about this option. With his free hand, he pulled three hundreds out of his pocket and handed them to me. I wasn't worried, he would play for at least half the twenty minutes he was paying for.

"She looks very happy." Colton commented from my side, watching the trio go.

"Yes, she does. I think she was looking for him for some reason."

Colton's ever-present frown deepened.

Carter ended up having to pay me extra, not having been able to help himself. He had to taste the girl. By the time he left, I started thinking they might actually have a chance at convincing him to take on a few pets.

I ended up booting the teens before midnight. They all had been very popular. The other two newbies were as well. I even realized I made a mistake in what their stress had been about.

One time they were picked together, more for show before eating, then playtime. They both enjoyed it more than most newbies would have.

I sighed with relief when the night was done. The week before had left me worried about Sundays. Last week they had been a bit more outspoken in their desires for my angel. It got bad enough that I had to make her stay behind the bar.

Colton's plan was working though. We both had our hands on her many times. We replayed the scene from earlier a time or two, minus the dancing.

My favorite time was when I pulled Colton out of his pants and rubbed him against my angel. I slid him right up that skirt. She gasped but was trapped between us. I kept her mouth distracted until I finished him. I could see the dents his fingers were leaving in her side as he released. She walked away on the edge, so close to getting what she needed.

If I did decide to share after all, Colton would be willing. I had no doubts about that.

A few hours later, I sat in a chair and propped my feet onto the table. Colton locked the door behind the last customer. Carrie walked over and I pulled her onto my lap.

"I am really glad so many donors showed up tonight. It was probably why they didn't get so crazy this time."

I chuckled at her naivety. She had no idea just how alluring she was. And not just from the scent of her blood. Colton gave me a look, telling me it was time to tell her. I sighed. I guess it was as good a time as any.

"Angel?" She must have heard something in my voice because her back straightened and her eyes had daggers in them ready to throw. I gulped. "I need to get an idea of what the roads are going to be like when I go on that supply run."

Her body wanted to relax, but she knew there was more. "Oh-kay." She drew the word out slowly.

"Since Mondays are not known for being too busy, I want to do it tomorrow. I'll go during the daytime, and try to be back before night falls, I promise." When did I start pleading with her? I usually made the decisions and others were expected to follow. What was this power she had over me?

My angel pushed off my lap and stepped away. "Are you going alone, or are you taking backup in case something happens?"

I stood and tried to follow her, she pulled away from my hand. She already knew the answer and didn't like it. Without a word, she turned and stomped up the stairs.

I growled. "This is why I never marked or mated. Women make no sense."

"She is worried about you, but for the wrong reasons. You need to tell her the truth, Deacon. You need to tell her what you are. What *we* are."

I pouted like the arrogant prick I was, not wanting to admit I was wrong. I roughly grabbed glasses and started to clean. Hopefully she would be asleep by the time I got up there.

Colton was staying in my apartment since his was taken, and I had been sleeping at her place. Not that she knew most of that of course. She assumed he was sleeping on my couch.

Colton silently started helping me clean up.

We took nearly two hours, giving her plenty of time to go to bed. Her breathing was soft and level, so I went in. I didn't pause to take in her beauty like I normally did, I just stripped and slid in with her.

Now that October was here, the weather was getting colder at night. With no heat running, she needed my body heat.

I barely touched her arm when she suddenly turned and curled into my chest. It took a few beats for me to realize she was missing a few things. My mind zeroed out, going completely blank, when she pressed her bareness against me.

"I'm sorry I got mad. I just hate the idea of you being gone. I worry about you getting hurt. And I feel safer when you are near."

Uh oh. "I thought you were asleep." I was trying really hard to not sound like a child who had just been caught stealing from the cookie jar. At least she hadn't caught me eating a certain cookie, something I may or may not have done in the middle of the night to her. "You're supposed to be asleep." How did I not know she was awake?

She gave a tired sigh, her eyes still closed. "I almost was. If you had just waited a few more minutes you would have been able to continue with your creeper status." I felt her small smile against me.

She wasn't mad.

I laughed softly with relief and wrapped her in my arms. "Creeper is a matter of opinion."

She snorted and held me tighter. "Molesting people in their sleep and not telling them you were ever there, is the definition of a creeper. No opinions needed. It's a fact. You've been a creeper for weeks. I just don't know why." She sighed again, deeply.

Maybe she wasn't as awake as I thought.

"How did you know?"

She laughed and rolled to her back, I didn't let her go far, her eyes finally opening. Aaaand maybe she was fully awake.

"You left evidence all over me." She waved at her chest, a knowing smirk on her face.

I did, I really did.

I grinned like a fool, completely proud of my work. Which she immediately pointed at with a sexy little scowl on her face.

"That right there, that was how I knew. If they had just randomly shown up, you would have freaked out, thinking someone had been in here with me. That someone was touching me. Instead, you get that proud grin when you see them. And you kiss them all the time."

I grimaced. She had me there. I would have gone on a murderous rampage if someone had been marking what belonged to me.

"Why did you come? Why did you do all this?"

I kissed her forehead. There was nothing I could say that wouldn't lead to the truth. "I needed to be near you, and I was marking you as mine."

"You could have done that while I was awake, in fact, you have a few times."

"That's not what I meant." I sighed, guess it was time. "My people, we have a way of marking those we are claiming. It blends our scents, a warning to others that they are spoken for. From the moment I saw you, I knew I wanted you to be mine. Whether it be to give me the son I've never been able to have, or as mine to protect and care for."

"I will withhold the comment about giving you a kid for now, seeing as how you maintained some decency while I was sleeping. You've respected most of my wishes. What do you mean, your people? How did you blend our scents?"

"My people." I licked my lips and rubbed them together. "We are few in number now, because of a curse that a witch placed upon us many years ago. We can only bear male children, and it is not easy to find a human strong enough to survive carrying our children or even birthing them."

Carrie started shaking her head and mumbling no, over, and over again, pushing away from me. I let her go, confused. I hadn't reached the part that should freak her out yet.

She paced away from the bed. I was worried enough about her reaction and what was going on in her head, that I was *mostly* able to ignore her perfect body. My angel rubbed her eyes with both hands, looked at me, cursed, and looked away.

"Carrie, angel. Talk to me. What do you have going on in your head? Let me help, love." I needed to help her. I hated seeing her in such distress.

CHAPTER 13

Carrie

The moment Deacon started talking about the curse, I heard my mother's voice. I could feel the ghost of her arms holding me as she told me one of her favorite bedtime stories. It felt as though it had only been yesterday.

"When she returned to her home, the witch pulled her coven together and told them what happened. Together, they put a curse on all the Vampire Borns. They would no longer be able to give birth to female vampires, they would only have sons. Each witch cut their hand and sealed the curse with their blood."

I kept looking over at Deacon, trying to place everything I knew. The vampires all respected him, some even feared him. There were times he moved faster than expected. He knew so much about their culture. But he went out during the day. One of the stories she told me had mentioned something about that.

I cursed for letting myself forget. And for not listening to my mother more often. I was vastly unprepared for this world when she left. Something I didn't want to admit while I still had her.

I wasn't even aware Deacon was talking to me until he grabbed my hand, a worried plea in his eyes. I let him pull me closer, placing me between his legs and holding both my hands in one, his other coming to my cheek.

My anxiety began melting away again. I had no idea how he always managed to do that to me. I should be irritated, I wanted to be, but it was nearly impossible to do with him around. With him touching me like this.

"Angel? Talk to me. Or at least listen, let me explain. I wasn't trying to hide anything from you, I was just afraid you'd hate me, and I could never live with myself if that happened." His sincerity was my undoing.

"You…you're a…a…Vampire Born. Aren't you? The cursed ones?"

His eyes registered his shock, but his body didn't move from mine. I was beginning to regret my decision in how I slept tonight, all part of my plan to catch him. I was done waiting. I needed to be with him.

"How do you know that name, that term?"

"I told you. My mother was full of stories. I, uh, haven't exactly been completely honest with you either."

His palm fell. "What are you talking about?" Awesome, he was getting defensive.

"Hey. None of that. You kept the fact that you were a day walking vampire from me and did whatever you wanted to me in my sleep. And judging by the dreams I had, I'm pretty sure you fed me your blood and fed off me. Is that how you blended our scents?"
Oh, good. There was the anger for all that.

At least he had the nerve to look ashamed. "I'm sorry. I needed you safe, and that was the best way to do it."

Sorry, my right butt cheek.

"Then what was all that BS with you and Colton having to touch me all the time?" I pulled one of my hands from his and waved toward the bedroom door, emphasizing his little friend in crime.

I was not going to admit I was starting to like it. Two hot guys paying so much attention to me, who wouldn't?

"That was true. They needed to see as much as smell. This generation of Nightwalkers has no respect for the law."

Right, I knew that was true. I always did. Deacon stood up, pulling my chin up to look at him as he made sure there wasn't an inch of air between us.

"And I *never* heard you complain about any of it." Dang, he already knew I liked it. "You saw tonight how they behaved better. Same with the last two nights. They won't cross us both. You are well and thoroughly protected between us both."

Umm, yes, it was nice between them both.

Deacon chuckled darkly, his eyes sparking flames, somehow knowing where my mind was going. His hand went to my butt again, forcing me to feel every blessed inch of him. He lifted my thigh, creating a pathway.

"Mate with me. Let me make you mine permanently. I love you, angel. I never thought it was possible. I don't know how, but you wrapped me around these fingers the moment I pulled you through that door." He folded his freehand with the one he was still holding of mine. "You were always meant to be mine. I know that now." He was moving just enough to tease me and keep me from thinking clearly.

"I... I can't. I don't… know." I groaned as he slowed, keeping me from reaching a place I had only ever been in my sleep.

"I know you don't, just follow me, love. Tell me you will mate with me. You will forever be protected by me and my people. I can't bear to lose you. I need you."

My heart swelled at his words. I couldn't doubt that he loved me and needed me. I had felt the same from the beginning as well. From the moment I first saw him, I knew I was finally safe, finally home. No one would ever hurt me again.

I wrapped my arms around his neck and kissed him. "I love you too, Deacon." I smiled at the happiness in his eyes. "Make me yours. Protect me forever."

He growled, spun, and dropped us on the bed. Somehow he managed to keep himself from crashing into me.

"You are going to need to drink from me again, angel. And me from you. Not yet though, I'll tell you when." He pushed my legs apart with his knee. "This is going to hurt, quite a bit, I think."

He looked down, my eyes following. Holy cheese and crackers. That thing was massive compared to my ex's.

"Don't worry, angel. The pain won't last long."

It didn't. I screamed like a freaking banshee, but it soon faded leaving room for much better feelings. When I was building up to scream in a different way, Deacon bit into his wrist and placed it on my lips. His blood was even better when I was awake. He tasted like caramel and honey.

I wondered if it was because of his skin tone. He was a bit caramelly on the outside.

Instead of screaming when he slowly sank his fangs into my neck, I bit down harder on his wrist. We both drank each other in, while we reached those pivotal moments. After a minute, before my body had even begun to settle down, I felt this woosh of air run through me. It was like someone had suddenly rolled down the window to my veins, while the car was going over a hundred on the freeway. My whole body shook, Deacon's was shaking nearly as bad.

On some level, I registered how good it felt, all other levels were freaking me the hell out.

We released each other and he wrapped his arms around me, rolling us to our sides. We were hit with wave after wave. The wave built us up without us doing anything, and once again I felt this fiery heat shooting through me from below. From him. He was enjoying the ride just as much as I was.

It was hot, very hot. Like stepping into the hot tub after swimming in the cold pool water, kind of hot. The kind of burn that felt so good, too. My body rocked against his, needing more of it.

He didn't ask why, he just reacted, moving us to my back again. It felt like hours before I felt sated. I collapsed on his chest, laying down on top of him, with exhaustion. I didn't even fully comprehend when, or how, we ended up in this position. It just happened.

"That. was. Awesome."

He laughed and rolled us to the side again, holding me close. "That it was, angel. I almost want to do it again, but not until after we sleep for a few hours."

"I'm good with that."

I was nearly there when he spoke again.

"Angel, what were you going to tell me earlier? What have you been hiding?"

I frowned. Really? Now? Ugh. I just wanted to get it over with and go to sleep. I yawned again.

"According to my mother, both she and my father were descendants of the coven that cursed your people. I'm sorry."

Deacon scoffed. "Don't be, it's not like you had anything to do with it. It was a thousand years ago. Neither of us were alive back then."

"That's true." It came out in more of a yawn. "Can we sleep now?"

He kissed my head, his lips turning up, oddly amused at my desire to sleep. "One more thing. Does your family still use magic?"

I shrugged. "Some, I guess. It changes with each person, with each generation. I'm not nearly as strong as my parents were. My mother was clairvoyant and had great control over it. My father could read minds when he wanted. Which helped him as a detective. I don't really know any other witches outside of my family."

"And you?"

I looked up at him, feeling a bit shy. "I can tell when people are lying, hiding things, and what kind of character they have. A few months ago, I started being able to feel intent. I always knew there was something you were hiding, but I also knew you weren't hiding it to deceive me. I felt how strongly you wanted to protect me." I giggled. "I can tell you a lot of things about this bar and your customers."

"Oh, yeah? Like what?"

"Hmmm, let's see." I tapped my chin playfully. "Ethan, one of the donors, has a crush on Chad, the vamp who always picks him. The feeling is mutual too. I'm waiting for the day Chad offers to keep him. Ethan is taking care of his siblings now, and Chad would be really good to all of them. The teenagers are cooking up something. Some type of plan, but it has good intentions, so I don't want to stop them. The two new guys, yeah, they have been best friends for years but were too ashamed to say anything to their families about their real feelings. Both their families are devout in their religions. They agreed to come so they could be together somewhere where they didn't have to feel guilty. I could go on, really." I shrugged. I only knew so many details because I was able to talk to them and piece what I felt together with that. For some reason, my powers had seen a major power boost over the last few weeks.

All this talking was waking me up more.

Deacon must have been thinking along the same lines, he kissed me softly, his hands taking possession of me again. He waited until I was in a very vulnerable spot to ask, very slowly, "what about Colton? What do you feel from him? Regarding you."

Nope, not going there. I didn't want him to be mad at his friend for something he was working to control.

Deacon stopped moving at *the* worst time. I whimpered and moved to get him back. Stubborn pain in my butt.

His chuckle was deep, evil-like. "Not until you tell me, angel."

"You'll get mad."

"Try me." He already knew the answer. I could feel it. But for some reason, he wanted me to own it.

"Fine." I laid back into the bed with a huff. "He likes me, he has since we first officially met. He had ulterior motives when he came up with his plan. He wasn't sure you would let him come near me. He knows he can't have more, but he is happy with what he can have. As you said, Colton would never hurt me nor betray you. He is loyal to you."

Deacon rewarded me handsomely, many times, until we both passed out from exhaustion. When I came to, the sun was up further in the sky than normal. Deacon was lying next to me, his head propped up on his hand. His other hand was circling me, the blanket pushed down to my waist.

“Good morning, angel. How did you sleep?”

I blushed and tried to hide my face. I was embarrassed by the strength of my need for him last night. I still felt it, but it wasn’t as overpowering. I felt something else, too. A fuzzy, happy feeling in my chest. I rubbed it.

“Deacon, I feel something right here. It feels good, like love, and happiness.”

His fingers spread out, allowing him to take all of me in. “Yes, it is the bond. Something I wasn’t expecting. By bonding with me, we have blended our scents to the point of mixing your siren blood, which I am thinking is the pure witch’s blood running through you, with mine. You will also now live as long as I do. Our souls have been sealed together. But this feeling is something I did not foresee, and I should have. It is the very reason we came so far, so quickly, at least by human standards. You are my one true mate, the one fate designed just for me. You are the other half of my soul. You always have been. We can feel each other, our emotions. If you are hurt, I will know. If you are scared, I will know. If you are… I will know.” His voice deepened at the end, responding to the feelings I was having at the moment.

It helped speed things along. I got what I needed two more times before he helped me stand and pulled his shirt from the night before over my head. He only put on his boxers.

Deacon, my fated mate of all things, made me French toast, while I sat on the counter. We talked more openly now. He could use more details about stories and places he had been. He carried me to a chair at the table, before bringing me my food.

“Deacon, how old are you?” He had just told me a story about the civil war, I had to know after that.

"I turned 446 years old this past summer."

My jaw? On the floor.

"Holy crap balls you are old." I giggled. "Look at you, robbing the cradle."

He shook his head at me. "Colton is more than twice that."

"No way."

He nodded, a glint of amusement in his eyes. "Yes, you were dancing between two really old men last night, angel. One of them to the point that he ran down your leg." He popped my nose with his finger. "And you liked it."

"No, I didn't." I answered quickly, with a scoff, shoving a bite in my mouth.

Deacon found my denial to be the funniest of all. "Angel, I'm a vampire, we can smell arousal. And I am especially sensitive to yours. And while I may not have your gift for knowing when someone is lying, I can feel your shyness, guilt, and a little bit of shame, right here." He tapped his heart with one finger.

At this point, I was pretty sure my blush was going to be permanent.

Deacon pushed his plate away and knelt down in front of me. "Angel, I'm not upset. I'm quite happy that you like him and that he likes you. It makes me hope that one day, we can do more than just dance together. I want to show you the wonders extra body parts can do." Deacon's face fell. "I will only ever consider it with Colton, though."

I couldn't even form a word. Was he suggesting what I think he was suggesting? Thankfully, he let the matter drop. Although the next matter made me want to go back to it.

“I need to get going. I had planned on leaving earlier than this, but someone kept me in bed this morning.” I was tempted to stick my tongue out at him, he was only trying to lighten the moment after all. It wasn’t working though, so he moved on. “I will get back as soon as I can. I just need an idea of what the roads are like.”

He moved to stand and step away but I grabbed his hand. “Don’t leave me.”

He dropped down again, fast enough to make me jump. “I'm not leaving you, angel. I will be back in a few hours. Colton will be here with you. You said it yourself last night, he will protect you. And with my mark on you now,” his finger grazed over a sore spot on my neck, “nobody would be stupid enough to come near you.”

I pouted as he pulled me into the bedroom with him and I watched him get dressed, on the verge of tears.

Before he left, he hugged me tight. “So much sadness I feel in you, angel. I will be back soon. You are safe.” His voice sounded like he was the one in pain.

Deacon didn’t turn to the door, open it, raise his voice, or anything, all he said was a calm “Colton?” And a moment later, Colton was standing in the doorway.

He looked at my neck and smiled. “I had a feeling this was the case. I ended up sleeping in the cellar last night.”

I grimaced, they both laughed.

“Take care of my angel, for me?”

“It will be my pleasure.” Colton winked at me, making me wonder just how much he had heard of our conversations. “Just don’t turn me into a frog, and we’ll be cool.”

I groaned and tried to hide in Deacon’s chest. He just laughed, kissed me one more time and disappeared into thin air. Not even a minute had gone by before I heard his truck start… before the backdoor to the bar had closed all the way.

CHAPTER 14

Grace

Deacon kicked us out of the bar around 11:30. We felt fine and could have probably stayed longer, the money was awesome, but we had already accomplished what we went to do. No one spoke until we were back in our stolen car.

"Was that him? Was that vamp our ticket?" Todd asked excitedly.

"Yes. I saw him in the vision, and I heard him talking to Deacon. He is a leader over others. And he has been proving himself. Plus, I got another vision while we were with him, he is definitely the one. That was why I teased him until he bit me."

"Man, that was hard to watch."

I understood what Todd meant. I reached over and held his hand. We both had accepted the sharing our partners part, but watching someone bite and drink their blood? Yeah, that was hard to do.

I didn't know when it happened, but somewhere over the last few weeks, I started seeing him the way he saw me. As my partner, not just in the spy sense, more like my equal, my person I could turn to.

"Oh, my gosh, did you see the vamp with the whip? He was swinging that thing around and hitting everybody he could." Rachel laughed.

"Which whip are you talking about? He was swinging both around." Scott mumbled. He had gotten poked more than once by men tonight.

"What was all that stuff Deacon was saying about Carter needing testosterone?" Todd changed the subject, not wanting to rehash the sore butt syndrome they both were suffering from.

Carter was a big vampire. Much bigger than Ryley. We won't even try to comparc Scott and Justin. It would just be embarrassing for them.

"What's tester one?" Rachel couldn't even say the word. Sometimes I forgot how young she was.

"Testosterone is a chemical that increases body mass and strength. Guys have more of it. Did you see those other two new guys? I bet Deacon was on the hunt for buff guys when he met us." I turned back to Todd to answer his question. "Carter was talking about being tired and worn out. Deacon basically sold him you like a pick me up drug."

"Ok, that I get. But why do all that other stuff?"

I giggled at his disgusted face. Some things he was never going to get used to.

"Are you trying to say you didn't enjoy any of it?" I teased him.

He gave me a playful scowl and moved our hands so he could pinch my leg. “You know those parts I enjoyed, it was his involvement that I didn't.”

I sighed. “Exercise can build the levels up. Testosterone works in the sex drive as well. It’s possible he just likes that too.” I tilted my head. “Or he was trying to lace his favorite drug with dopamine.”

“Yes, that. That is what I need to know more of,” Rachel leaned between the front seats. “This one vamp kept chanting over and over again, for me to raise my dopamine. Then when I reached a certain point she cheered and dove into her dinner.”

I laughed again. Finally meeting the vamp who we were going to use, and getting started on this path, was putting me in a good mood.

“Dopamine is a chemical your body creates. It is what heightens the *pleasure*.” I let the last word roll slowly off my tongue, making them all laugh.

We were swapping stories when Rachel got excited over something she remembered. “Oh my gosh, did you guys see behind the bar, Deacon, Carrie, and that other large guy?”

“Colton?” I turned to face her again.

“Yes, him. Thank you.”

“No, what happened?” Todd asked for us.

I missed it too, and judging by the look on Scott’s face, so had he.

“Oh. My. Gosh. So. The two were dancing again, while Deacon was off dealing with customers, and I mean like, all up in each other’s business dancing. The guy was like way into it. When Deacon went over there, he just stood there watching. I thought for sure he was about to punch the guy. I mean, his hands were just barely under the rim of that tiny shirt she wore, which looked totally cool, by the way. I have to get one. Anyway, Deacon just stared at them, and then started smiling. You know how he kissed her when we first got there?" She didn't even wait for our answers. "Well, it was like that, only this time, he did a whole lot more. He worked that guy right against his own girlfriend's butt until he was dripping all over her. She was totally into it too." Rachel let out her breath and folded her arms as she leaned back. "I bet they are all together, like together, together."

Scott leaned toward Rachel and placed a hand between her legs. "We can't exactly talk, love, now can we?"

"Dude. I am so sore right now it is not funny. Those guys were part animals and three times your size. You are going to have to back off tonight." She lightened her tone with a wink. "Catch me in the morning."

I laughed. I already knew Todd wasn't going to let me wait that long. Every time we had to share with others, he needed to have me close. Sealing our partnership again. We got quiet as we pulled up next to the school.

We left the car parked nearby and snuck over a fence and toward a back door to one of the halls that would lead to the gym. Todd unlocked the door and stepped aside. Rachel went in first, and I followed, bumping right into her frozen back.

I looked up to see why she wasn't moving, then shoved the door closed before the boys were seen.

An irate man of about fifty stood in front of us. His hair gray was falling out, his stomach more of a beer gut now. He had his hands on his hips as he looked at us up and down. The scowl on his face did not match the tent in the pajama pants he was wearing. He wasn't wearing a shirt, but he had enough hair on his chest to look like he was.

"Where the hell have you two been? Do you have any idea what time it is? There is a curfew in place for a reason, and you two are out galivanting all night dressed like a bunch of hookers! I bet you were just hoping to call a vampire over so you could get a thrill! I should be kicking you two out right now. You know the rules. If you are not back by sundown, you are not back at all. Well? What do you have to say for yourselves?"

I sighed to myself. I didn't need a vision to know that if I didn't act right now, he would kick us out tonight. We knew we couldn't stay here for much longer, but we hadn't started scouting for a new place yet. If I didn't act now, he'd kick us out before we could get our stuff and figure out the next step.

I stepped to the right and pushed Rachel behind me. I was the one that got us into this after all.

"I'm so sorry, Mr. Ryan." I pulled out my pathetic childlike voice. "It's all my fault. I forced her to go with me. Please, don't punish her, just me." I forced a tear out of my eye. I learned how to fake cry and pretend to feel bad when I got caught sneaking out of my foster homes. "I'll do *anything* but please don't kick us out, Mr. Ryan." I pushed my bottom lip out in a pout, his eyes were going lower than that.

I may have also had to beg a store manager or two not to call the cops after I got caught stealing. Mom taught me how to do it. Hell, she used me as the diversion so *she* wouldn't get caught. She didn't care that some of them wanted payment in forms that didn't involve cash. I was 12, and an early bloomer. Thanks, mom. At least I knew how to play this.

"Hmph. Looks like you and I need to have a talk about responsibility, young lady. Rachel, go put some clothes on and get to bed. If I catch you out late again, you will have to face punishment as well. Grace, come with me."

Rachel waited near the door as I followed him. I knew she would let the boys in as soon as the coast was clear. I just had to hope she could keep Todd from breaking down the door to the office Mr. Ryan was using.

I pretended to cry harder as I heard him close the door roughly, locking it behind us. He walked in front of me, leaning against the principal's desk, his arms folded once again. Probably going for some relaxed but still held the power pose. Little did he know…

"What are we going to do about this, Grace? What would your father say if he were here?"

Ha! Jokes on him. I never knew my father. He was just one more in the line of morons my mother got paid to sleep with. His cheap condom broke and boom! Nine months later, here I was.

I sniffed and wiped my cheek. "My daddy would just sigh with disappointment and say it was time for another reminder. He didn't like punishing me like this, but it was the only way I would learn. He used to make me pull down my shorts and underwear and bend me over his knee and spank me when I was naughty." At the spark in his eyes, I knew I was on the right road. My mother taught me very little, but she did teach me how to read men. She always knew what I needed to do to get the managers distracted enough. "He always took care of me after, though, being all nice and rubbing me to make it feel better. He even had special lotion that took all my pains away. He rubbed it everywhere on me, to make sure there was no pain left. The first time I was naughty rubbing hurt really bad, but he was right, it stopped hurting and the lotion made everything better." I sniffed again. "Daddy hasn't been around in a while to punish me when I am naughty. I guess I forgot." I shrugged pathetically and started crying again.

"What did your mom say about the punishments?"

Ha! Like she would have cared.

"Daddy said mommy told him how to take care of me, it was the way all good girls had to learn to be good from their daddy's. But we couldn't tell her. She would be very disappointed and mad at me for being so naughty. I just can't help it, Mr. Ryan. I didn't mean to be naughty. I promise!"

"Well, I'm sorry you lost your daddy. It sounds like you need a reminder of why you should behave. I will help you this time, but next time, I won't be so nice. And I'll let you keep it between us."

He sat down on one of the chairs and waved me over.

"Thank you, Mr. Ryan."

He grinned up at me, with those yellow teeth of his. "Think nothing of it, darling. And I think I even have some of that special lotion your daddy used to use."

I grinned back, like a complete idiot. "Oh, thank you, Mr. Ryan!"

"Now, I think you need to take that skirt off there, Miss Grace. It's one of the reasons you were so naughty tonight, wasn't it?"

I let my lip tremble and looked at the ground. "Yes, Mr. Ryan. I stole it from someone's house."

"Well, now. Stealing is awfully bad. I think you will need to take it all off for your punishment to mean something. I'll let you wear it back to your bed later, but you have to promise never to wear it again."

I shook my head. "I won't, Mr. Ryan. With you here making sure I behave; I know I will do much better."

I let the skirt slowly drop, then carefully untied the top before pulling it off. He was practically salivating.

He grabbed my arm and pushed me over his lap. "You have been a *very* naughty girl, haven't you?"

"Yes, Mr. Ryan."

"No. When I punish you, I want you to call me daddy, that way you'll feel like he is the one teaching you again. Understand?"

"Yes, sir, Mr.... I mean, daddy. But this isn't the way daddy did it." I looked over my shoulder at him, his eyes glued to his hand rubbing over my bare butt.

"No, what am I forgetting?"

"Daddy made sure he was poking me in the stomach, so I felt the pain more. He said it was a reminder."

"What did he poke you with?"

I looked down like I was feeling shy. "Himself. He said only really naughty girls had to feel that. And I have been very naughty tonight... daddy."

"That's it? You only have to feel it on your belly?" He totally wanted me to feel it somewhere else.

I nodded and nibbled on my fingernail. "Yes. He only put it somewhere else if I was naughty too often." Well, looked like he was enjoying hearing it as much as doing it. I could work with that. "One time, he had to punish me four times in the same week. I couldn't sleep, so I kept sneaking out of my room for things. The last time, daddy said I wasn't learning my lesson good enough. He made me lay on the bed, with no clothes on. He tied my hands and feet to the bed, so I wouldn't accidentally move away from him. It hurt so bad, and there was so much blood. At least the first time. He said I was only allowed to yell because mommy wasn't home. He left me tied up all night. In the morning, he came back and kissed it all better before using his magic lotion on me."

Mr. Ryan could barely speak by that point. "Did you tell your mommy when she got back?"

I shook my head, forcing a small blush. "No. Daddy said mommy told him to do that. It would help me sleep and remember not to sneak out of bed."

"And how often did your daddy have to tie you up?"

"He tied me to my bed the rest of the weekend, coming in to remind me why I had to stay in bed. By the time mommy came home, I wasn't bleeding anymore, but it still hurt. Daddy was so much bigger than me. But he always made it better. I lost daddy not much later. I have tried really hard to remember, daddy. I promise."

"Well, why don't you help daddy with his pants, little darling? Since this is the first time we'll start out small. The next time though, I will find a place to tie you up, so you remember better."

"Thank you, daddy." I stood up and leaned over him as he lifted up enough for me to slide them down.

I let my fingernails drag along his skin, and let other things hang practically in his face. My goal was to get him so worked up he blew before he could really make me regret this. He struck me as the kind to be a "quickdraw McGraw," as my mother always put it. I was sure he wasn't far from losing it just from my story.

Too soon, I was lying over him again, feeling sorry for his wife as that sad thing pushed against me. He started telling me every bad thing I had done since I stepped foot inside *his* shelter. The man had apparently watched us a little too closely.

In between each infraction, he smacked my butt. After the third, I realized he was trying to hit me hard enough to make me move forward, so he could catch me and keep me from falling. The parts he grabbed wouldn't have stopped anything, but I just thanked him and called him daddy.

I was really bored while I waited for him to decide I had had enough. It was better than what I'm sure he was hoping for. I could deal with him being the grabby one if it kept me off my knees.

"Now what, little darling? How does daddy make you feel better?"

I pulled another chair over and held onto it. "I hold on like this, while he… you, punish me and then take the pain away."

"That's okay, little darling. I have plenty of time. But we need to keep this our little secret, alright? I don't want anyone else misunderstanding and thinking you are still being naughty. It's my job as your daddy to punish you."

I nodded again. "Yes, daddy. Am I allowed to go to bed now? I'm really tired."

"Of course, little darling, now cover back up so no one tempts you to be naughty again."

I dressed quickly and left. My group was all sitting on the floor near our cots. I waved for them to pretend to lie down, as I knew Mr. Ryan was watching us. We laid quietly until we were sure he was asleep.

As quietly as we could, we crawled into the hall and into a classroom, the one we had pretty much adopted as our own. Many lessons had been taught in there. Just not the ones you would expect in a high school.

Todd was livid still. I made them all laugh with how I played the shelter manager and kept him from doing something I would have really regretted.

After some time, I broached what we all knew was coming.

"We need to leave. Tonight. We can use the car and move."

"Why tonight? Why not tomorrow?" Scott asked with a yawn.

"Because most of us are still underage and were told we had to stay with the adults. Plus, I don't want anyone here knowing where we are going. No trails to follow. We just disappear. If they catch us, they will break us up and make us sleep closer to the rest of them. Possibly even in different shelters. Somewhere they can keep a better eye on us."

“Where will we go?” Justin asked softly. I didn’t have an answer for that.

The twins exchanged a look, then Layla spoke up. “We know a place. We hid there before. It’s an apartment complex. The vamps cleaned it out. There is a three-bedroom suite towards the top. The guy had a bunch of canned goods, maybe they are still there.” She ended in a shrug.

We all agreed and twenty minutes later we were sneaking out through the outside basketball courts. The car was only a five-seater, but we shoved the twins on top of laps in the backseat. We still had all the bags of food Todd and I had scrounged. At least it was a start. We even had money now, we could buy more as we needed it.

This was only temporary, until we could see Carter again. We needed to be there every time he was. We needed him to get attached enough to want to keep us. We needed him to get us closer to Curtis and his men.

CHAPTER 15

Deacon

For once, I almost hated the idea of leaving the bar for a day. Even though I had been curious to see what damage had been done to the city and surrounding areas, I still would have preferred to stay behind.

I charged my phone every day, while the generator was on. But there hadn't been a lot of time for me to search the internet for news stories. Most of what I heard came from the Nightwalkers when they came in at night.

From what I have been able to put together, Curtis had been planning this for quite some time. Long enough that he was able to change a navy pilot or two into one of them. It wasn't hard. He just had to hit up the military hospitals, looking for recent wounded who were not expected to survive. The ones that were desperate to stay alive. Their clearance hadn't been deleted yet. With their help, he was able to steal a few bombs and hide them away. Then, when the time came, they stole a plane and dropped them, three nights in a row. One night per region.

In the meantime, Curtis and his team managed to get a bunch of other bombs made and placed them just right, and for the right times. Then came the systematic cleansing of neighborhoods. Fewer humans to fight back. Fewer humans to maintain. But plenty of food for the vampires in the state.

I hadn't heard anything, but I was assuming that he had taken over a few of the military bases as well. California had quite a few to begin with. With all the drones that I saw the other day, and the stories I'd been told, it only made sense. I couldn't help but wonder if he gave all those soldiers the option of being changed or being donors. They would have been like espresso for vampires. A quick pick me up.

The biggest piece of the puzzle came from my last conversation with Carter, before he checked out for the night last night. He was happily satiated in his booth, a small frown playing on his face when the teens got picked up by someone else. I didn't want any problems, and I had a few burning questions, so I sat across from him, drawing his attention away.

"Well, you look a lot better. I told you that you just needed a boost." I teased him.

He chuckled and rubbed his belly. "Hit the spot, that's for sure. You really have an eye for donors. I've never walked away from here unsatisfied. But those two just might be my favorites. Where did you find them?"

"I found them, and their friends, in a shelter a few nights ago. They were just lying around, bored." While I was sure he would love the specifics, I didn't feel like going over them. "You said you finished your part of the wall. Just how big is this wall? Did Curtis lock us all in here?"

Carter chuckled and shook his head. "Nah. We could climb it without a problem. The strongest might even be able to jump it, with a good run. But it's supposed to go around the whole state."

I gave him an incredulous look, knowing his ego would insist on more information to prove him right, and the psycho he chose to follow.

"You all built a wall nearly 200,000 miles in length, in less than a month? With debris?"

Carter laughed, like I was being dimwitted. "No, of course not. Curtis had walls started months ago. Real ones, too. Mostly in the more hidden areas. The mountains near the Oregon border, Yosemite, and the deserts near Arizona and Mexico. I don't know how he's gotten it built during the day. Maybe he hired a construction company or something. Humans will do anything if you pay them enough."

Or he found Vampire Borns and pulled them to his side. I wondered…

"Anyway. I don't know if the whole wall is done yet. I am only in charge of the Mojave and Death Valley sections. We even built small ramadas, and put up those collapsible tents far enough away, for those on duty."

"Curtis has you all monitoring the walls?"

He grimaced. "Yeah. We usually only do 24-hour shifts but with the roads being such a disaster, it ain't easy getting there. We've been camping out in a few deserted houses. I only come back when I have more than a few hours off at a time. I wish I could come back more often. That area was already pretty deserted. Whoever the bombs didn't get, ran away before the wall could be finished."

"No wonder you came in tonight looking like a mess. Sounds like you might need to find a few humans of your own. I bet your guards would work better with food close by as well."

"Eh, maybe. I'll think about it." He glanced around, keeping an eye on things. Or maybe certain humans.

I turned my eyes to my angel. She was walking around the bar, her hips swinging to the music. Colton went up to her as soon as she rounded the bar, grabbed her hand, and spun her in a circle. Her head fell back as she laughed and went with it.

"How are you guys getting back and forth? Are most of the freeways there and back intact?"

He snorted lightly. "Yes and no. There are patches of clear road, but then they suddenly give way. Plus, there are a lot of abandoned cars on them, blocking traffic. We have cleared what we can. I took over ownership of a Humvee, I don't need a road with that sucker!"

He talked for the next few minutes about the various adventures he had been on with his new love. I listened, gathering details for the trip I was planning, while watching my angel dance with my best friend.

"You going to kill him or pull him off her?" Carter asked with a grin, tipping his chin at Carrie and Colton.

I chuckled and stood up. "Neither. That would be counterproductive. I may join them though." I winked at him as I walked away, leaving him laughing.

Last night was the best night of my life so far. I never dreamed my angel was actually a witch, a pure blooded one at that. I felt a bit stupid now that I had time to think about it all the way through. I should have known the magic in her blood would create an enticing scent. I had known many witches in my time, but none had ever called to my primal side the way Carrie did.

Most curses called for a touch of blood from the caster, it added strength. Maybe that was it. Maybe her blood called to all of us because it was used in the curse that was laid upon us. That could be why so many in her family were killed and why they hid in the sun. And she had it from both parents. She was double the sweetness. Double the temptation.

Would the curse keep her from giving me a son? Or would the purity of her blood make her strong enough to survive it?

I pulled onto the 10 and drove for a few miles, my eyes peeled for a random drop off. I transferred to the 5, thinking this wasn't so bad after all. Then reached the overpass and exit for the 14.

Where once sat two roads, one over the other as they turned, now was a gaping hole. Very few pieces of the freeway filled it. Very few burned up cars remained. All the big pieces had probably been carted off to build Curtis' wall. It was one giant, burned out, pit. It almost looked like it had been a bonfire at one time.

Was that how they cleared the bodies, after taking what they wanted?

I pulled to a stop and groaned.

The pilot had even taken out the truck routes too. While those were originally carved into the hillside, they now gave way to deep fissures and had been overrun by giant rocks. More than one car lay flattened under them.

I ran through my memory bank for the way we traveled before the freeways were built.

I turned around, not caring which side I was driving on since I was the only one there. I took the exit to Sylmar. From there, I took the long way to Newhall, and was able to jump onto the 14. Finally.

I went as far as the Antelope Valley before I found the next hole.

The cities here looked mostly intact. I pulled up to a gas station, next to a McDonalds and some rundown apartment buildings, refilled my tank, then went inside the convenience store. Prices were higher than normal but everything else looked the same. They even had power.

“I’m trying to get to Mojave. Is the 14 drivable, minus the big hole down the way?”

“Nope. It got hit a few times. Sierra highway should get you most of the way there though. What you wantin’ to go to Mojave for? Ain’t nobody there.”

I shrugged. “Had a friend out that way, haven’t heard from them in a while. Thought I might get a look at this wall too.”

“Suit yourself.” He gave me directions and I left.

I didn’t go the way he told me to. I had what I needed. I had also been gone for nearly four hours already. I should be able to make the trip back faster, not having to backtrack this time. Still, the sun would be going down and vamp hour would start before I got back home.

I was going to be in so much trouble.

I would happily take it though. My angel was now my mate. My fated one at that.

Everything I had been feeling for her from the beginning finally made sense now. I didn’t remember the last time I heard of someone finding the one person meant for them. Not since we went into hiding anyway.

Which was probably why I didn’t recognize the pull. I knew barely anything about it. Rarely did anyone talk about fated mates, or mates in general. It didn’t matter how much time had gone by as a mate was a mate. They were missed. Their absence was felt. Which was why when one died, the other usually went with them. We were still stumped on how not one of the men mated when the curse hit survived, while their mate was killed.

For me though, my life was looking up. My bar was busy all the time. I had my mate. I had my best friend. One day I may even have both at the same time (crossing my fingers). If I were to share her with anyone, it would be Colton.

It wouldn't be the first time he and I shared a woman, but it would be the first time we both liked her. It was always just helping each other spice up a redundant life.

Growing up in a nearly all male society, your options were limited. There was a reason most vampires didn't care about genders. We had our preferences of course, but we accepted anyone that could get the job done.

I would never complain about it being just my angel and me, I loved my mate. I would also never dream of betraying her like that. And not just because the last thing we needed was another curse. I just couldn't stand the thought of hurting her. I didn't know how anyone would be able to hurt their mate like that.

Her fear and sadness over me leaving today was hard to take. I had to leave before I caved to her pleading, if only to make her feel better.

I would be thrilled if Colton joined us though. Sharing someone I loved with someone I trusted and cared about would be fun for me. My mate was perfect in every way, and I wanted Colton to see that. To appreciate that. I wanted to show her off to my best friend.

My life was better than it had ever been before. I mean, yeah, the whole deal with Curtis killing lots of humans and closing up California sucked, but it hadn't affected me negatively. On the contrary, I never would have met Carrie had she not gotten trapped in that bus station and then chased to my doorstep.

As long as Curtis didn't find out that I was still alive, and here, or about my mate, I could continue living the way I had been. Only better. I wouldn't have to work to ignore the scent of the constant arousal in the air from the Nightwalkers and the donors. My mate and I could join in the fun. Colton too. It had been some time since he and I shared a woman. Since we did anything together, actually.

We always tried not to use the donors, at least in the beginning. If we did, we shared her together. Right there in the bar. We both fed, at the same time. And got our other needs met. The last one got really clingy after that, though. We accidentally turned her into a blood junkie. A week later, the cops found her body. She had started seeking out the Nightwalkers a little too often, ignoring her own health.

After that, we never used the donors again. If the scent got to us, we just helped each other out. It was rare when it was just us. But I had tired of using human women a long time ago. As had Colton. It was actually better just us and without them. Sundays were always the harder days.

The cab of my truck filled with my own laughter when I remembered one particular Sunday. Colton had been gone for many months. He had lost the habit of ignoring the overwhelming scent. Every VIP room was full. The scent of the alcohol and cigarette smoke did nothing to cover it up for us. The moment the last human was out of the bar, Colton had his pants down and pushed me to my knees. I laughed all the way up until he made that impossible. Then I took a turn.

That was many years ago, and possibly the last time we had been together. Having him and my angel at the same time would be heaven. Just the thought of how good that would feel filled my heart. One day. One day it would happen.

If only my angel would get pregnant, and give me a son, then my life would be better than perfect.

I slammed on the brakes, the truck swerving to the right, as the next thought hit me.

If Carrie were to get pregnant, we would need to leave. A vampire being born from a human would draw Curtis' attention my way. There would be no way to hide her from him then.

My son would not survive that. Neither would my mate, who smelled like heaven.

I slammed my foot back down on the gas pedal, feeling the need to get back to her as soon as possible. I needed to see her, to smell her, to feel her. I needed to assure myself that she was still here. Healthy and happy.

I was only a few miles from home when I felt a sharp pang hit my chest. I gasped for air, rubbing the sore spot, trying to figure out what happened. It only took me a minute to realize the pain wasn't coming from me.

My mate was scared, really and truly scared.

CHAPTER 16

Carrie

Was it me or the room that felt beyond awkward after Deacon left? Colton obviously overheard the witch conversation, which meant he overheard *everything* else. I twisted the rim of Deacon's shirt in my fingers and bit the corner of my lip.

"Exactly how good is your hearing?"

Colton moved closer, slid a hand on my waist, and kissed my forehead, before he moved to sit on the couch.

"Let's put it this way. If I wanted to focus, I could hear Mr. Garcia talking to a customer."

My jaw dropped and I released the shirt. "He is next door, and in a whole different building!"

Colton just shrugged like it wasn't a big deal. To him it probably wasn't.

"Can all vampires do that, or just the ones like you and Deacon?" I sank onto the other end of the couch, my body turned to face him.

My curiosity was helping me ignore the original embarrassment.

"Nightwalkers have good hearing, compared to humans. Vampire Borns have double that kind of range. Between all the talking and the music in the bar, they won't pick up much of anything." He reached over and stroked the side of his finger along my bare legs. "Deacon and I will catch everything, well, if we want to. We learned the hard way to not focus on everything going on around us on some nights."

"Did you really sleep in the cellar last night?" I would feel really bad if he had.

He laughed and pulled my leg from where it was curved under me and set it on his lap. Then he started grazing his fingers along the inside. I could feel that he was perfectly content, like this was normal for us. I guess, in a way, it was. He tended to take advantage of the loose rules when we were in the bar. He was getting braver with his hands lately, since it was obvious Deacon didn't care so much. And when I got lost in the moment. I wasn't even sure last night whose hands were under my shirt, while we were dancing together. And I wasn't sure if I cared about that, at least, not at the time. Colton had a way of drowning out the world for me too. Not quite the same way as Deacon, but enough.

I did care when I felt Deacon place Colton against me, under my skirt, but even that flew out the window pretty quick. Hence, my not knowing who was in my shirt. I barely registered my shirt zipper being pulled down halfway.

I was pretty sure Colton knew where my mind was going, as he smiled softly and dared to move his fingers a little higher. Just high enough to make my breath catch.

"No. I was just being dramatic. You both weren't that bad. And for the record, I don't mind that your ancestors were the ones that cursed us. I lived during that time, too. I was still very young, but I do vaguely remember my mother. She was a Vampire Born. One of the last females."

I couldn't help it, I reached over and set my hand on his. Not the one on my leg, his other one. "I'm sorry, Colton."

He rolled his eyes and shook his head. "It's not your fault, sweetheart. What's done is done. Now we are here, and" he lifted an eyebrow at me, "you are now fully mated to my best friend." He gave a small sad laugh and took his hand back. The one I hadn't wanted to disturb. It was probably a good thing.

"Yes. I am." It was quiet for a few minutes, until I stood up again. "I'm going to go get ready for work." I bit back the laugh at his pained expression.

While part of me wanted to play nice for Colton's benefit, the other part wanted to make Deacon happy when he got back. I pulled on the black top, the one that hugged my breasts, and only my breasts, from behind. It was Deacon's favorite, that and the white one. Although, he did seem to enjoy the one with a zipper too. I paired it with one of my black pencil type skirts. It rolled up easily when he moved my legs. Almost to my waist.

The entire outfit provided him with more access to more fun places. After being gone all day, Deacon was going to be all over me. And I was perfectly fine with that.

It only took one look from Colton, and I knew I had picked right. Knowing he found me so attractive made me feel giddy. He was still sitting on the couch, his eyes watching my every move like a hunter preparing to strike.

I walked over and picked up his hand, pulling on him.

"Come on, lazy. You came to work, and we've got work to do. Sunday vamps always leave a giant mess behind."

He grumbled disgruntledly from behind me. I couldn't hear him, but I felt the intent. He was jealous, probably over the way the mess was made.

I loved how much stronger that power was getting lately. Both of them really. Maybe all I had been missing was stepping fully into the world of magic, depending on my powers more, and accepting what I was. I may have been more willing to accept my powers the last few years, but I still had barely been walking the line.

Even though it was obvious the two of them had cleaned up the bar last night, it was not good enough. They did the basics, but Sunday calls for more than just the basics. Men, especially vampires apparently, may not care about certain types of messes left on benches and floors, but I sure did.

We spent the next two hours giving that place a proper scrub down. We might have finished sooner, but Colton seemed to get distracted anytime I bent over. I didn't do anything to mess with him on purpose. I didn't bend over from the waist, knowing my skirt would move up enough to give him a peek. Or even shake my butt with the music, while bent over. And I certainly didn't fix my shirt with him watching.

I would never mess with a man like that.

As one of my dad's favorite songs, by Collin Raye, when I was a kid said, "that's my story and I'm sticking to it." He used to say that to my mom, and then break out singing the chorus. If she still didn't crack, he'd grab her hands and start dancing. Worked every time.

Once we opened the bar, the humans began trickling in. Colton took that as his sign that he was allowed to touch me again. He put a hand on my stomach, from behind me, and reached around me for a bottle of scotch. Since the music was playing I leaned over just enough to rub against him, dancing. He growled in my ear and pressed back. My eyes closed as the memory of what that felt like ran through me. He sniffed my neck with a sigh and kissed it gently before moving on.

For the most part, it was quiet. The humans were there to drink and forget. Not there to drink and have fun. Every day they talked less and less. Every day we asked fewer and fewer of them to pay.

"How you doing, Jack?" I asked an older man sitting at the bar.

He huffed and turned his glass in his hands. "I've been better, Carrie. I'm still here though, still kicking."

"Good for you, Jack. Just don't give up, this has to end sometime."

"I doubt it. There is a rumor going around. Saying the big bad vampire boss will be in town next month. He is going to each city and town in California. He is organizing a vampire government and getting a census of all the humans still living within *his* walls." Jack snorted and took another drink of his scotch.

My eyes flicked up to Colton, who I knew now was most likely listening. He came over and put a hand on my back, trying to soothe my fears. His comfort helped, but he wasn't Deacon, so I was only partially calmed. Before today, I didn't understand how Deacon was able to affect me so easily. Now I did.

"That actually might be a good thing, Jack." Colton said. "It means he is done spreading destruction. We can start building some semblance of a life again. He will want to keep all the humans fed and healthy. Not everyone will become vampire food. Some will need to farm and work in factories and other jobs. California is a big state, with lots of places for people to work."

Jack stared at my new friend like he had grown another head. Colton had meant well. I set one hand on his lower back and patted his chest with the other, placatingly.

"What? What did I say?"

"It's not really what you said, so much as how you said it. You sounded like you were rooting for the vamps, Colton."

"No, no. That is not what I meant. I was just trying to tell him that, with some sort of organization, things will get better than they are now."

"I don't care what kind of organization he puts in. He wants to boss around the other vampires, fine. All for it. But he wants to boss around humans too. That ain't right. Humans should be in charge of humans and vamps should be in charge of vamps. They want a home? Then they should buy some land and go make their own. Leave our home alone." The older man stated firmly.

Colton looked like he wanted to argue, but the man was not going to be swayed, and frankly he was right. I put my hand on Colton's arm and shook my head when he looked at me. It wasn't worth the fight. Jack wasn't going to change his mind, and neither was Colton. He sighed, deflated, and walked away.

"Tell me more about this great-grandson of yours." I changed the topic with Jack, bringing a small smile to his face.

The day shift dragged by slowly. We didn't have many human customers, and those we did have didn't have very much at home, or the shelter. Especially food. We were more than happy to provide that.

We only had a few patrons left in the bar, and I was bored enough to do extra cleaning. Colton didn't need to put on a show as much with the humans. They knew I was taken, and they knew they had a good thing going in our bar. They didn't want to ruin that. With less than an hour until we sent them home to safety, I gathered the large trash bag.

"I'm going to take the trash out to the alley." I informed Colton.

He swiftly blocked my path. Thankfully the few humans in the room weren't paying attention since he let some of his facade slip.

"No, save it. I will do it soon."

I scoffed and rolled my eyes. "I am perfectly capable of taking out the trash. I used to do it all the time before I came here. It'll be fine."

I tried to move him, but he was thicker than a stone wall. He folded his arms, his face telling me there was no way in hell I was going out there.

"You are not to leave this bar alone." His voice, his vibe, and especially his stance, backed up his statement.

I groaned and practically dropped the bag. I lifted a hand toward the window, where the sun shone through. "Colton, the sun is still up, and I am going only two feet from the door. If something happens, I'm sure you'll hear me before I even scream." I pleaded.

He refused to budge. I left the bag where it was and leaned against the wall, pouting like a teenager.

He smirked at me and returned to the bar to help Fred, who was now watching us carefully. With a silent laugh of triumph, I picked up the bag and ran for the door. Colton didn't have a choice but to let me go this time. If he used his full speed in front of the humans, especially while they were paying attention to him, the word would spread of vampires that walked in the sunlight.

Even still, I heard the low growl, which made me laugh more. I was really beginning to love making them both growl like that. Didn't matter the reasoning, it was just fun.

I didn't know what the big deal was, I would be back before he was even done with Fred, a heavy drinker. He watched his wife raped and murdered in front of him by vampires. I couldn't blame him for turning to the bottle. And if Colton did run in front of him, he would lead the mob, holding the biggest pitchfork.

I walked out the back door, looked around to be safe, then stepped out. It took me maybe twenty seconds to put the bag in the dumpster and head back to the door.

It took three seconds for a hand to wrap around my mouth from behind. I never heard him coming. I never *felt* him coming. I should have searched with more than just my eyes. I should have paid better attention to my surroundings.

"There's my pretty birdie. I knew if I was patient long enough you would come out of your cage."

I recognized that voice. One I only heard once, a few weeks ago, another lifetime ago. That one time had been enough to sear it to my brain.

Victor was back.

I tried to scream, but it was pointless. I had to hope Colton could somehow hear my muffled scream. I could feel Victor's nose moving along my neck, as he inhaled my scent. Then his tongue licked the same spot Deacon had marked me just hours before.

"He ruined you!" Victor yelled in a low voice. "He tainted your blood with his own. I will kill him for this." I could feel the vibrations in his chest as he growled out the threat.

I didn't like his growls nearly as much.

I opened my mouth and tried to bite the palm covering me, it only made him laugh. His other hand retaliated by squeezing various parts of me. It felt like I was a used car, and he was kicking the tires to see if I was still any good.

I tried to kick behind me to hit him. It didn't work. He wrapped his free hand around my waist and arms and lifted me in the air. Victor made it look as though I was nothing but a doll.

"Since he tainted what was mine, I will have to taint what is his. Well, was his. There won't be much left of you by the time I am done. Hopefully, by finishing you off, it will take him out too. Serves him right for taking what was mine."

As Victor pulled me further into the dark places of the alley, my eyes overflowed from the fear and soaked his hands. I stopped kicking him, it was fruitless anyway. My fear quickly bled into depression.

I should have listened to Colton. I should have stayed in the stupid bar. Why didn't I listen? I knew I was safer inside then out. That's why I had never come out by myself.

Victor stopped walking as he neared a dark van hidden down a separate alley, no windows in the back, and a black moving blanket hung like a curtain behind the two front seats.

I had thought all my adrenaline was gone, but seeing this, it came flooding back.

I started screaming into his hand again, kicking my legs behind me. I lifted them up to the van, placing one on each side of the opening, trying to push us back. Anything to keep from getting inside there.

I knew if I went in, I was never coming back out.

Victor growled again while trying to push my legs off the car. Unfortunately for him, both his hands were busy restricting my arms and my mouth.

Suddenly, he gave a grunt and released me.

I screamed with shock and fear, again, when I randomly fell. I landed on my butt and fell to my back, hitting my head against the pavement.

"Ow." I whimpered in a groan.

I didn't let myself have time to recover, I rolled to my knees and took off running, screaming for help. I was going to use every advantage I had to get away from him, and to get Colton's attention. Anybody's attention. The other vampires knew who I belonged to. Surely they would help get me back to Deacon.

My scream hit a new pitch when two of the hottest arms I had ever felt caught me from behind and swung me up until he was holding me bridal style against his chest. I was too busy freaking out for it all to register, until I heard his voice.

"Sh, now angel. I've got you."

My eyes flew up and met the glowing pitch-black eyes of my mate. The fire behind them looked more orange than yellow tonight. Even his glow was darker. He was beyond ticked.

I immediately threw my arms around his neck and sobbed into him. I felt rough kisses run across my forehead and down my face as the wind rushed over us. I kept my face hidden, needing his comfort, until I was being laid on a bed seconds later.

"What the hell happened?" he growled.

I tried to find my voice to answer. But it wasn't coming. Someone else answered for me. Well, to the best of their ability anyway.

"I don't know, alright! She wanted to take the trash out. I told her no. She acted like she was going to wait for me, so I helped Fred. Next thing I know she is laughing and running out the door. I didn't hear anything from outside. When she didn't come back after a few minutes, I went to check on her, and that was right as you ran by." Colton's voice stopped, taking a breath to calm himself. "What happened out there?"

Deacon stayed lying next to me, holding me tight to him. "I felt her panic when I was down the street. I was prepared to run inside. But the second I got out of my truck her scent hit me. I followed it. I could hear muffled screaming. I barely got there in time. Victor was trying to put her in a van. He had her mouth covered so she couldn't scream. I could hear it through that, why couldn't you?"

He was bordering on accusing his friend of being at fault. He shouldn't, it was mine. All mine.

I felt the bed dip, and one of Colton's hands landed on my leg. "I don't know. The music, maybe? Did he hurt her?"

His intent for touching me had changed this time. It wasn't about wanting me this time. His only intent was to provide comfort. And to reassure himself that I was alright.

I felt a pressure in my chest lighten, followed by a sigh from Deacon. Was this extra pressure from him? We hadn't had time to figure out the whole feeling each other thing before he left this morning.

"Not physically. I would know if he had. She was trying to fight him off, that much I could tell. I think she is just traumatized for the moment." Deacon's hand pushed the hair off my face, and I looked up at him. My sobs were slowing, my tears weren't. "What happened, angel?"

I hiccupped, opened my mouth to say something, and then started crying again.

"I think she's still in shock." Deacon told his friend calmly.

He slid an arm under my head and held his wrist in front me, just as he did the night before. Through my blurry eyes, I watched as he bit into his wrist.

"Drink, angel. Let my blood heal you. You have bruises from that fall, those are my fault. I'm sorry. I just reacted. I didn't think about how you would fall when I killed him."

He pressed his wrist to my mouth, and without thinking, probably a reflex by this point, I took him in. I shook as the first few drops went down. Deacon rubbed his hand on my bare stomach. Colton rubbed his own hand up and down my leg. I shivered from the contact.

My eyes closed, rolling to the back of my head. I sighed with relief as the warm blood flooded through my system, smoothing out the pains I hadn't yet noticed, soothing me like a warm blanket.

CHAPTER 17

Deacon

I almost didn't make it. If I had been a minute later, she would have already been under him in that van.

It had been a long time since I last killed a Nightwalker with my bare hands. Something only Vampire Borns could do. A silver dagger to the heart would have been fast enough, and I would have had time to catch my angel before she hit the ground, but in my anger, I needed to make him suffer.

I needed to use my hands. I needed more.

When my angel's eyes closed, I felt a stirring of pleasure in my chest. The same place I felt her fear earlier. She brought her right hand up to my wrist, holding it tighter into her mouth.

Where I could once feel the pain coming from her, now I only felt a new need. One I was more than happy to fill.

I slid my hand up, pushing the small material off her. She let out a small moan. I lowered down and teased her with my teeth. I lifted my head up and looked at my friend. He was still rubbing her legs, one hand on each now. His glowing eyes were locked on my mate's luscious body, the fire bleeding through them.

I had been extremely ticked that she was alone, but that had been my fear. I knew him well enough to know he was beyond just simply liking my mate. It was easy to see the worry in his eyes, the self-condemnation when I brought her back.

Colton needed to soothe his fears, he needed to feel her. And she didn't seem to mind his touch right now.

She needed to know she was safe. That she was protected. That no one would ever touch her again. Besides us.

She was my mate, but I felt like, in a way, she belonged to both of us. And the idea didn't bother me as much as I thought it would.

"Wanna play?" I whispered to him. I didn't want to ruin the zone she was in now. A small part of me might have also been a little worried she would put a stop to what we were already starting if she came out of it..

"Are you sure? Won't she mind?"

I looked down at her, paying attention to the feeling in my chest. I had stopped moving, but he hadn't. She was still soaring.

"No, she is enjoying your touch just as much as mine right now."

"She may not know it is me, though. She will be mad later."

I chuckled. "She will be embarrassed, but not mad." My laugh fell away. "She needs a distraction. Let's give my mate what she needs."

"And you don't mind?"

This whole thing started because I refused to share what I deemed mine from the moment I saw her. I could understand his worry.

"With you, no. I trust you."

"But today…"

"Was not your fault. I am as much to blame. I never thought to warn her that Victor stalked the alley every night. I never thought she would feel safe enough to step out even that much on her own. I should have known better."

"It's not your fault either." Colton insisted.

"We all made mistakes, but the full blame lies with Victor. Now, help me to soothe her fears."

Colton nodded once and let go of her legs to stand up. A faint whimper came out of the angel in my bed. I laughed. I knew this was the right call. Colton quickly removed his clothes, then crawled over her legs, starting again, moving himself higher. My angel shook at the touch, her body registering it.

I slowly pulled my wrist back, knowing she had had enough. If she took much more, she would be dangerously close to that last change. Something I would never do without her permission.

For the first time, my angel didn't want to let go. Comatose Carrie was more obedient. I pulled harder, forcing her to release. She grunted her disapproval.

Her argument was cut off, as Colton distracted her with his hands sliding between her thighs. I watched as he worked, watching her body react to what he was doing to her. Watching his body as it reacted to her. I couldn't decide which one I enjoyed more.

She was far enough gone that I was able to extricate myself from her while I removed my own clothing.

Upon my return, I pushed the material off the other side of her chest. Colton had moved up enough that her skirt was now around her waist. We had a nearly perfect view of her body. Colton paused, right as he was about to make the last move, his eyes looking at me.

“Only my seed will spill into her down there.” I warned him.

With the slightest nod of agreement, he moved. My angel’s back arched into the air. I continued leaving fresh marks all over her, enjoying the uninterrupted time. When my lips met hers, she turned to press back, her hand holding my head to her lips.

Colton reached a hand down to me, and helped me out, while we both helped her. I was right on the edge when he released me and moved away from my angel.

“Headboard.” I instructed him.

He crawled to the top of the bed and sat against it.

She yelped a laugh as I flipped her over, smacking her butt as she moved. I placed her right in front of him. When his hand slowly petted the back of her head, she lowered, she knew exactly what to do. While she was busy, I took my rightful place. It wasn’t long before we all finished.

My angel collapsed next to Colton, her head on his lap. I went behind her, pulling her into me. Colton’s hand stroked the side of her head, combing his fingers through her hair. I kissed the back of her neck, and she sighed. We waited as she slowly came back to awareness.

We weren’t disappointed.

Carrie’s head lifted a little, her eyes trailing from Colton’s lap, up his chest, and onto his face. It took her a few seconds before her eyes widened and she jumped back with a small yelp of surprise.

When she heard both our laughter, she rolled into me, hiding once again. This time was more fun though.

While I held her close, Colton slid down and cuddled up to her from behind, his arm wrapping around her waist, just barely below the one I had around her back. I laughed harder when she squeaked, feeling him pressing against her. Our soldiers were never fully at ease, and with her still being in the state of undress that she was in, they were already starting to salute again.

Her adorable squeak did nothing to hide, or distract us, from the shiver his lips brought out of her.

"Why?" She mumbled into the crook of my arm.

"You needed it. You wanted it. But you would have never asked for it." I stated simply, as though it were no big deal. Because it wasn't. It was only the beginning.

She tipped her face back and glared at me. It might have been scary, had she not yawned in the middle of it.

"Rest now, sweetheart. You can have your tirade in the morning." Colton kissed her shoulder one last time before getting up. "I am going to go down to the bar. The donors are all here and I can hear clients arriving."

I nodded at him, appreciating his help. "I'll be down soon."

He was dressed and out the door less than a minute later.

"I don't know if I will ever get used to how fast you two are." My angel relaxed in my arms, moving to her back to look at me better. "I should get dressed and come down with you." She yawned on the last word again.

"No. You need to sleep." I told her firmly. "You have had a rough time, and you need to rest. My blood healed you. We helped you to relieve the remaining adrenaline, now your body and mind must heal naturally." I softened my voice. "Please, angel. Rest." Her lip trembled and I felt a spike in my heart. "I won't be far, just downstairs." I kissed her cheek and held her head against my heart. "Would you like me to stay until you fall asleep?"

She sniffled and nodded her head against me. I helped her remove her clothes, so she could rest more comfortably, then pulled her back into my arms. Quietly, I petted the back of her hair softly, holding her until I felt her breathing even out. It seemed as though it would take more than just a sip of blood and a pleasurable round to get her over what happened. Not that I even had many details yet.

I would get them tomorrow when she was feeling better.

I quietly made my way out of the apartment and down to the bar. I breathed with a sigh of relief that we had mated. Despite the level of music, I would be able to feel her. For now, it was a low, warm, burn. It was comforting. Like the feeling of holding your hands over a fire to warm them. Well, I assumed so at any rate. Vampires didn't chill easily.

"Hey, how's she doing?" Colton asked, the minute I stepped behind the bar. There weren't too many people in the bar yet at least.

"Sleeping now. She got scared again when I started to leave. I'll know if she wakes up."

"How? We may not hear her over this music. I barely heard you coming."

I grinned as I looked at my long-time friend and tapped my chest. "Because I can feel my mate right here."

"Is that what you meant when you said you felt her panic?" I started nodding before he even finished, so he kept going. "I thought that was only possible with fated mates. I'd never heard of a chosen mate having those benefits."

"It's not. Carrie is my fated mate, Colton."

Why hadn't he realized that yet? His brain was not working up to its normal par. Maybe it was the effect of my mate on him. I knew that I frequently had brain malfunctions when she was around.

"It explains why I felt the connection to her so strongly from the beginning. The feeling when she sealed herself to me was… there are no words to describe the feeling. It was unexpected, that's for sure."

Colton looked around the room, making sure no one was paying us any attention, then lowered his voice.

"What will you do if she cannot survive after giving you a son? It will take you both."

The idea of her leaving me hurt my heart. "If I have to avoid getting her pregnant then so be it. I will not lose her. However, I don't think that will be necessary. You heard her last night, yes? About her true heritage?"

I gave him a minute to think about it as I intercepted a man approaching one of my donors.

Colton waited until I returned to respond. "You think being a witch will make her body stronger?"

I shrugged, placing the money in the register, and adding it to my tally sheet. "I don't know, but it gives me hope. If I could have my mate, and a son, I would be a happy man."

"A happy prince?" He added with a teasing smile.

I shook my head with a small huff. "That is not my life anymore, and you know that. Curtis has more power than us these days. Now more than ever, it is important for me to stay hidden. I will not put my mate at risk."

We went our separate ways, cleaning up the messes left behind - the kind my angel would get upset if we left until later. I grabbed drinks for tables, and a few food items from the kitchen, where my new cook, Marty, was.

Colton monitored the donors and the bar.

“I forgot to ask you, did you want me to collect Victor and make a warning out of him?” Colton asked as I reached into the fridge for two beers.

“No.”

His head spun to me with surprise, not expecting this response. I scratched the bottom of my chin awkwardly, feeling embarrassed for my lack of control.

“I, uh, I didn't use the dagger. I was too angry for that.”

Colton’s eyes widened, catching my meeting. “I need to go. Now. We can’t risk someone else finding him first.” He was gone before I could even respond.

He was right of course. Leaving Victor there for so long had been sloppy. I should have sent Colton as soon as I had my angel safe. Not pull him in with us. Even though I didn’t regret it at the time. Or now, my only regret was not using the right brain.

I remembered enjoying the times Colton had joined me before, but I forgot how much I enjoyed his touch. Just hours ago, I had reminisced on the days it was just us. I remembered liking it, but I didn’t remember liking it this much. And I was right, with my angel in the mix, it was even better.

With the possibility of having them both, I must have wiped all logic out of my mind.

Our kind were stronger. We didn't need a silver dagger or a sword to kill. We could remove the Nightwalkers of their heads on our own. A headless corpse would be suspicious.

Colton was gone for half an hour. A very long half hour.

He walked in the back door and started working again like nothing had happened. He gave me the smallest nod, almost like a greeting.

"Hey, Deac?" I turned toward the voice and walked over to the table I had passed while having my silent discussion with Colton. "You're cute and all, but not nearly as cute as your girl. Where is she?" Lou, an old friend, was grinning at me.

"She wasn't feeling well, so I told her to stay in bed and rest. Guess you're stuck looking at me tonight."

"Ah, that's a shame. That is one thing I definitely don't miss about being human. Illness." He laughed, like it was the best joke in the world.

Considering he had been dying of smallpox when he got turned, I let it slide. Many Nightwalkers were created during mass pandemics. Plague, smallpox…COVID. Wars were another time. People who were dying, and were in immense pain, were more likely to accept the changes. Well, they didn't always know what they agreed to. Some were so far gone, they thought it was medicine, and then struggled to stop. If done right, the changeling believed they were experiencing the epitome of pleasure, all the way up until the hunger hit. And then the real pleasure never ended.

Colton and I had fun over the years, going to the movies and watching the ignorant human's version of our species. We both got a good laugh at it. There was no burning when we hungered. We felt weaker, just like a human did when they had not eaten. Unlike a human, it would not kill us though. For a Nightwalker, they would eventually go crazy and attack the first human to come near them. For Vampire Borns, we could eat food to help stave it off for some time. We get only a little weaker, but we rarely lost control. Unless they were a psychopath, they never would have let themselves get that hungry in the first place.

I smiled at Lou's attempt at a joke. "Any news? I trust your word more than some of these other yahoos around here." Lou wasn't known for embellishing a story to make it better.

"Let's see." He scratched his jaw in contemplation. He had a lot he could share. I slid into the booth across from him. "Ah. Got it." He snapped his fingers, pointing at me. "Curtis is building a government. He is starting up North and moving down this way. Word is that he is going to be moving all the humans out to the smaller cities, leaving the bigger cities for us. With all these large buildings and alleyways, we can get around pretty good during the day. Plus, it will help the humans to learn their place. Curtis and his men are creating a list of all the humans, and then will direct them to live in certain areas, working specific jobs."

"What about feeding?"

Lou shrugged. "Not sure, nothing definite on that front yet. Rumor is that he is going to assign that as one of the jobs, making groups for each area. He will probably take volunteers, use it as a punishment, or just as a job. The man is a creative genius. Just look how far we've come in such a short time."

I was preparing to ask more questions when I felt a small rise in anxiety in my chest, followed by those lovely tingles. Somebody was waking up.

"Lou, I need to go check on my angel upstairs. Thank you for the information. I prefer being prepared." I shook his hand and walked away.

Colton heard me and gave me one of those looks. I held up a hand trying to reassure him, before taking off for the stairs. Once out of sight of the others, I bolted.

“Angel? What’s the matter?” I sat on the edge of the bed, pushing a sweaty strand off her head. She was burning up.

“Deacon. Need. Now.” She demanded, grabbing my arm, and pulling me down. I laughed and let her do whatever she wanted to me.

It was sometime later before her body fell onto my chest. She was still burning, just not as hot.

“Are you alright, my angel?”

“Yes. No. I don’t know. I was sleeping fine, but this need kept growing, invading my dreams, to the point that I woke up expecting you to be here like before, and you weren’t. Normally I sleep deeply after you feed me.”

I rolled us to the side so I could hold her better. “Yes, but you were always asleep already. My theory is that my blood enhances what you are doing, or feeling, at the time. If that makes sense.”

Her brows took on a slight frown. “I was upset this time, so wouldn’t the blood have made it worse?”

“Yes, and no.” I said slowly. “My blood was healing you. As you are my mate, my blood can do that. By the time that was done… um…” Why was I feeling shy about this next part, when a few hours ago I was proud of it? “You were reacting to both mine and Colton’s touch, angel. We just gave you what you wanted.” I shrugged, hoping if I acted like it was nothing, she would as well.

“Yeah, we will talk about *that* later.”

I smirked, and she smacked my chest. Then she got distracted feeling up my chest. The tingles were building again. I kissed her neck, her scent driving me mad.

“Let me feed, angel. You smell divine with your need for me. Let me have you in every way.”

She didn't speak, but her hands gripped my hair tightly. I sank into her completely, filling her as I drank from her. By the time I pulled away again, she had cooled. I chuckled proudly.

"Guess we figured out what you needed."

"Apparently so." She yawned and curled her body into mine. "I love you, Deacon."

"Hmm. I love you, too, angel." I rubbed my hand softly on her back and waited until she was asleep again.

As I did a few hours before, I snuck back down the stairs.

Colton had a bemused expression. The bar was nearly empty, the last donor taking care of the last client. Alicia was thorough, that's for sure.

"Feeling better?" He grinned.

I chuckled and licked my lips. "Much. Apparently, my blood intensifies whatever she is doing. When I feed her in her sleep, she sleeps like the actual dead. When I feed while, I, or in this case, *we*, are doing certain things with her…."

He barked out a laugh. "What was she like?"

"She was literally burning with need. At first I thought she was sick. She proved it otherwise. I ended up feeding. The mix seems to have done the trick. I kind of want to do it in the morning to see what would happen during the day, but I know she would kill me if I did. Maybe if we feed at the same time it will take some of the extra off." I was mostly talking to myself by this point.

"Well, if you need help with any of it, just holler." His eyebrows raised suggestively, and I laughed.

"I'll keep that in mind. She did warn me again that we would be having a certain talk in the morning."

My friend grimaced. He didn't want her to be upset with him. He also didn't want her to say no to another round.

I handed Alicia her money and she left, the client right behind her. He was watching her walk but would hopefully let her go unmolested.

"Is she going to hate me, now?" We had been alone, cleaning, for nearly ten minutes before Colton brought up his fears.

"No. She is in her own head too much. She feels something for you. She let me take care of you against her yesterday. On some level, she knew you were involved tonight. She wasn't caught up in her own head." An idea came to mind, the kind that guys rarely thought through, and often got in trouble for. "I think I have an idea of how to convince her. If you're up for it, that is."

Colton grinned from ear to ear. "Anything."

See, I knew he more than *liked* my mate. I was pretty sure she returned his affections. Which was how I knew this plan would work.

CHAPTER 18

Carrie

I half expected Colton to be in bed with us when I woke up the next morning. I vaguely remembered feeling his hands on my legs last night, and slightly aware of extra body parts. I was too far gone to think much of it though. I never would have imagined, even in my wildest dreams, that my overprotective, possessive mate would invite someone into our bed, especially without talking to me.

At least, I was assuming it was our bed since he brought me here after the incident with Victor. We were mated, basically married - in human terms, it was only fitting that we lived together.

I heard Deacon grumble to the late hour, well, late for us, and hold me tighter.

“Good morning, angel.” His voice was still rough with sleep.

“Morning? More like afternoon. I don’t remember the last time I slept this much.”

"You needed it. How are you feeling?" He was more awake and alert now.

"Better. A bit sore. Not sure I'll be able to walk right away."

Deacon's eyes filled with mischief and my heart spun in circles. He was excited. It made me feel giddy. I laughed and rubbed my chest.

"This is going to take some getting used to."

"Hmm."

I was already losing him, he was kissing and licking my neck.

Oh. Oh. That was good too. A little lower and it would be even better. There we go. I shivered and sighed contentedly when he rolled us over, at the same time, possessing me in a way only he could. I couldn't say *in only the way he had*, because I had a sneaky suspicion that Colton was down there at one point too last night.

I remembered being upset with someone leaving and then someone else taking over. Don't ask how I knew the difference, I just did.

I had planned on insisting that from now on, we not feed during certain activities. Instead, Deacon took advantage of his position and put his wrist to my lips. I forgot my argument the moment his blood touched my tongue. Seriously, the best flavor in the world. I would never be able to get enough of it.

When his fangs broke through my skin, I soared higher and higher.

I pouted when he disengaged from my neck and removed his wrist a short time later. Watching him lick his wrist did something to my insides. I had no idea what time it was before he pulled one of his shirts over my head again, put boxers on himself, and carried me out of the room.

Colton was there, wearing about the same as Deacon, cooking breakfast.

“Good morning.” He called.

Deacon and I responded. Deacon’s was cheerful, while mine was more mumbled, my face heating up.

Seeing Colton like that reminded me of the up-close view I had the night before. Colton had very strong thighs, an eight-pack chest, with just the right amount of hair. And we won’t talk about what else I got an eye full of. And, if I was remembering correctly, a mouth full of.

As though it could feel my heated stare, his boxers twitched. I closed my eyes and shook my head. They both laughed.

Deacon set me on my feet near the kitchen, holding me in front of him. I turned and faced him, hugging him back. Which was a bad idea, this man looked even better. I felt a tingling in my chest and looked up to see him staring at me hungrily, like we hadn’t just spent the last hour together in bed.

I licked my lips, my skin beginning to feel like it was burning up again. He did this on purpose, I knew he did. And I was going to kill him when this passed. Deacon slammed his lips on mine with a low growl and backed me into a hard wall.

That’s what I thought it was at least, until the wall grew a sharp stick and began poking me in the back with it.

A pair of hands sprouted from the wall and slid up the shirt I was wearing. Soon I was feeling the wall without any barriers between us, nor were they between Deacon and me.

“Can’t…” I started, trying to tell them no.

"Can." Deacon argued as he kissed down my neck, falling to his knees in front of me. Colton held one of my legs up, one hand on my chest, the other working with Deacon down below.

My skin didn't start cooling again until we were all on the floor, lying in different directions, panting.

"Good call." Colton said, lifting a fist to Deacon.

"I hate you both." I grumbled, rolling over to crawl away from them.

I squeaked when someone grabbed my hips and pulled me back over to them. My yelp quickly morphed to something much better.

I wasn't even thinking when someone else appeared on their knees in front of me. They barely had to push my head down before I took over. I was already starting to burn up again. The next thing I knew, I was being filled with heat from the top to the bottom.

Deacon's was still the hottest. Colton's was close but a few degrees off. My body shook from it as parts of them both flowed through me. As a result, I was heated from the inside a second time. They had both reacted to my shaking. Oddly, their heat cooled mine down.

I fell to Colton's leg again, not having the energy to move away from him. Deacon crawled up behind me and helped me roll into his chest. Colton formed his body around mine.

"I still hate you both." I told them.

They laughed. Jerks.

"No. You love me. And you like him. And you like doing this. So do we. So, why can't we enjoy it? Enjoy each other?" Deacon reasoned.

"You purposely did the blood exchange this morning, knowing what it would do to me. Then you both trapped me and made it impossible to move away. You bloodwashed me!"

Colton rubbed a hand down my arm, and the heat began again. This was going to be one very long day.

"We helped you shut your brain off. That is all. Tell me you don't want me here, sweetheart, and I will go. Not once have you said no."

Yeah, because they wouldn't let me. His hand was going down my outer thigh, then moved under my knee, lifting my leg. Still making it impossible for me to say it.

Deacon's hand took over from there. "Say it, angel. Tell us you don't want to do this anymore." Soon he was kissing down the front, while Colton kissed down the back.

"Not. Fair." I mumbled. My breath was coming out in pants, my skin on fire.

Colton lifted my leg all the way up and knelt behind me. Deacon continued kissing me. I gasped at the next feeling, my sore and extra sensitive body reacting beautifully to him. I tried to hold back the complaint when Colton moved away.

Judging by the laughs, they knew they had won.

I expected Colton to come back to me when Deacon took his place, instead he stood by Deacon. Who then did what I had done earlier. Colton's hands were holding on to Deacon's hair this time. Deacon didn't give me much time to dwell on any of it, he made sure to pay just as much attention to me.

"Jerks." I mumbled again.

They didn't argue. Just sat on the floor, no one moving this time. When I could speak again, at least part way, I tried to clarify what was happening.

"You don't share."

"Normally, no. But he has been my best friend for hundreds of years. I trust him with you. There are still some things I won't share. My seed is the only one that will get a chance to take root inside of you. And I am the only one who will share your blood, or their blood with you."

"I am going to my apartment, finally, and showering. I will see you both downstairs." Colton leaned down and kissed my head, where I laid on the floor, before leaving. "Good luck." He told Deacon with a small chuckle, patting his back as he passed.

Once he was gone, Deacon crawled over me. "I'm sorry if you feel like we ambushed you this morning. It's still your choice, angel." I nodded, and one traitorous tear fell out. "I don't understand these feelings. I am trying, angel. But I need your help, this is new to me too."

I huffed and wiped at my eyes. "I'm not sure I understand them either. I love you. You are my mate. My soul. Why do I desire Colton as well?" There I said it. "I was raised in the human world. Where we are monogamous. Desiring someone besides your significant other is frowned upon. I don't want to betray you."

He balanced his weight with one arm and wiped my tears with his free hand. "Nor would I want to betray you. If it were anyone but Colton, I would have a problem with that. I was raised knowing that monogamy was only something between mates, and even then it was up to the couple. They do not sleep with others, but they have been known to invite someone to join them. Colton is the only other man, vampire, or human, that I have done this with. I've had no desire to do so with anyone else. I enjoy seeing his desire for you. I am proud of how perfect my mate is. I also like seeing how you react to him. Tell me part of you didn't like watching him and I moments ago."

I couldn't. I wanted to, but I couldn't. "I never have liked watching that before. Why would I like watching my mate with another man?"

I felt his leg push mine apart, then I felt something else much better.

"It's not just anyone, it's Colton. Normally, we will let you do that, but there are times when you might need a break from servicing two of us at once. And times where we might want to do it. You have to remember, angel. There are no Vampire Born females. The female Nightwalkers are not the same. They are as bloodthirsty and violent as the males. Yes, we use humans. No offense, but most humans are not able to handle us, let alone two of us."

I laid my arms over his shoulders, my back arching. "I'm not exactly human though, am I?"

"No, my mate. You are not. Which gives me hope that one day, you will give me a son, and live by my side forever."

We didn't talk again for a while. We took things slower and reveled in the feeling of the two of us.

"I know you would probably like to shower, angel. But I love how much you smell like me right now. The hint of Colton mixed in adds a nice spice to it. The blend of the three of us is very satisfying to me. Something he and I both need after what happened yesterday."

I nodded and walked like a newborn fawn to the bedroom. I had already started for the other apartment, but he informed me that they moved my clothes over the night before.

Deacon laughed at my imbalance and caught up to me to help. I pulled out a skirt and top from the new dresser, not paying attention to what they were.

"Aren't you forgetting something, angel?"

I stopped and stared at the clothes I had just put on, then looked back at him. "No. I don't think so." Was I?

He chuckled softly and opened the top drawer, pulling out a thin strip of material. He held them up, a big grin on his face.

"Would you like me to help you put them on?"

I ripped them out of his hand and put them back in the drawer. "That would be counterproductive, dear. Besides, I didn't forget them, I just chose not to wear them. After this morning, and last night, I'm more than a little tender. Those do *not* sound comfortable right now."

Deacon growled like a hungry lion and looped a finger through the top of my skirt, pulling me closer.

"No." I told him firmly, my finger in his face. Well, it was supposed to be firm.

Deacon knew he already had me. He pulled me to the bed and turned me to face it.

"I have been dying to do this since the first time I saw you in a skirt." He pushed the skirt up and roughly took over my body again.

Needless to say, he had to carry me down the stairs.

By the end of the day shift, I told Deacon, in no uncertain terms, was he allowed to trade blood with me again during the day. My skin burned on and off the entire day. Which always affected him, and he had an even harder time controlling it. I blamed it on centuries of self-gratification. He was spoiled, plain and simple. And I blamed part of that on Colton, seeing as he had been by Deacon's side for most of it.

As soon as the humans were out of the building, Deacon had me bent over a table. Colton thought it was hilarious. Until Deacon told him I was going to need more. Colton gleefully came over and sat on the chair next to the table, pulling me toward him.

My skin was slightly cooler by the time we finished.

Deacon had been right about the scent. The other vamps didn't make comments or try anything. But their eyes were on me a whole lot more. Which led to Deacon feeling more possessive, which heated me up faster.

I slapped his hands off me many times. There were still some things I was not going to accept about vampire culture.

Like voyeurism.

I ended up having to ignore the feelings I had that were coming from Deacon. Which meant trying to ignore my own as well. It was getting easier, for me at least. I didn't see how bad the problem was becoming until one of the customers winked at me. Deacon nearly lost it.

Colton had a grip on both his arms when I returned to the bar and told me I had to get him upstairs and help him work this out. That was when I let the feelings roll through me again, consciously. I thought he had only been responding to my own side effects of the blood trade. Looked like I was wrong.

"Ok, um. Block him." I told him as I took off down the hall and up the stairs.

I had barely made it halfway when I heard loud laughter from the customers and a growl at my back. I tried to run faster, but a Vampire Born was the fastest there was. And with him taking my blood regularly, he was even stronger and faster than his own people.

He caught me with one arm around my waist. “Hold on.” He growled in warning.

I gripped the rails hard as he was a lot rougher than normal. Something I wasn’t complaining about. As soon as he was even remotely under control. He spun me around and lifted me up. He carried me to the bed, his lips not moving from mine.

When he came back to his senses, I again insisted on no more day trading.

“No promises, angel.” He laughed when I hit him in the chest. “How about, I promise to make sure it's on a day when I can keep you in bed all day?”

I rolled my head to look at him. “When do we ever have a day free to spend in bed?”

He chuckled and kissed my forehead. “One day, love. One day.” I rolled into his arms and started falling asleep. “After everything today, I used a lot of energy. I am going to need to feed. Do you want me to wait until morning?”

“No.” I yawned. “You can do it now.”

“Hmmm. I think I should feed you first, heal your body after what I did to you today. It will help you sleep.”

“No.” He flinched back like I offended him. I gave him a small smile and placed a hand on his cheek. “I only meant that I don’t want you to put me to sleep like that. I will sleep fine on my own.”

He nodded and bit into his wrist. There was something about the way his warm blood flowed down my throat that heated me all over again. In an effort to not give into our desires, which were still slightly heightened, Deacon bit down into his other fist. I tried to reach for him, but he grabbed my hand and wouldn't let me go.

The logical side of my brain understood, the other side did not.

When I finally released his wrist, I attacked him. He kissed me but refused to do more. Instead, he dove into my neck. That felt good enough to keep my inner demons at bay. At least until he finished. He pulled away and rested his forehead against mine. We lasted about one minute. Maybe.

I definitely did not need his blood to knock me out after that.

One of the benefits of sleeping naturally, I knew when Colton came in.

I vaguely heard the sounds of his clothes hitting the floor before he lifted the blanket and slid in behind me. I sighed as his body molded to my own. I also heard the soft chuckles next to me.

"I guess that means I can stay."

Deacon snorted. "I told you it would be fine. How was the rest of the night? Sorry we didn't come back."

Colton laughed softly. "It was fine. They all got a kick out of watching you chase her. I swear Neil winked at her on purpose. Everyone could tell you were losing it down there. He laughed the hardest. Everything alright, now?"

I felt Deacon's hand rub up and down my arm, as though he knew I wasn't completely asleep.

"Yes. She wanted me to promise no more trading during the day. I don't know what happened. I thought I had gotten away without whatever was affecting her, but the first time one of the humans looked at her too closely, I about lost it. Everything just got worse from there."

"Trading blood like that is what you do when you are mating, you were already mated. And she is your fated. Maybe it just strengthened for a while. Did you feed again? This isn't the time to get weaker."

"Yes. We both did. I, uh, wasn't very gentle once I caught her. She didn't seem to mind, but I was worried I hurt her. It was very hard not to touch her, or her me. You know the effect feeding has on us. I nearly called you up here, but I wasn't sure if that would have helped us avoid any repercussions. I couldn't make the promise to her, but I did promise to wait for a day we could stay in bed. It was the best kind of torture."

I felt my mate kiss my head and I burrowed deeper into his chest. I felt Colton's grip on my waist loosen, like he was preparing to leave. Unthinkingly, I put my hand over his and held him there. I felt his body relax behind me and his grip tighten again.

"I told you." Deacon said smugly. I wasn't sure who he was talking to. Me or Colton.

CHAPTER 19

Grace

I awoke with a start, the incoming visions ripping me from my dream. One minute, Todd and I were alone on a beach, no one around for miles. Next thing I knew, we were back in the bar.

Deacon was saying goodbye to his girl, getting ready to go somewhere. Alone. Fast forward a day or two, and new vamps arrived at the bar. The vision was more detailed than I had ever had before this.

Carrie backed up the moment they came in, somehow knowing why they were there. Deacon's friend looked at her, seeing some sign, and stepped between them. The new vamps were headed straight for her.

"Colton. How lovely to see you again." A syrupy voice said, as it entered the bar.

Colton spit on the ground with a curse. "Curtis." My inner eyes widened. "How did you find us?"

Curtis laughed. His face was blurry, I couldn't see him clearly for some reason. "The little princeling was a little too confident. Did he really think my guards wouldn't see him driving back through the gate, after the sun rose?" Curtis sighed, like he was disappointed. "All these decades he has been hiding from me, from the world, and that one little slip up was all it took. My guards called me, confused. They never heard of a vampire who could withstand the sun. You royals have hidden better than any of us." Curtis moved closer to them both, sniffing the air, an evil laugh coming through. "Imagine my surprise when they told me about the bar owner who took a mate."

He breathed deeply then paused, his body tensing as though he received a shock. "She carries the old blood. She will be able to do what no one has in centuries, bear a child, and even survive. I see why he mated her, calling a claim to her. But he is of no consequence anymore."

With one swift move, he pulled a knife from his back pocket and stuck it in Colton's chest. He moved so fast. You didn't even know he was moving until he was holding the knife there.

Carrie screamed, and tried to run to Colton, who was gasping for air, very much alive, but unable to move. Curtis stepped in her way though.

"Don't worry, little witch. I will leave him alive. Someone has to take the news back to the King, and their little clan. Let them know that I have finally won. I will be taking over the throne. The rest of the Vampire Borns will have no choice but to fall in line now. Imagine how much we can get done with the superiors of our race? The super soldiers if you will. We will no longer be restrained by the sun."

Curtis waved an arm and Carter walked around him, toward Carrie. With a small sad smile, he picked her up and threw her over his shoulder and walked out. My last shot was of Colton's murderous eyes on the backs of the others as they left the bar. His fingers already starting to twitch again.

"No!" I yelled, my back shooting up.

Most of that did not make sense. That led to the end of the war, and it was not a good end. What was Deacon going to be doing? When was this?

"Gracey? What's wrong? What's going to happen?" At least Todd was smart enough to know that this was something in the future, and not immediate.

"I don't know. Hold on. I need to focus. That can't be the only possibility, it can't be." I moved to sit up, curling my legs under me. He kept one arm around my shoulders, keeping me grounded.

It took a few minutes for my heart to calm down enough for me to pull the next vision. We were in the bar again. Deacon was saying goodbye. Only this time he didn't leave alone. This time he took Todd with him. They came back the next day. Everything continued on like normal.

Fast forward a week, and Carter was back. But when he left that night, we all went with him.

I pushed away from Todd and jumped off the bed. "Get dressed. We have to plan."

I threw a pair of sweats and a t-shirt on, one of the few things the twins picked up for us the day after we moved in, running out of the room. I ran down the hall and opened doors, yelling at them to get up.

Raya had been right about this place. The three bedrooms were perfect. Todd and I took the master suite. Rachel and Scott shared the one next to us. And the last one held the twins and Justin. The pairings we had unconsciously made in the shelter flowed smoothly into the apartment. Everyone just broke into their pairings on their own, choosing rooms together.

“Family meeting, now.” I said in each of their rooms, not caring about what I interrupted or who I woke up.

Todd was already making coffee for us in the well-stocked kitchen. We did have to clean out the toxic waste from the fridge and freezer, which had had the entire apartment reeking. The stove was gas, so even without power, we were able to heat up water for the instant coffee garbage that the last owners had on hand.

We had particularly enjoyed the liquor cabinet. What the man had lacked in coffee taste, and life choices (the twins had told us about the woman they had met), he had made up for with his choice in liquor. There was also plenty of soups, beans, canned fruits and veggies, noodles, and jarred sauces. It wasn’t much, but it was better than what we had at the shelter.

We’d been here for a few weeks now. And we had already used some of the money we earned at the bar to buy more food, candles, and matches. The nights were getting colder, and we didn’t have the generator from the shelter anymore. But we did have thicker blankets, and plenty of body heat.

I sat at the table, while the others shuffled in. Todd started passing out the poor excuse for coffee, then sat next to me.

“What’s going on?” Scott asked, pulling Rachel onto his lap.

“I had the vision of all visions this morning. Something big is about to happen, something really big. And it looks like if we don’t play our parts carefully, things will get worse than we ever thought possible.”

The room was silent as they listened. I explained every detail I could of both visions. When I finished, a pin could have dropped in the neighboring apartment, and we would have heard it.

“So… Deacon is some kind of vampire royalty?” Todd asked slowly, trying to make sense of it. “The kind that can walk in the sun. What did Curtis mean by super soldier?”

“If he can walk in the sun, then that means his kind are stronger, right?” Justin asked. “Sounds to me like this Curtis guy would want all of them on his side. The humans won’t stand a chance then. I mean, that guy took a knife to the chest and was still alive!”

“When is this supposed to happen, Grace?” Layla asked softly.

“I think the bar thing is tonight or tomorrow, I’m not sure. We need to be there. More importantly, Todd needs to be there.”

“How is my going on this trip with him going to change anything?”

“Easy. You do the driving once the sun is up. He hides, acting like he is hiding from the sun.” Rachel added. “That’s what Curtis said got him caught in the first place, right? But why is he going through the gate and then coming back?”

“I don’t know. But whatever happens, it somehow leads to Carter taking us all with him later. Now we know why he was our target. He is close to Curtis. We need to use Carter to get to Curtis.” I explained, feeling a little excited that we were getting close to where we needed to be.

“I don’t like the sound of Curtis.” Raya whispered.

Justin put an arm around her and held her close. I was sure their trio was mostly them two. Layla didn’t care much for any of the guys, at least not that way, but she loved her sister.

During our first training, just the girls, Rachel asked them if being together weirded them out. I nearly died at Layla’s response.

“Not really. I mean, I think of it on the same level as taking care of business yourself. It all looks exactly the same. Only, you have more hands.”

Raya just giggled and nodded her head.

Then they very kindly demonstrated their meaning. That was a whole new level of weirdness, even for me.

“We always knew he would have to be worse than the rest. But that's why we need to do this. No one else can get close to him.” Justin said into her hair, gently trying to comfort her.

“We weren’t planning on going to the bar tonight, it’s only Thursday. Carter won’t be there for a few more days. The last few Sundays, he has been there, I think that’s his normal day. I say we split into two groups.” A few started to protest, we were supposed to all start going now. I held up a hand to stop them so I could finish. “Deacon and Carrie won’t let us in the bar two nights in a row. If we all go tonight, and he leaves tomorrow, we are screwed. I will go tonight with Scott and the twins.”

This time it was Todd that tried to jump in. I put up a hand to cut him off.

“If it is tonight, we can come get you. I need to be able to listen in and see what I can hear. Or just tell them about my visions. I’ll have to play it by ear. If it’s not tonight, then you will need to be ready to go for tomorrow. He won’t take you if you are low on blood. We already know Carter is in charge of the wall. What if your going is what seals the deal with Carter? If he is there, you will be what he wants. The testosterone boost.” I winked at him at the end. He scowled at me.

Just because he was used to certain things now did not mean he liked them. He was also a pro at shutting himself off though, something the rest of us had struggled with. It did make me question from time to time if he was starting to like those certain things.

With our plans made, the seven of us sat back and waited. Everyone divided into killing time however they chose. The idiot who lived here before us had a decent thriller and mystery selection of books. Not that we needed much of those in our life right now, but at least it was something to pass the time with.

After we all ate lunch, Todd pulled me into the bedroom. This would be the first time we were going to be apart since before we woke up to an empty house. He was not happy about it at all. I wasn't exactly thrilled with the idea of him leaving to go to the wall with Deacon either.

When the time came for us to leave, he was full on pouting. Rachel held his hand, trying to give him some comfort, her watery eyes were on Scott. We all stood quietly at the door. The tension was high. Things were amping up, things were going to change.

"You guys know you are here by choice. If you want to back out, no one will think badly of you. We all get it. When we leave with Carter, if anyone wants to stay behind, you can. We have a decent set up now." I told them carefully.

We had become a family, depending, and caring for one another. A very odd family, but a family, nonetheless. More of a family than I had ever known.

"Someone has to take them down. What we have here is only temporary. This is still just the beginning. We've seen more drones flying overhead during the day. If anyone acts out, they get shot. We've also heard the rumors at the bar. Curtis has plans. We are going to be treated like cattle and shipped off to who knows where. I think it's better that we get into the position that we chose. I hate not knowing. Not having any control. We're in this." Layla stated firmly.

Everyone else agreed with nods.

"Well, alright then. Let's go feed some vamps and spy on the ones we didn't know existed." I leaned in and kissed Todd one more time, just in case.

The elevator ride down was quiet. Scott drove us over to the bar, parking in the front. We still had an hour until sundown. We arrived early not wanting to miss anything.

CHAPTER 20

Carrie

It had been almost two weeks since the incident with Victor. The morning after the day of the bloodlust, what we were calling it, I woke up to both men holding me possessively. They were both also awake and waiting for me. I didn't even have time to say good morning before their hands started moving along my body.

Over breakfast, they made me finally spill all the details of what happened with Victor. Since then, I always had at least one of them by my side. Colton slept with us every night. Every morning, he returned to the apartment I had apparently kicked him out of when I showed up, to shower.

Which was when Deacon and I had some alone time.

If Deacon and Colton had been overprotective before, it was nothing on what they were now. Something the other vamps picked up on. Even Carter had commented on it, nearly a week later.

"What's going on? You two look like you are expecting a fight." His voice was uncharacteristically serious.

"No. Just being cautious." Deacon told him. "You know what you want tonight? If you want both of them, you're gonna have to wait five more minutes. Grace is busy."

Carter frowned, looking at the table she was sitting on. A female vamp was feeding from her thigh, while her hand was up Grace's skirt. He turned back to Deacon, putting in a giant effort to not watch. I was sure if he watched much longer, he'd be ripping the other female off her.

"I know you better than that, Deac. What's going on?" His eyes traveled over the room, stalling on me. Which made Deacon tense up.

I laughed and answered for him. "Someone cornered me in the alley the other day. They are both still a little sensitive about it." I walked over and patted Deacon's butt.

He playfully growled at me.

"Ah. Yeah. Well, we do get a little territorial over things we consider ours. Hate to break it to you, but they are both going to stay like this for a long while." Carter chuckled.

Deacon wrapped an arm around me, holding me tight.

"That's okay. I don't mind too much."

Deacon gave me a swift and rough kiss, appreciating my words.

"Do you know what you want?" He repeated to Carter. Probably hoping Carter wouldn't ask about why the message hadn't been posted outside. My boys eventually told me about what they normally would have done.

There were still a lot of things they didn't tell me. But I did learn that they both liked pillow talk. And if I was careful, they would assume I had already fallen asleep, and speak freely. I heard all kinds of things.

Like my mate being a prince. Yeah, that one was a shocker.

I also learned that they didn't like to keep their hands to themselves while I slept. Which was exactly why I put my foot down and insisted on no more putting me into a coma at night. I loved it when they woke me up. And I really loved not sleeping through it anymore. And it always made me giggle when I woke up to them messing around. I didn't think they even noticed how their own relationship had changed. It wasn't usually much, just one or the other with a hand across me, while the other laid on his back, the hand moving. The mouth belonging to that hand usually landed on me not much later.

Bed wasn't the only time I've caught them either. Deacon was kissing me one night, the bar packed full of Nightwalkers, and Colton just walked up behind him. Deacon kissed me harder as Colton unzipped his pants and pulled him out. Deacon lifted my leg, and this time Colton worked Deacon against me. At one point, I thought they were trying to push the connection, and it freaked me out. Again, bar full people! Deacon must have felt it though, as he pulled back. Colton followed his lead.

Tomorrow was going to be a rough day though. Tomorrow, Deacon was leaving to go on that supply run. Anytime I felt anxious or worried, Deacon would come and try to make me feel better.

Which was exactly what happened when the humans began to file out after the last call before sundown.

Deacon put both hands on my face and looked into my eyes. We were getting better at not using words. Of course, we had had the same conversation over and over again for days. So, it was just a repeat now. Instead of saying anything, he just kissed me deeply.

These were the times that Colton kept his distance from us. The times when Deacon couldn't share. And neither could I.

"I will be fine. You will be fine. Trust me, please?"

I just nodded my head and wrapped my arms around him. I did trust him. It was everyone else I didn't trust.

"Hope we're not interrupting anything." An amused voice said from the door.

I laughed but kept my head against Deacon. "I think you got your days mixed up. It's only Thursday. Sunday is still a few days off."

Grace tskd and waved her hand. "Neh. We just got bored. I never realized how much our lives revolved around technology until the power went out. We figured we might as well make a little money. I brought some different friends this time. Hope you don't mind."

I sighed as Deacon moved away from me, needing to get the newbies prepped. Although I was sure Grace had already done that.

"No Todd tonight?" Deacon asked curiously.

"No, he is back at the apartment with a few others. They will come tomorrow."

I tilted my head, there was a lot she wasn't telling us. A whole lot. Her eyes met mine, then rolled over to Colton.

Grace was scared for us. She knew something we didn't. I opened my mouth to ask her what was up, when I was cut off by a squeal of excitement.

"Carrie???"

I turned, finally taking in who was with Grace. I covered my mouth in shock.

“Holy crap!” An identical voice said.

I frantically ran around the bar and met them halfway.

I gave them both hugs and then started running my hands all over them.

“You’re okay? You're both, okay? I was so worried! I wanted to go find you, but I wasn’t sure where to look. And I worried I would lead him back to you somehow. It wasn’t exactly all that safe for me to leave either.”

Once I was satisfied they were both in one piece, I pulled them both in for another hug. The twins held onto me tight in return.

“We thought you were dead! We saw that vamp chase after you.”

“When you didn’t come back, we were so scared. We even went to the bus station the next day, hoping you had hidden in there for the night.”

“We were going to keep looking, but the cops showed up and insisted on taking us to a shelter.”

I kissed both their heads one more time before pulling away. Deacon had come up behind me, responding to my intense feelings, no doubt.

“What happened? How did you get away?” Raya asked. She had the slightest dimple on her chin. That was how I learned to tell them apart.

I glanced up at the face behind me. “Victor chased me down the back alley. Deacon heard me and stepped out. He saved me.” Deacon winked and kissed my head.

The twins giggled. “So, I guess you took our advice, huh?”

I looked back at my girls and Layla winked at me too.

I laughed. “He didn’t give me much of a choice.” I turned back to them and grabbed their hands. Pulling them to the bar. “What have you been up to since? Are you still in the shelter? I was there with Deacon, all those people made me sad, and the manager was creepy, so I waited outside. If I had known you were in there, I would have come over and dragged your butts out that day.”

“Mr. Ryan was the worst!” Raya exclaimed, rolling her eyes. She looked at her twin and they laughed. “We, uh, actually moved back into Bryce’s place a few weeks ago.” She shrugged, like it was no big deal. “It was a little closer than the shelter, more comfortable, and more food.”

I grimaced, walking around the bar to get them waters. “Please tell me someone got rid of the bodies.”

“Yeah, but I don’t know who. I do know the cops were going to places those first few days, looking for survivors, and cleaning places out. We don’t know what they did to them though. Sorry.”

“Eh, not a big deal. Honestly, it feels like another lifetime ago. Ya know?”

I leaned back as Colton set two plates with giant burgers down in front of them. He winked at me and rubbed a hand on my back. Something neither of the twins missed. They just giggled. From what I had seen of their little group, they were not going to judge me for how I was living now.

“Yeah, we get it. All of it. Looks like you are in a *much* better place now.” Layla said, dramatically leaning to the side to get a good look at Colton’s retreating frame.

Grace came and sat on the other side of them, digging into her own burger. I always insisted on feeding the donors first. Deacon insisted on it being something with iron.

“This the girl you were talking about?” She asked vaguely.

I could tell she was hinting at something. I could feel an underlying question.

"Yes. She and I were trapped in the bus station together." Raya proudly answered the verbal and nonverbal question.

Grace appraised me with new eyes, something hidden. She and I were going to have to have a long talk. I could feel that she wanted that too but wasn't sure how to go about it.

"Your ex had crap taste in coffee."

Layla nearly choked on her burger. Raya spit out the water she had just taken a drink of.

"He had crap taste in a lot of things." I responded in a deadpan voice. I could feel Deacon tensing up. I could see Colton's fist by his side. "It's a good thing I always knew there was something off about him. I chose better the next time." I winked at both of them. Deacon huffed in amusement and shook his head.

"Yeah. A vampire prince. Talk about moving up in the world." The whole world froze at Grace's comment. "Huh, interesting. I'm not really sure what it means, but whatever it is, you all just confirmed it."

"How the hell did you hear that? And from where?" Colton moved to stand in front of me, between myself and Grace, on the other side of the bar, a second later. Well, he was more to her side, but prepared to jump between us if need be. Scott quickly moved behind Grace, acting as back up. Raya and Layla leaned back, looking around warily.

"Don't worry, we have about ten minutes before anyone else gets here." Grace said, taking another bite like she didn't just give two vampires a heart attack.

"You're clairvoyant." I whispered.

It was all that made sense, especially if she knew how long we had. Deacon and Colton both looked at me. Deacon took a big sniff of the air, moving closer.

"I knew that day in the shelter that she smelled similar to you, but it was weak. So, I didn't give it another thought." He sniffed again. This time close enough to make Grace flinch away from him. "You have witch's blood in you. Not as strong and pure as Carrie's, be grateful. She has had no end of trouble because of it."

"Is that why that vamp didn't even give us a second look and went after you?" Layla whispered.

"Most likely, yes. He talked a lot about my scent." I could feel Deacon getting angry again, so I reached out and held his hand. I put my other across the bar to hold Colton's tight fist. So sensitive. "It's not a topic they like much. Victor came back a few days ago. He was waiting in the alley for me. We don't have to worry about him anymore, but vampires, of both varieties, can be territorial."

We needed a change in subject, and we were running low on time.

"Grace, did you have a vision about Deacon?" She nodded, a little scared now. "Don't worry. My mother was a clairvoyant. A very powerful one at that. I'm sure the twins already told you what I can do."

"Yes. If I had known you were the same person, I would have come to you sooner. I woke up to one hell of a vision this morning. Deacon was going somewhere, through the gate." Her eyes looked up to Deacon. "The vamp guards will see you driving in the sun. They will call Curtis. I don't know exactly what happens to you. But he does tell your friend here that you are of no more consequence. He puts some type of knife in his heart, paralyzing him, and takes Carrie. He says she is of the old blood and that he can see why you mated her." At the deep growl from both of them, the humans all jumped back. "Yeah, it didn't sound like a good thing."

“What else did he say?” Deacon just had no control over that growl.

“He said he was leaving Colton alive to tell the king and other Vampire Borns. He said he was taking the throne and was excited to have the rest of your clan with him. He wanted them to be his secret weapons, his super soldiers.” Her voice trailed off into a whisper.

“What was the other path Grace? What is our other option?”

Her eyes widened, apparently she hadn’t fully believed me when I said I knew how it worked.

“Deacon has to take Todd with him. The vision didn’t say why. We think Todd needs to drive back, while Deacon pretends to hide from the sun.”

No, there was more. Much more.

“What else is there? What are you hiding from us?” She exchanged looks with the smug twins. “There is no need to keep secrets anymore. We can help each other. What is your plan?”

When Grace refused to say more, Layla answered for her, much to Grace’s dislike. “We are trying to place ourselves as a harem to Curtis. We are using Carter to get us there.”

“Why would you do that? Curtis is the most dangerous being on this planet.” Colton asked in confusion.

Grace growled. “Two minutes. I’ll talk fast.” She gave Layla the evil eye, who just shrugged at her. Not apologetic in the least bit. “I had a vision two nights after the roads blew. The government will fail to save us unless someone can get closer to Curtis. Real close. Todd and I survived that night because my visions told me what we needed to do in order to survive. We distracted Ryley enough that he said he wanted to keep us as his secret harem, he was too low for a real one or to get any confidential information.

His friend had said something about only Curtis and his top men getting them. The visions came piling in after that."

Colton smirked. "Ryley still complains about the pets that ran away."

"Yes, we had planned on starting here a night earlier than we did, but I had a vision of him going postal. It would have made Deacon act out in a way that would have gotten him caught sooner. So, we waited. And then we met Carter. Somehow, if you take Todd, it will lead to Carter taking us with him. Which is what we need."

I looked up at Deacon, pleading with my heart. If he didn't take Todd, he was surely going to die.

"I could just leave earlier. I could make sure I do not drive during the daylight." He was only talking to me, and the others knew it.

"If that was a possibility, the visions would have shown it. I know how these work. I watched my mother use them my whole life. She told me not to be late to dinner that night. She said I had to be on time. I was going to be late, so I blew off the whole night thinking it would make a difference. That was the night they died, Deacon." I stood up, getting closer to his face. "You are taking Todd with you. End of story. If not for your own safety, then do it for Colton and me. Would you risk Curtis getting his hands on me?"

Colton leaned over the bar. "I second this. Either you take the boy, or you do not go at all, your highness. It is my duty to protect you. I am only staying behind because she needs me more."

Deacon looked between both of us, then sighed. Alicia and Ethan walked into the room.

"Fine." He spat quietly. "Tell him to be here an hour before sundown."

CHAPTER 21

Deacon

I stood back most of that night, reviewing everything that happened with Grace. Carrie was so happy to see her friends. She had lamented to me many times, worried about where they were, if they were alright, or if they were even still alive. I was glad she no longer had that worry. But it was going to be replaced with another one soon.

When she let it fully sink in as to what their plan was.

These teenagers were still kids, and they were planning to work their way up to spy on Curtis. I had to hand it to them. It was ingenious. Curtis spoke freely in front of his pets. He had cycled through many harems for centuries. He only fed from the primest cuts. He would love these kids.

Until he lost control and killed them.

Curtis thought of his harem as nothing more than animals. They had no brains of their own. They were only there to serve his needs. He also used them as incentives and rewards for his most elite, his closest companions.

He would speak plainly in front of them, assuming they wouldn't understand anything he said anyway. Of course, it was possible they didn't. The way they were abused, eventually their minds shut down. Lucas in particular enjoyed breaking them in.

I didn't know what all they had planned, and I wasn't sure I wanted to. I didn't want to take the boy with me. It would be too dangerous for him. But I couldn't escape the image of Curtis stabbing Colton and kidnapping my angel.

If Grace hadn't said anything, that's exactly what would have happened.

I was planning on meeting Eric at sunrise. He said the U.S. had soldiers based around the wall, especially at the gates. Coming with the sun up would help them feel more comfortable around me.

I figured it would be safe enough to pass through the gate again because Carter and his men would be hiding from the sun. My arrogance would have gotten not only me killed, but it would have put my angel in serious danger.

I watched as the twins became very popular with the Nightwalkers. Vampire or human, males always had a thing for twins.

Many years ago, I had male twins as donors. They were just as popular. It was how they paid their way through med school. My usuals were sad to see them leave. Last I heard, they were both doing well, both married with children of their own now. One of the brothers decided he preferred men after their time here. But they were all happy, and safe. In Florida.

Grace sat back, not advertising herself to the extent she usually did. Her eyes kept moving to Colton and Carrie, the fear in her scent permeated the air around us. It made me want to grab my mate and best friend and run for the hills.

Which was ridiculous.

Carrie hugged her friends goodbye, a few hours later, a big smile on her face. I could still feel the relief and joy she felt every time she saw them. I caught Colton watching her as well. He had the concerned look, the planning one. He was making back up plans. No matter how long we had been away from our clan, he could never shed the habits of a soldier.

"If I am not back by noon, get her out of here. I don't care where you have to go. Just get her out." I told him, with both our eyes on her as she locked the door. "Promise me."

"You have my word. I will not let harm come to her. In return, you have to promise me something." He turned and gave me that deep stare. "If there is even the slightest chance they will see you in the sun, or anything else that will give you away, you hide on the other side of the wall. I will protect her, but you need to protect you. The two of you are sealed. That is the one thing that did not match in the vision, if you had been killed, she would have died along with you. Curtis may not want to kill you. He may just lock you up and torture you for the next century. You have to keep yourself alive, and free, to protect her."

"Will both of you knock it off? Grace said as long as Todd goes, everything will be fine." We turned back to my mate, who was standing across the serving bar from us, her hands on her hips.

"And how do we know we can trust her? It is not easy to trust in the vision from a witch. They have been known to lie and twist things to get their own way."

I inwardly hissed. Colton was a braver man than I. Especially considering the look he was being given. I took a step away from him, putting distance between us. This was his fight not mine.

"First off, keep in mind that I am a witch too."

"That's not…"

She waved and cut him off. "Second, trust me. I grew up with a clairvoyant witch, not all of them are untrustworthy." Carrie put a hand to her chest. "I felt her sincerity. I felt her concern and terror at what she saw. I also felt her anxiety over telling us about her gift."

Colton leaned across the bar. "Yes, but how do you know where the anxiety stemmed from? She could have been anxious about lying!"

Carrie sneered at him. "I am much better at sniffing out a lie than I am at reading intent. For example, your whole touching me to help protect me thing…yeah… lie!" She waved her hand at him while speaking, then pointed at him harshly when she accused him. "You just wanted an excuse to touch me."

Colton was the one hiding the smirk now. "Yeah, and you pretending you didn't want it was also a lie."

She shook her head, dropping both hands to her hips. "No, that was called denial and being human. You both just couldn't leave well enough alone and had to do the vampire version of drugging me to get me to cave. Jerks."

We all laughed. I felt a little better now that they weren't arguing so heatedly. And a little excited for what had the potential of coming next.

Carrie sighed and stepped back. "Grace has had no one to help her with her gift. I could feel the anxiety coming from that. While I spoke with her earlier, I could tell that she was terrified at the idea of Todd going with Deacon tomorrow. He is nothing but a human child. And I don't think she handled him not being here tonight very well. From what Raya told me, he didn't like her leaving him behind either. But she didn't want to risk him being low on blood, just in case. She's also scared because she is the one who convinced the rest of them to follow *her* plan. If anything happens to any of them, she will be to blame. That is a lot to put on the shoulders of a 17-year-old girl."

"Then why is she doing it? Why doesn't she just hide in that little apartment, and stay safe?" I made my way around the bar and stepped closer to my mate.

Carrie waited for me to reach her before answering me. She clasped her hands around mine after I encircled her.

"Because the visions came to her. She feels a duty to be the one to follow through. She has the warnings, the tools. Can she trust anyone else to do it right? Grace will put herself in the lead. She will be the one to take on Curtis, just like she is the one to take on Carter. And Todd will follow her, keeping an eye on her. It is the burden that goes along with the gift. My mom got lucky, she was married to a cop. If she saw something, she told him. He would play it off as a tip from an informant. Grace doesn't have that. And in this case. Who would she call?"

Colton deflated and walked around the bar, coming up on my angel's other side to hug her and kiss her head softly. "I'm sorry I got upset with you. I wasn't trying to offend you."

She patted his cheek. "I know. I could feel the intent behind your words. It didn't change that they still irked me, but deep down, I knew what you meant."

I just chuckled. "Are we ever going to be able to surprise you with anything?"

She was getting better at reading the intent from others. She even warned us a few times, since we all came clean, when a certain client was going to go over on time on purpose or would be too rough with a donor. One time, she told us when a Nightwalker planned to force the donor for more than they were volunteering.

Colton stopped them before they made it to the table. I told Alicia to take the girl's place.

Colton's theory was that my angel's powers had been getting stronger because of my blood. Her whole body was stronger, her health. The same way she had made me stronger. For the first time in my long life, I could probably beat Colton in a fighting match.

She shrugged her shoulders. "Don't know. Guess we'll have to wait and see." She grinned and looked at me and then Colton. "You are always welcome to try though. I do love surprises."

I could feel that tingly feeling, the one coming from her. I was debating on how to act on it when she spoke again.

"What are we?"

Colton brushed his fingers through her long blond hair. "What do you mean, sweetheart?"

She nibbled on her lip, her eyes bouncing back and forth from one man to the next. "I don't think I know how to say it. Deacon is my mate. Which is supposed to be like a marriage thing in the human world. Also in the human world, Colton would be considered my boyfriend, or my side piece, or Deacon's side piece, our pool boy, handyman, cable repair guy, or whatever, but we are all together in this. So, what are we?"

Well, I guess that explained some of the confusion I still felt from her from time to time. She needed a label. I looked at Colton. He didn't look like he was going to be of any help.

I moved a lock of hair behind her ear, causing her to turn and look at me. "What do you want us to be, angel? Nothing will change the fact that you are my mate. You carry my mark. In the *vampire* world, that is not always needed to claim someone. What do you want us to be?"

"See, none of that makes sense to me." Her face twisted like she was in pain.

She laid her head against Colton, and I felt the sting of guilt come through her again. Was she feeling guilty for dragging Colton into our relationship?

"Angel, a vampire can have more than one mate at a time, even when they aren't marked. As I told you before, it is up to the mated pair what they want to do."

I looked up at Colton, seeking his thoughts, his permission, before I verbally tied him to us. It wouldn't be as permanent as the bond between Carrie and I, not physically anyway.

Colton looked down at her and then back at me. He nodded. He was willing to do it.

"Angel," I took her head and turned it to face me, stepping in closer, trapping her in the way I knew she liked. "Colton can be our mate as well. *If* that is what you want. I told you before, he and I have always been close."

Now her guilt was turned toward me.

Was this how she felt reading everyone's intent all the time? I was glad I could only read hers. It was handy when it came to understanding my mate, my angel, but it would be annoying on a regular basis. Having no choice but to always think about the feelings of others? Yuck.

"I would not be jealous or offended if you care for him as well. I know you love me, and I know you share part of my soul. Nothing will ever change that."

Colton rubbed a hand up and down her back, doing what he could to soothe her. He knew her as well as I did now, even without the added connection.

Carrie turned her face to look at Colton.

"I would be honored to join your mating, sweetheart. I love both of you. I know Deacon comes first in your heart, which is as it should be, as he is your fated mate. The fact that I own even a little bit of this beautiful heart of yours is enough."

A small tear slid out of my angel's eyes. I caught it with a kiss, and she smiled.

"I love you both, too. And, as long as you don't mind. I think I would like the whole mating thing with both of you."

I laughed as Colton kissed her for the first time. He'd been afraid to do that, as it spoke of a closer intimacy. Something he was afraid she would shy away from. As soon as he released her, I stole my angel back. I kissed her hard, then threw her over my shoulder.

A moment later I was dropping her on our bed.

"Do we have to do the whole blood trading thing again, because if you are leaving tomorrow, this would not be the best time for that." She said with a grin.

We both laughed.

"No. I will not be trading blood with you sweetheart. There are some things a fated mate would not be able to share, even if he was willing." Colton knelt in front of her, pulling the little zipper on her top down. "Besides, we would run the chance of weakening the bond, which would weaken both of you. We need you both at full strength. We will continue as we have been. Nothing has changed for us, just the knowledge that will help you feel more comfortable and accept what Deacon and I already have. That you are ours."

He stood up and moved to the side, both her clothing items in his hands now. Mine were already on the floor.

The next morning, we took our time lying next to each other. Internally, Carrie was a ball of anxiety. I think on some level, we all were.

We went through our morning routine in silence. Everyone lost to their own thoughts. Even through the human shift, we were all subdued.

Once they were all gone, Carrie couldn't hold it in anymore. She broke down crying into my neck. I just held her close, while I could.

"Bad time? I seem to always be interrupting things when I come in."

I laughed as the small hand left my chest and raised her middle finger at Grace. Grace laughed.

"We need to go, angel." I kissed her head softly. I dragged my knuckles down her neck as she picked her head up off my chest.

"Do you want to feed one more time before you leave? You won't be home tonight. I don't want to risk you growing weaker."

"And what about you?"

She gave a small, amused huff. "I will be fine. Technically we don't have to do that every day now, remember?"

"Oh, but I think we do." I lifted my eyebrows a few times, teasing her.

She scoffed and hit me. I loved the small blush that covered her cheeks. My smile dropped. The idea of feeding from her in public was an intoxicating thought. But I didn't want to risk leaving her weaker.

"If you don't mind, angel."

"I never mind, Deacon. At least not now that you do it while I am awake and with my permission."

Colton barked out a laugh. It was my turn to flip him off.

Carrie tilted her head and gave me the access I needed. Instead of taking her up on her offer, I left soft kisses there.

"I don't want to risk it with you. As I said, I will be fine. But thank you." I kissed her one more time, then looked up at Colton. He was already close by, so he took her in his arms.

"If I'm not back by noon." I reminded him.

He bowed his head slightly. "As you wish, your highness."

I pointed at them both sternly. "You will not leave this bar, and you will not go far from him. Do you understand, angel?"

Carrie rolled her eyes. "Yes. Pretty sure I learned my lesson with that already. Now go, so you can hurry up and come home already!"

I chuckled and turned to leave. Todd and Grace were in a similar position near the door. I smacked him on the back.

"Let's hurry up and get this over with."

I led him toward the back of the bar, and out the back door to where my truck was waiting. I froze for just a moment, as I felt something new run from my angel to me.

Anguish was the only word I could even come close to describing it. The pain nearly took my breath away. I rubbed my chest and looked back at the door that was now closed.

"Deacon, she'll be alright. Grace checked again this morning. That first vision is gone." Todd said, opening the passenger door and climbing into my truck.

I followed him. When I had the truck backed out, I responded. "I know that. But it doesn't change the pain that my mate is going through right now."

"How do you know what she is feeling?"

"One of the perks of being magical beings. Vampire Borns are born with only half a soul, which is why we are not hampered down by all the morals the humans put on themselves. Our fated mates are born with the other half of our souls. When we find that person, and mark them as our mate, we seal our souls together. We can feel what the other feels. I can feel the pain my angel is in, and the fear she has knowing that something may go wrong."

"But she's human." His voice could have either been of disgust or just confusion. Considering the work he did for me, I was sure it was the latter.

"No. She's a witch. Just like your girl is, or part anyway." I shot him a small grin as I merged onto the empty freeway.

He didn't look surprised, so they must have shared with him what happened already.

"There was a time when our fated mates were only of the same species. Eventually, my people started finding them in others. It took a lot of adjusting too. Mixed matings were frowned on in the beginning. So much so, that one vampire, caught up in the moment, bonded with his mate, who was a witch. Then he betrayed her because he was too afraid to say something to the female vampire he had been seeing. The witch found him, then put a spell on all the vampires in the kingdom, putting them to sleep. Her and her coven went through and killed all the females in our kingdom. The next morning, her mate woke up to a headless corpse and a note, telling him what they did. And about the curse they put on our people. See, my kind are born as vampires, we are not created. Their curse made it to where we were unable to birth females."

"So, what happened to your people with all the females gone? Why was that curse needed if you didn't have women to get pregnant in the first place?"

"We can procreate with all species. All bodies are biologically the same. It is the magic within them that is different. Humans do not have that magic. Their bodies are weaker. We tried using them to continue our line, but most died in the process, or during childbirth."

"Are you worried about Carrie getting pregnant? Is that what Curtis meant in the vision about the old blood and why you mated her?"

"Yes. His type does not understand the call of a mate, or love in general. But he is old enough that he would know of her importance. Carrie is a pure-blooded witch. The odds are good that she will survive. And if not, she will take me with her to the grave."

Todd gasped in shock and disbelief. "You would kill yourself and leave your child behind? Knowing it would be in danger?"

"It would not be a conscious choice. Or a choice period. With our souls sealed if one dies the other dies."

"But in the vision, Curtis said you were gone. And she was still there."

"But did he say I was dead? He would know that if I had bonded with her, she would have been dead too."

Todd thought about what he had heard for a minute. "I don't think he did. I think Grace said he said that you were of no consequence."

"I think, in that reality, Curtis would have kept me somewhere. Curtis and I have battled many times in the past. I was tired of all the fighting and hiding. Since I can be in the sun, I wanted to live a normal life. Many of my kind are living among humans."

"Why can't the other vampires walk in the sunlight?"

"They were created. They once lived as humans and were turned into vampires. For most, it was a choice they made. They have to drink a certain amount of our blood to make the transformation. I can't say for sure, but I think they get close enough to death that they lose their soul entirely before the change finishes. I have never heard of one of them finding a fated mate. Nor do they have the capability of compassion and love. All vampires, no matter the breed, are territorial and possessive by nature. Remember that with what you all are doing. If you manage to convince Carter to fall for it, remember that what he feels is nothing more than a desire to control and possess. I saw it on Sunday, he is already struggling with the idea of sharing you both with others. He will not easily hand you over to Curtis. You will have to do something to draw Curtis' attention. He is not like those he commands. The older a vampire gets, born or not, the smarter and stronger they become."

CHAPTER 22

Carrie

I barely made it until Deacon was out the door before I collapsed into tears. My butt never hit the floor though, something I didn't realize until later. Colton was just as hard as the floor, but much warmer.

I was crying so hard I couldn't even put two words together. Not that I needed too. Colton already knew. So did the others.

"You might want to take her into another room until she calms down. The other donors will be here in a few minutes. We'll keep an eye on the place." Grace's voice echoed as though it were coming through a tunnel.

Wind hit my face, and I vaguely caught the sound of a door opening. Colton was already sitting, with me on his lap, before I heard the sound of the door closing. He just held me and let me cry, his hand rubbing my back as he tried to soothe me.

I probably should have felt guilty that I was being held by one of them, while crying for the other. I was too caught up in my own pain to care though. I knew I needed him, so I let him try to comfort me.

When the sobs started to subside just enough for me to hear him, I realized he was talking.

"Sweetheart, Deacon will be alright. The psychic witch has seen it. They will both be fine. They will be back tomorrow."

I hiccupped. "You don't know that. The future is always changing, it is not set in stone. One slight misstep on their part, or our part, or, hell, on Carter's part, and everything changes. I never liked him going in the first place but knowing how close it came to him being captured or killed. I… I…"

And I started again.

Colton kept his lips to the edge of my hair, holding me tight. "That was only a small piece. It was not the whole story. You were alive, which means Deacon was still alive. We only had the ramblings of a mad man in that vision. I would have been after him in a minute, to get you back. They never would have been able to keep Deacon down, if they even had him in the first place. We would have had you back before they could touch a hair on your head. I promise. Deacon and I have made multiple plans on how to get out of here if need be. We are all safe, sweetheart."

It wasn't really the words that he used, but the feeling behind them. Colton believed what he was saying. Wholeheartedly believed it. Yes, part of him was trying to reassure himself as well as me, but it didn't change the fact that what he said was true.

I pushed my head back, still resting on his chest, and looked up at him. "I know. But I'm still scared. I'm still worried about him. And it's still the longest he's been away from me. It doesn't feel right. I can't even feel him anymore." I put a hand to my chest. "Last time he left, I was still adjusting to it, I was still learning about it. Now I'm used to the feeling of him always there. Now it's gone. He's gone." My voice cracked on the last word. I was teetering on that edge again.

Colton's arms tightened around me. I lifted mine up and put them around his neck, laying my head on his shoulder.

"He's not gone. He's just too far away. If he were gone, you would feel it. It would feel like the dagger was going through your own heart. Like you were being ripped in two. Up until it took you with him. I won't let that happen to either of you. I won't lose either of you." He was practically growling, making sure I knew how determined he was.

I lifted up and leaned back. Colton wiped the tears from my face, before pressing his forehead to mine.

"If I didn't believe he was safe, I wouldn't have let him leave. Deacon is more than a duty to me. He's my best friend, my brother." He smirked and chuckled lightly. "And apparently my mate now too."

I was surprised when the small laugh left my lips as I tucked back into him.

"Are you ready to go back up now?" He asked after a few minutes of silence.

My eyes were closed, and I sighed. "No. Not yet."

Colton moved his head away, but replaced it with his lips, kissing my forehead softly. "We only have a few more minutes. I don't know how well a bunch of teenagers will be able to handle a bar full of vampires."

I giggled. His lips moved further down my cheeks. His intent now was vastly different, he no longer sought to comfort me.

"I think you have that backwards. I don't know if a bar full of vampires can handle a bunch of teenagers."

Colton dropped his head to my shoulder and laughed. He wasn't one who smiled too easily, at least not in front of others. He was hard and serious. But when it was just the three of us, he would soften. His lips brushed mine softly.

"I love you. You know that right? I know I'm not Deacon. I'm not your fated mate, but I still choose to be with you."

I nodded and slid my fingers up the back of his neck and into his hair. "I know. I love you, too." I closed my eyes briefly and shook my head. "It's still a little weird to me that I can love you both. It's not the same, but it is. I'm not sure how to describe it."

"You don't need to. It's natural in our world. As I said before, I consider myself lucky to have even a small part of your heart." Colton put his hand over my heart, his thumb rubbing back and forth.

I turned in his lap, moving my left leg over him so I could face him.

"It's not just a small part, Colton." I whispered fervently, wanting, and needing him to understand that he owned more than a small part of me.

His eyes came back up to meet mine, having been focused on his fingers and where they were threatening to go next. With a small growl, his lips were on mine again. I reached down between us and released his beast that was banging on the gate to get out.

I learned a lesson down there, besides the fact that we were sitting on the bottom of the stairs in the cellar, Colton had a *lot* of beast in him.

He was careful to leave me before it was too late. Even without Deacon here, he was going to honor the boundaries in our mateship. Mating? Whatever the hell we were in, he was not going to betray Deacon's trust. Not now, not ever.

When we emerged from the cellar, it was to a few whistles, which made me blush. Grace just laughed and winked at me.

“Feeling better?”

“Shut up.” I told her with a partial laugh. “I’m surprised you came tonight. You know I can’t let you work.”

She just shrugged. “I wasn’t planning on it anyway. I just can’t stand the idea of staying home right now.” Her voice had gone soft long before she finished.

I put a hand to her shoulder and smiled gently. I felt a little guilty for my breakdown. She had the vision. She knew what would happen if they failed. She was still a kid, and her one comfort in this new life had gone to face off with vampires. Something she sent Todd to do.

The night dragged on slowly for me. A few asked where Deacon was, donors and vamps, we just told them he had some things he had to do tonight. To the vamps, this made sense, seeing as nighttime was the only time they could do things.

The humans were just confused. Why would anyone want to go out at night?

Grace and I picked up where we left off the night before, talking on and off, during my down times, about her power and how it worked with my mom. There was only so much I could tell her, but she was thirsty for anything I was able to share.

Once the place was locked up, I kept cleaning. Colton worked along beside me without a word. When the place sparkled better than it had in years, he practically dragged me up the stairs with his arm around me.

“Do you want me to stay with you tonight, or would you rather be alone?”

I looked at him like he had grown a second head. "What the hell kind of question is that?"

He tried to hide how happy that made him by pressing his lips together. "I didn't want to assume. I don't know how much of this is you and how much is us pushing our will on you."

I just rolled my eyes, grabbed his hand, and pulled him into mine and Deacon's apartment. He practically lived there with us anyway.

Unlike Deacon, Colton gave me space to get ready for bed on my own. When I was ready, he lifted the blanket up so I could crawl in next to him. Deacon usually just stripped me and threw me on the bed. Both ways were nice.

I snuggled into Colton's arm, noting the difference there as well. I missed sleeping in Deacon's arms. I sniffed and a small tear slid out. Colton silently wiped it away.

"It's not the same is it?"

I shook my head. "No. There's too much room on the bed."

Colton barked out a laugh and held me tight.

"Maybe we should put it to some use then." He turned to cover me with his body, and I laughed, which he cut off by kissing me.

Moments like this made me glad I had both of them. Lying there alone would have been hard. My imagination would have taken control, and I probably would have cried all night. Instead, Colton kept me thoroughly distracted. It still wasn't the same without Deacon, I could still feel the emptiness in my heart that was left behind just minutes after he left.

CHAPTER 23

Deacon

Todd and I drove in silence for a time. I wanted him to think over everything I had told him, give him time to process it all. I gave him a lot of information. A lot of new information. Information they needed to know to go into this with an open mind and not blinded.

It was dark outside, and hard for him to see all the damage done to the roads. I knew tomorrow would be another story altogether. Sometimes we didn't think about the full scope of the damage, only the parts we saw on a regular basis.

"So, what are we doing? Why are we going to the gate?"

"I am running low on supplies, as are the stores. I have a man who usually delivers to me, who was willing to at least meet me at the wall. He is human, and no, he doesn't know that I am not. I agreed to meet him at sunrise. There are soldiers on the other side. If I come at night, they will assume that I am a vampire and will kill me on sight. On our side, there are vampires guarding the gate. I had thought I would be safe driving back over with the sun up. Your little witch tells us otherwise."

"Is this Carter's gate? Will they just let you go through without any problems?"

"Yes, and probably not. I had planned on negotiating with Carter for passage."

"Negotiate with what? They raided the banks. And they never seem to worry about money."

"No, when you walk the earth for as long as we have, and I am older than him by the way, you invest, you work jobs just for something to do, or you steal. No matter your choice, you accrue quite a bit of money."

"H… how old are you?"

I chuckled at the waver in his voice. "I'm over 400, Todd. Carter has barely passed his first century."

I heard the faint sounds of him mouthing woah, and dude that's old.

"Colton has seen ten centuries." I laughed at the stunned look on his face.

It took him a few minutes to form a sentence again. "What could you negotiate with Carter over?"

I just raised an eyebrow at him. His eyes widened. Now he was freaking out.

I waved a hand at him. "Calm down. I was going to negotiate covering his tab, nothing more. Although, with you here already, he might just want that payment now. He has told me more than once how limited the feeding options are out there."

Todd nodded and blew out a breath roughly, his cheeks puffing out. "Yeah, we already wondered if that was the case. Especially with how quickly our plans are supposed to escalate with him after this. Any human could have driven you, why else would the visions suggest me?"

Todd glanced at the clock glowing in the darkness. We had already been on the road for two hours.

"Shouldn't we be passed the Antelope Valley by now? Have we even reached Santa Clarita yet?"

"No. You can't see much because of how dark it is without the lights. But we have to take a lot of side streets, and different ones at that. I made a practice run through after we arranged this. About Palmdale, we will be able to stay on the freeway until we reach Mojave. With only one detour, and then back on again. We still have a few hours to go. Why don't you try and get some sleep? You will have to drive us back tomorrow."

"How am I supposed to drive if I don't know the way?"

I chuckled at his rising frustration. "I will be able to guide you from the floor. Vampires have terrific memories."

Todd nodded and leaned against the door. I put my arm to the back row of my extended cab and picked up the blanket Carrie insisted I bring. She said I would need it to hide under. The idea of hiding made me chafe, but I did not want to risk her life. I had a feeling she would be able to convince me to hide in those rotten caves again. I handed it to Todd. He bundled it up like a pillow and laid on it, against the window.

We drove in silence for the next hour. I was taking my time this time around. Anything could have changed. And I didn't want to miss something in the dark. Besides, I had plenty of time.

"How do you kill a vampire?" His question was soft, barely there.

"A silver dagger to the heart will kill a Nightwalker. They cannot heal from that. You can also cut off their heads. If you come across a Vampire Born, the dagger will only paralyze them for a few minutes. So, you better move quickly to cut off their head."

"Is that why Colton couldn't move in the vision? Was the knife a silver dagger?"

I shuddered at the thought of it. Colton would have been scared, not for himself, but for Carrie, as he watched them carry her away. I didn't like the idea of him coming that close to death either. Both of them being put in peril because of my thoughtless actions chafed.

"Yes. If Curtis had planned to kill him, he would have cut his head off too."

Silence rained down on us again, and soon I could hear the slowing of his heartbeat and his breathing. It reminded me of my angel. I smiled when I thought of all the times she pretended to still be asleep. Even if she forgot how well we could hear, she should have remembered that I could feel her curiosity, her alertness. It was the easiest time to tell her things. I knew she would internalize everything we said, she wouldn't jump up and start arguing with me.

Eventually, Todd and I entered the smaller cities. The ones that still had power. It was nice to have streetlights again. I could see fine in the dark, but after decades of living with electricity, you get used to it. It was comforting.

The lack of power at night, not using the heater, was another benefit to Colton sleeping on my angel's other side. She would be warm no matter what. Of course, according to her, we warmed her up on the inside as well. I had never noticed it before.

I still didn't feel a temperature change between Colton and myself. Nor have I noticed the difference when I have cleaned the tables and booths after they had been used. Colton and I theorized that it was linked to the magic in her blood.

Whether it was her personal magic, or because she was a witch, I had no clue.

I looked up at the glowing clock on the dash. It was nearing two. The bar would be getting ready to close. Colton would make sure my angel was safe and comforted tonight.

I was grateful that she accepted him, that she cared for him. And that he cared for her. I knew she was safe. I knew she was loved. And I knew she wouldn't be lonely. I was sure she was still missing me. I wished I could feel her from so far away.

It was odd, but I missed both of them.

Colton and I had been together for a long time. Over these last two weeks, we'd grown closer than ever before. My angel brought us together. She was the gravity that pulled us together. And now she was the glue that kept us that way. He hadn't planned on staying this whole time with us. Just the time for me to make this trip and the practice run. But he didn't want to leave. We didn't want him too, either. He was part of us now. From that first time, right after Victor tried and failed to take her, he became part of us. Maybe even since the morning he suggested to double team her. The moment that door started opening, he became part of us. We were not meant to be a mated pair, but a mated unit. All this time, we had just been waiting for her to piece us together.

My eyes widened when we drew closer to a large dark shape. It was as long as the eye could see. It wasn't high by vampire standards, but it was high enough. Straight ahead, I saw a break in the wall. One that was just large enough for a semi-truck of vampires to get through.

I reached over and hit Todd in the shoulder. "Todd. Wake up. We're here."

I heard him rubbing his eyes and starting to move around. I knew he was really awake when a curse word flew out of his mouth. A few of them actually.

"Is that the wall?"

"So, it would seem. Be ready, there are quite a few Nightwalkers out there."

Three vampires stood in the road, blocking our path. I slowed down until I came to a stop and rolled my window down. Another vampire stepped up from the side.

"Where do you think you are going? And why do you have a human with you?" He practically snarled at me.

Todd's fear spiked, even though he kept his cool on the outside. The new vamp grinned when he smelled it. Lovely.

"Get Carter for me." That was the only way I was getting through this gate, especially without someone killing the human boy next to me.

"Why?" His eyes came back to mine warily.

I glared back at him, pushing my door open. He jumped, not expecting it. "You need to knock off the attitude and do as you are told. How old are you? Ten?"

The vamp tried to straighten his shoulders. "No, sir. I'm twenty."

I scoffed and shook my head. "You're a baby. An infant." I looked over his shoulder, to where I could see more vampires moving around. One bald head stuck out more than the others, mainly because of the way the moon shined off it. "Carter! Get your sorry butt over here before I relieve you of one less child."

I heard the sounds of deep laughter, and then the footsteps jogging closer.

"What's wrong, Deac? You gettin' so old you don't have patience for the little ones anymore?"

I scowled at the insufferable child. "He hasn't even reached puberty yet. I don't have the time or patience to deal with someone who doesn't know when one of his elders is talking to him."

Carter slapped the infant on the shoulders, making him jump. "We need to work on you telling the difference in a vampire's age, Private. Take a big whiff. The older they are, the more they stink." Carter barked out a laugh at his own joke.

"Har, har." I kept my face straight.

The infant sighed with relief when Carter let go of him and dismissed him.

"He wasn't doing anything wrong you know. What are you doing out here?"

"I need supplies. For some reason, my delivery guy doesn't want to come through the gate. Even if it would open for him." I acted shocked and Carter laughed.

"And what makes you think I will let you through? For all I know, you won't come back over." He was struggling with the straight face.

I chuckled and scratched my jaw. "You really think I would have left Carrie behind if that was the case?"

He scoffed. "You would if you ticked her off. That girl would stab you in your sleep."

"Man don't give her any ideas. She's scary enough. Now. How about it? Are you going to let me through or what?"

He folded his arms across his chest and sighed. "It's against the rules, Deac. Why can't you get supplies within the wall?"

“Eventually, I will be able to, but I don’t have the contacts right now, nor the idea of how to do that with the roads the way they are.” I sighed, acting like I was frustrated. “What will it take, Carter? Name your price.”

He grinned, that was the opening he was looking for. “Twenty minutes, on the house, both of them. Playtime included.”

I pretended to think about it for a minute. “I don’t know, Carter. That’s a lot. Hmmm.” I looked him up and down. “What about, one of them. Todd. Ten minutes… right now.”

Carter opened his mouth, ready to argue, then froze, his eyes widening. They darted to the truck, where he could see a figure in the cab. Then he took a big sniff.

He grinned. “You brought me a treat?”

I laughed. “Well, someone has to drive me back with the sun up. You think I want to be stuck out here with all these babies until sundown? I figured he could drive me, and maybe help convince you to open that gate for me, both times.” I held a hand toward Carter. “Deal?” He didn’t even look at me, he only had eyes for Todd,

“Make it thirty.”

“Twenty, and that’s as high as I’m going.”

His hand finally met mine. “Deal.” He was already working on his pants as he made his way around to Todd’s side.

I leaned against the truck to wait, chuckling softly.

“Hey, stranger. Long time no see.” Todd laughed, acting happy to see him. At least he didn’t smell like he was scared anymore.

“You have no idea how happy I am to see you. I’m starving.” I heard a new zipper as Todd laughed.

“That’s why I’m here. Don’t tell anyone, but you are my and Gracey’s favorite vamp.”

“The feeling is mutual, pup. Now, turn around. I only have twenty minutes, and I plan on making every minute worth it.”

I heard the slightest grunt from Todd, then he turned them into more. From the scent in the air, he wasn’t just acting.

It didn’t take Carter long to get what he needed from Todd, and to build up the dopamine. As soon as he let him turn again, he had Todd sitting in the seat, and drank from his thigh while he kept building the addictive chemicals up.

At twenty minutes, I knocked on the side of the truck. Todd was outside of the truck now, on his knees. He released Carter and stood back up. Both of them were still hanging free.

“Will we see you on Sunday?” Todd asked, hopeful.

“Yes. Make this pick up take longer, and you can visit me in my tent before you take him home. Deacon will be trapped in the truck. We can have more time together.”

Todd pouted. “If you brought us back with you, we would have all the time we wanted. We have friends who could help with the others.” Todd reached a hand down, softly stroking Carter’s ego.

Carter sighed sadly, sounding like someone who had had this conversation too many times already. “And where would I keep you?”

Todd pointed at the houses not far off, with his chin. “Are any of them empty?” His hand stopped being so gentle. “You could even stay there with us, when you are off duty.” Carter growled, pushed the kid against the truck, and grabbed him in return. I decided to play nice and give them an extra minute.

I knew Carter's growl when he finished by now. Surprisingly, the kid growled with almost the same intensity.

I opened my door. "Time to go." I climbed in and pretended I couldn't hear Carter lean in and whisper in his ear.

"When you come back, turn right as soon as you come through the gate. Pull up to the first tent. I'll be waiting." He dropped to his knees in front of Todd, apparently having difficulty saying goodbye. Todd didn't seem to mind either. He was all in it, and it most definitely wasn't an act.

The scent coming from both of them was making my life difficult. And it made me want to get back to Colton more than it used too. Huh. Interesting.

"See ya later, Deac!" Carter laughed as he released the shaky teenager and stepped away. He knew perfectly well that he basically got the thirty that he wanted.

I laughed and shook my head. Todd fixed his pants before climbing in and closing his door. I waited while Carter signaled for them to open the gate back up.

"Are you going to do what he said? Pull over to his tent? It won't be paid."

Todd grunted. "I know. We aren't doing this for the pay though, that just helps. We need him. And if this is what it takes, then so be it. I just want this over with."

"Why are you doing this? I know why Grace is. Carrie explained the place Grace is in, with the visions coming to her and all. But why are you?"

He shrugged, and for a moment, I didn't think he would answer. "I didn't want to let her do it by herself. I had a crush on Grace for years. I thought I won the lottery when she was moved into the same foster home as me. I managed to get her into my bed a few times, but it wasn't easy. I have her now, and I'm not letting her out of my sight. I hate the fact that I have to share her with every vampire out there, but it is a means to an end. When this is all over, I am going to hide her away somewhere. Just the two of us."

"Well, good luck then." I had no idea what else to say to all that. Especially since he reminded me a little of those twins I had before. One of them in particular. It took him a while to accept his change of opinion as well.

Those boys worked for me for ten years, it took nearly that long for him to figure it out. He came back to my bar, just for a drink, after a date with a girl he had liked for a long time. He was confused. They finally did the deed, but there was something off. It just wasn't the same as it once had been. A Nightwalker that he regularly serviced came in not much later and approached. The new doctor figured, why not. He was there anyway. He had his problem figured out long before any fangs came out.

Sometimes, tastes change. I knew mine seemed to be. Well, mine were more like expanding. Growing to include things I hadn't paid enough attention to before.

Within minutes, we were pulling up to another guard shack. This one was less than half a mile from the other side of the wall.

I rolled my window down again as a real soldier stepped up this time. "Who are you and how the hell did you get through that gate?"

"My name is Deacon. I run a bar in Los Angeles. This is one of my employees, Todd. I'm meeting a man by the name of Eric Anderson here at dawn. I am taking a truckload of supplies back with me."

A look of absolute confusion crossed the younger man's face. "Why would you go back? You're free."

“No.” I shook my head and sighed sadly. “I’m not. I could only come if I left my wife at home. Todd’s girlfriend and family are back there, too. If we don’t go back, they will pay the price.”

“How do we know you aren’t one of them vamps?”

I chuckled. “Why would I meet my contact at dawn if I were one of them?”

The soldier nodded like that made sense. “Alright. But I have to check with my CO first. Stay here.”

Todd made a whistling sound as the soldier walked away. I just nodded. Ten minutes later, a young Captain approached the car. I sniffed deeper at the new scent and rolled my eyes.

The shifters always had been better at blending in than we were. He sniffed me in return and his eyes widened. He looked around to make sure none of his men were close enough to hear.

“What in the hell are you doing here? And don’t give me some BS about supplies.”

“It’s not BS. I am here to get supplies. I brought the kid so he can drive me back during the day.”

The Captain frowned at me. “You can drive yourself back.”

“Not without alerting the Nightwalkers into what I really am. The kid’s girl is part witch. She had a vision of it not going so well if I tried that. My mate is a pure-blooded witch. The Nightwalkers know all about her, their captain is a regular in my bar. Right now, all of them think I am just old and that’s why I smell different.” It was the Captain’s turn to roll his eyes. “I know, but you know it’s not safe right now for us either. Especially if Curtis finds out that I have a mate. A fated one at that.”

The Captain’s eyes widened again, as he took a step back, rubbing his face. “She can carry your son?”

I nodded. “We think so. The magic in her blood is strong. The vision showed Curtis taking her if I got discovered. We need the supplies. Curtis is still working things out up North. The roads are shot to hell. People need to eat.” I cast a look at Todd and nodded.

“I am not just here to cover for him. My girl and I are spying from the insides. We have a plan to get close to Curtis, but we need to know who to contact with information when we have it.”

“How old are you, kid?” The Captain asked.

“17, sir.” Todd had a decent backbone on him. Not everyone could look an alpha wolf in the eye without blinking. Even when they didn’t know what he was. Their aura was not one you messed with.

“And how in the hell do you plan on getting close to the scum who is behind all this?”

Todd gave him that trademark grin that teenagers all over the world had perfected. The one that was all smug and attitude.

“By creating a ready-made harem full of teenagers who are willing to give them what they want. We are young enough that we will last longer, and we are strong enough that we have the chemicals they need.”

The Captain was truly shocked and had no idea how to respond. That quickly changed though. He turned a murderous gaze to me. I raised my hands in surrender.

“Don’t look at me. They started all that before I found them. I brought him along for cover. Things are different over there right now. You do what you have to in order to survive. It’s a long shot, but I can guarantee that if they find their way close enough to Curtis, they will get the information no one else can get.”

The captain paced away for a few minutes, then came back. “I have to run this up the chain of command. Pull your truck up to that building. You both can wait inside." He pointed to a small shack of a place just down the road, on our right.

Inside, we found water bottles and an array of snacks on a table tucked off to the side, across from a couch. A soldier near the door told us to help ourselves. Todd dug in. We waited silently for a couple hours in the small, worn-out furniture that they had in there. At one point, Todd fell asleep, stretched out on the couch.

Just before sunrise, the Captain walked in. I stood up and met him. I left Todd sleeping.

"Well, what's the verdict? Am I free to grab my supplies and run back, or am I going to be locked up?" I grinned sarcastically.

He just shook his head at me, a tired smile on his face. "You will be free to go. So long as they all see you in the sun, they will believe you are human. I wouldn't make this a regular thing though. The President is planning an invasion soon. Any humans coming out will have to stay out. As for the kids…" The captain closed his eyes and shook his head. He pulled a small box out of one of his many pockets. "I was told to give them this burner phone. I've already programmed my number in it. Teach them how to be careful with this please."

I took the box with a resigned sigh of my own. I had really been hoping that the army refused to accept their help.

"I will. Grace, the girl, may only have a little bit of witch's blood in her, but her power is strong. My mate's mother was clairvoyant as well. The gift seems nearly identical so far. And my mate comes from a long line of pure bloods. In fact," I shook my head slowly, "they trace back to the coven that cursed us."

The Captain hissed then cursed fate. I grinned.

"At one time, I may have agreed with you, but not now. I wouldn't trade her for the world. I didn't even know what she was to me until I bonded with her. It's been a long time since my people have met fate."

"That's how it goes, sometimes. Part of me longs for the day I finally meet mine, but the rest of me, fears it." We both heard the unmistakable sounds of a large diesel truck pulling up. He extended a hand to me. "Good luck. Get your mate out as soon as you can. Neither of you are safe in there."

I thanked him and then woke Todd up. I gave him the box, and he thanked the Captain.

Eric had a trailer he was willing to part with, for extra money of course. I laughed as I slid my card through the small Square card reader he had attached to his phone. The man was prepared. He knew what he was doing when he loaded up.

The Captain and I both laughed as we watched a few of the men trying to lift the hitch from Eric's truck and move it to mine. They got it off, and then promptly dropped it in the dirt.

The Captain and I walked over and lifted it up. One of us probably could have done it on our own, one handed, but we didn't want to stand out *that* bad.

I tossed my keys to Todd, then grumbled as I sat on the floor of the truck. The Captain threw the thick blanket over my head, laughing still. He wished us good luck again and we were off.

Todd slowed at the gate and waited while it was opened, probably by remote. He pulled to the right, parking outside a large tent, and mumbled that he would be back.

He was gone for over an hour.

I was getting restless, debating on going out there to check on him. But that would put Carrie at risk. It wasn't just him being gone that worried me either. The longer he took, the later we would be getting back.

I sighed with relief when he got back in the cab and started driving.

When we were far enough away, I pulled the blanket off my head.

"How much did he take? Are you alright to drive?"

Todd chuckled and waved me off. "He didn't drink much." Todd shifted uncomfortably in the seat, making a face. "I may have convinced him that once a week was not enough. We'll see on Sunday." Todd shrugged.

Now that he was more awake, he asked about the Captain and how he knew about me. I had to explain about shifters and our history with them. Apparently, they were better at passing down knowledge than the vampires were. Which was good. It was kind of sad that the only magical species to forget about my people were the vampires themselves. The witches remembered. As did the shifters. I couldn't help but wonder why that was.

When we returned to the city, I offered to drop him off at home. He insisted on seeing this all the way through. He parked in the alley behind the bar, leaving me enough shade to make it from the truck to the bar.

CHAPTER 24

Carrie

Somehow, I managed to wake up before Colton this morning. I never managed to do that with Deacon. He was almost always awake before me. Maybe it was from weeks of him having to wake up and be out of my bed before I caught him. Maybe he could feel when I was going to wake up. I didn't know.

What I did know was that I couldn't lay in this bed anymore. I needed to move. I needed to do something. I didn't know what time Deacon would be home. I didn't know what he meant when he told Colton something about noon if he wasn't back.

I did know that I didn't like the sound of it.

I slid out of the bed quietly and tiptoed to the dresser. I wasn't sure how well the hearing on a Vampire Born worked while they slept.

As carefully as I could, I pulled my shorts and tank top out of my drawers, the ones I used to sleep in. With the bar already spotless, that left only one place for me to clean. Upstairs.

I was halfway done scrubbing the floors, by hand, when I felt someone watching me. I turned my head, looking over my shoulder, and noticed Colton standing in the doorway, a Cheshire grin on his face.

“Morning, sweetheart.”

I didn’t need my gift to know what he was thinking, I could see it. The boxer briefs he pulled on weren’t even trying to hide it, in fact, I was willing to bet that he was hanging out on purpose. I rolled my eyes and shook my head, then started scrubbing again. He gave a deep, resigned sigh and pushed off the door.

“Hey! I just washed there!”

He ignored my warning as he crossed the room and sat on the floor next to me. I scowled at him.

“I hope your butt gets all wet.

“That wasn’t the part of me I wanted to get wet this morning. Close, but not quite.”

I scoffed and kept scrubbing. “Wow. The two of you have really gotten comfortable in this relationship. Neither of you can come up with anything original anymore, or even slightly smooth.”

I pushed harder on the sponge that was probably as old as Deacon and falling apart in my hand.

“When was the last time anyone washed these floors?”

Colton shrugged, not paying any attention to me. At least not to what I was saying. I threw a look at him and sure enough, his eyes were zeroed in on one part of me. I sat on that part with a huff but kept scrubbing.

Colton finally caught on to my irritation and put his hand over mine, stopping my movements. “The floor looks good. The whole place looks good. How long have you been awake?”

I tried to move my hand again, but he was stronger than me. Stupid vampires and their stupid extra strength.

"I don't know. A while I guess. I couldn't lay still anymore. I had to do something. As soon as I am done here, I am cleaning the extra apartment."

I saw the grin he was fighting when I didn't call it his. I gave a small smirk myself. It had just come out. Somewhere along the way, I stopped thinking of him living separately from us.

"Why didn't you wake me?" He lifted my hand off the germ-infested sponge and folded our fingers together.

I shrugged, afraid to speak. I knew if I did, my emotions would get away with me again.

"He's fine, sweetheart. He will be here soon."

I glanced up at the clock and noticed it was already well after ten. Less than two hours until Colton whisked me out of here. I'd had lots of time to think about it this morning. I was pretty sure that's what Deacon meant.

Less than two hours before we had confirmation that something went wrong. My stupid bottom lip quivered.

I yelped when I went from sitting on the wet floor to sitting on a nearly bare lap in the blink of an eye, facing a completely bare chest.

"Should I be offended that you woke up early, didn't want to lay still, and chose to clean instead of waking me up? Do I come in second place to dirty floors now, too?"

I pushed against his chest with both hands, but he didn't let me move even an inch. "Don't start that."

He sighed and kissed my forehead. Then grimaced. I laughed.

“You smell like Clorox.”

“Yes, dear. That is what happens when you spend a few hours cleaning. You start to smell like the product.”

His frown deepened. “I don’t like it. It’s disgusting and hides your unique scent, and ours.” He stood up, swinging me completely into his arms.

“Where are we going? I haven’t finished yet!” I tried to kick my legs and push away from him. Stupid strong vampires. Why couldn’t my ancestors have passed down super strength as a power?

“I need to do a little cleaning of my own, and then we are going to work on getting these floors dirty again.”

“You're relentless.” I folded my arms and acted like I was still irritated with him.

The way he dropped me on the bathroom counter and crashed his lips to mine, told me he already knew I wasn’t.

After a long shower, and an even longer time drying off, I went to put on a clean outfit for work. I was trying really hard not to look at the clock. Colton had walked into the front room to take a call, so I took a minute to steady my nerves in peace. At least he couldn’t feel the swirling of nerves in my stomach.

I also picked out one of Deacon’s favorite outfits. The black and blue checkered skirt, and the black version of the top that was little more than a scarf looped around my back and neck.

I was sitting on the bed, zipping up my boots, when Colton came back in with a duffle bag. He dropped it on the bed next to me, with a sad and worried look. My eyes drifted to the alarm clock on their own.

12:05

“No!” I stood up and walked out of the room. “No. I am not leaving. Not yet.”

“Carrie, we have to. I promised Deacon that I would get you out of here if they were not back by noon.”

I spun around and glared at him. “I don’t care. I’m not going. We still have hours before the Nightwalkers, or even Curtis, would be able to come after us. I am not leaving. Not yet.”

Colton ran two hands over his face. “Sweetheart, we need that time to make sure you are far away from here. Long before they start looking for us. That’s the only way to make sure you stay safe. You think I want to run away? You think I want to leave him behind? I have spent the last 400 years protecting him! It's my job to take care of him.”

I shrank away, knowing he was getting mad. He wasn’t trying to scare me, but I was already terrified.

“I can’t leave, Colton. Not yet. Just two more hours, please?”

He shook his head and turned back into the bedroom. He grabbed the bag and started throwing my clothes inside.

“We don’t have any more time. I just got a call. I’m needed elsewhere. I have to leave. And I am taking you with me.”

I grabbed his arm, he let me stop him. “You’re leaving?”

He softened his face and put a palm on mine. “No, *we* are. I don’t know where Deacon is. I don’t know when he will be back. The time is up. It's time for us to go.”

I shook my head. “We can’t leave, not yet. Please, just a few more hours? If he isn’t back by then, I will go with you. But please, don’t give up yet.”

"Sweetheart, I know you are scared. I know you are worried. But we have to leave. We need to go. Now!"

I stepped back, curling inside myself, tears falling down my face. I could feel that Colton wasn't trying to be mean, he was worried about all of us, and in a hurry to get me out of there. And he was worried about whatever he was being called to do.

I walked slowly back to the bed and sank onto it. Colton left me to cry this time while he ran to the bathroom to get my bathroom supplies.

Like a blast of hot air through my system, I felt him. My mate, the one that fate designed for me. My chest warmed and the tightness eased. I felt his worry and then his happiness when he felt me too.

"Colton, Colton. Stop!" I shouted, jumping off the bed.

"No, Carrie. We have to leave."

"No. We don't!"

My laughing seemed to catch his attention. He turned just in time to see me running out the door. I ran straight down the stairs, just in time to see my mate start running up. As soon as he was close enough, I jumped into his arms, wrapping my legs around his waist and my arms around his neck.

Deacon laughed happily at my exuberance. I heard Todd laughing from behind him, with Colton's relieved chuckle from behind me. I ignored both of them and started leaving kisses all over Deacon's face.

"Are you okay? What took so long? Did you get hurt?" I threw questions at him right and left, which made them all laugh harder.

"Hold on, angel. I will tell you everything, just give me a minute." He grabbed my waist, like he was going to put me down, I tightened both my grips. He didn't try again, he just turned enough to look back down the way.

"Do you need help getting home?" Deacon laughed. "Never mind. I'm thinking your psychic sent someone to get you. I just heard a car pull up."

Todd pushed the door open and looked outside. "Looks like she did. Scott just pulled in. We'll see you tomorrow." He was out the door before we could say goodbye.

Deacon carried me back up the stairs and into the apartment. Colton waited for us to pass him, a hand rubbing Deacon's back softly. He needed to feel him for himself, to reassure himself that Deacon was in fact safe and home. Colton turned behind us and followed us in.

Deacon made a face as Colton closed the apartment door, spinning in a circle, looking for the root of the smell. "What is that horrid stench?"

Colton laughed like it was the funniest thing in the world.

"That would be the smell of a disinfected apartment." I grouched at him.

"That would be the smell of a mate who was going crazy with worry." Colton added.

I stuck my tongue out at him over Deacon's shoulder. He laughed at that too. Deacon stopped spinning, his body tensing on whatever he saw sitting on the floor.

"Guess I cut it close then."

I let him lower me this time, but I didn't move away. He didn't seem to mind, his grip on my waist was just as tight as the one I had on him.

"You might have missed us altogether, but someone wanted to act like a child and throw a fit about leaving."

I flipped Colton off. He just laughed and stepped close enough to wrap his arms around both of us. I got squashed. And I loved it.

It wasn't long before hands started roaming, and not just on me. Colton got his wish from earlier; we dirtied up the floor.

A little later we were all leaning against the foot of the couch, both of them sitting next to me, they each had a hand in one of mine. With our reunion out of the way, Deacon told us the story of what happened, and why it took so long.

My head sagged onto his shoulder, my heart finally at peace. Just in time to be shattered again.

"I have to leave." Colton told him quietly.

I closed my eyes, my heart sinking. I had forgotten that part.

"Why? What happened?" Deacon asked, not nearly as concerned as I thought he should be.

"Your father called. He has a meeting with the human government officials. He wants me there with him."

Deacon seemed taken aback by this. "My father? Why is he getting involved?"

Colton shrugged. "This battle has been building for centuries, Deacon. He has stayed hidden in his own little cave while the rest of us fought back. Don't you think it's about time he got involved?"

"Yes, of course. You know I do. I'm just surprised. How long will you be gone?"

Colton moved my hand between both of his and held it tight. I looked up at him sadly.

"I don't know. A week, maybe two. It depends on what happens and what all he needs me to do. You need to get her out of here soon. Don't wait until it is too late."

"I'm not even sure where we would go. Where she would be safe."

"Our clan will protect her." Deacon shot him a disbelieving look. "Yes, she has more potential to bear a healthy child than any in the past, but she is bonded to you. No one would dare to step between that bond."

"Except you." Deacon teased him.

Colton grinned and kissed my hand. "Except me, yes. Which just means she is doubly protected. As was the point all along."

All was quiet for a few more minutes, then Colton stood up to leave. We stood up with him. By the time my clothes were straightened out, as neither of them had seen fit to remove them earlier, he was back in the room, fully dressed.

I let go of Deacon and stepped forward to hug Colton. He had a different idea. I was practically panting by the time he released me again.

"Be safe. Come back to us soon." I told him.

"Please be careful, stay inside." I rolled my eyes at him. "I love you, sweetheart."

"I love you, too." I whispered, stepping away. He then hugged Deacon, his hand on the back of his head.

"What? No kiss for me? Sheesh. I see how…" Colton cut him off by giving him exactly what he asked for.

I giggled. It wasn't nearly as deep or as long as mine was. I was special that way.

"Take care of each other." Colton added before walking out the door.

Deacon came back to me and held me tight, while I once again cried about one of my mates leaving. Deacon didn't give me long to cry though, he just picked me up and carried me to the bed.

"We're going to have customers waiting." I reminded him.

"They can wait. I missed my mate." He started kissing up my legs. "I was worried about you every minute. The last thing I felt from you was the pain and suffering I caused you by leaving. I need to remedy that. I'm sorry if you are feeling sad again, over Colton leaving."

My fingers played with his hair, preparing for what I knew was coming next. "I'm sad, but not nearly to the point I was with you. The emptiness in my chest was unbearable." My voice cracked with the memory still fresh. "Please don't ever leave me again, Deacon. I can't stand it."

"I can't promise that. I wish I could. You have no idea how much I wish I could. But until this war is over, I can't promise to not be gone for small bits of time." He had stopped on my thighs and looked up at me. "I can promise that I will always return to you. I will always come back for you."

I didn't have to worry about what to say to that. I wasn't given the chance.

All in all, the bar opened nearly two hours late, seeing as it was supposed to be open at noon. The human cook had already arrived, and just waited outside. Deacon paid some of the humans to help unload the trailer he had bought off his contact.

I insisted that he stay inside just in case someone was watching.

CHAPTER 25

Carrie

The day ran smoothly, vamp hour was as busy as it normally was for a Saturday night. Something had them all energized and excited. Which had me worried.

As the night went on, Deacon's obsession with my neck grew. He was constantly kissing it and stroking it. It wasn't until one of his fangs grazed it that I realized he had not fed since the night before he left.

"Do you need to feed?" I whispered to him. None of the donors were sitting at the bar, they were all occupied elsewhere.

"It seems so. I haven't gone this long without feeding from you in over two months. It's been even longer since I fed you. And with the scent in the room… I feel like a druggy going through withdrawals."

I rubbed my lips together and looked around the room cautiously. "Do you need to feed, now? Or are you alright to wait a few more hours?"

Deacon was heading into a trance. He didn't even hear me. He just stood at my side, his fingers caressing my neck.

"You're going to need to feed him now, darling." I looked up and saw Deacon's friend, Lou, standing across the bar from us. "How long has it been since he fed?"

"Um. A little over two days, I think. I thought you all could go longer?"

He tilted his head side to side. "Typically, it depends on what our bodies are used to. How often does he usually feed?"

"Every night."

Lou looked Deacon over. "Either you feed that boy now, or he is going to cave to his desires soon. If he caves, he will not have the control to stop. Which would kill both of you." Lou laid two twenties on the counter and grabbed a donor on her way back to the bar.

"I can wait, angel. Don't let him scare you. My kind aren't like theirs, remember? I'm just enjoying your scent and the smoothness of your skin."

Ya huh, he totally sounded in control right now. And nothing like a creepy psychopath.

"Feed, Deacon. Please. Take what you need."

His eyes refocused, the glow receding, and he looked at me. "I thought you didn't want me to feed in public."

"You need it." I bit my lower lip, like I was confessing a sin. I kind of was. "I missed the feel of your teeth last night, Deacon. Please?"

Deacon looked around the room, no one was watching. I knew he could still feel my trepidation. Deacon didn't know how to feed without doing other things. He hated it.

Two things I swore I would never do in public.

You know, kind of like I swore I would never be with more than one man, and certainly not at the same time.

A grin slid over his face, the kind that said he had a plan I was going to both love and hate. He kissed my neck and slowly made his way down my chest, between the shirt that only covered the bare necessities, and down my waist.

He knelt on the floor, moving inside the small alcove that held the water pipes for the bar sink. I shivered when his lips met my thighs. I had to bite my tongue when I felt his fangs slowly sinking into my thigh. His fingers took position a little higher than his teeth. The resulting feeling was both terrifying and spectacular.

Lou winked at me, as he released his donor. He knew very well what was going on behind the bar. They could all probably smell both my panic from them noticing, and my pleasure. I stopped being able to control my expressions, and let my head fall back.

I felt the intent rolling off Deacon, he did that on purpose. I felt his tongue sealing my thigh right after, immediately followed by going somewhere else.

He came up a few minutes later, his eyes back to normal, the wicked grin still in place.

"Feel better?" I asked sarcastically.

He kissed me and laughed. "Much. I should be asking you the same thing. That was…I don't even know how to describe it. Your fear of being caught, mixed with your desires, it was intoxicating. I almost didn't want to stop. Then when you caved to the feeling…" He kissed me again. I could taste my blood still on his lips, among other things from me.

I didn't get it. His blood was addictive to me, it was sweet, and easily the best thing I'd ever had. My blood, on the other hand, tasted like blood. He laughed at the grimace on my face when I tasted it.

The way he was looking at me, his eyes roving up and down my body had me scowling at him. His intent was shouting at me. I lifted a finger and pointed it at him.

"No. Not happening again. This was a one-time only deal." I spun away and practically stomped off.

He followed me, begging like a puppy.

"Come on, angel. You can't lie to me. I know you enjoyed it just as much as I did."

I picked up a bucket and a cloth and went to a table that needed to be cleared. "I never said I didn't. I just said it wasn't happening again."

Deacon stood behind me, sliding his hands on my waist seductively, leaning in to nibble my ear.

"Why not? I can feel how much you want to. You learned how good things were with Colton. You know this can be too. Just let your guard down, angel."

I frowned. I helped keep him from losing control one way, just to swing him in a whole other direction. I turned in his arms and glared at him. It didn't faze him in the least bit.

"I am not talking about this right now. You are not in control of yourself, the wrong brain is in charge."

Deacon bent down and started kissing my neck. I knee'd him in the nuts. He dropped like a rock, laughing, and wheezing at the same time. The few vamps around us groaned louder than he had. I just stepped around my mate and walked off. It was nice to know that vampires were still sensitive there too. Possibly more so since they were almost always at least at half-mast.

By the time they had all left, Deacon was walking back over to me with an apologetic look on his face. “I’m sorry, angel. You were right, I got a little out of control.”

I lifted a questioning eyebrow.

“Yes, only a little. I backed off, didn’t I?”

“Fine.” I threw the dirty towel in the sink and turned off the lights.

I heard the sound of the cellar opening and closing, then all the power went off. Deacon was behind me again before I even made it to the stairs. He stopped me on the third step.

“Angel, come on. Please talk to me. I get that I pushed, that I let your blood get the better of me, but what is the big deal, really?”

I folded my arms and stared at him. “Why do you always have to keep pushing me? Why do you have to keep trying to change who I am? First with feeding me in my sleep, and you feeding from me. Which is ironic since you won’t let anyone else feed from an unwilling donor. Then you and Colton gang up on me when you already knew I was extra sensitive and would be unable to say no properly. And now this? Why, Deacon? Why can’t you be happy with who I already am?”

I tried to step back as he came forward, but I tripped over the next step, his arms caught me before I could fall on my butt. Stupid heels.

“I was never trying to change who you are, Carrie. I love you exactly as you are. I love your innocence. I love your purity, your spunk, the fire in you. I love your heart and how you care about everyone, whether they be vampire, human, or witch. I’m sorry if my actions have made it seem like I was trying to change you. I just want to make you happy. I want to share things from my life with you. You know I just wanted to protect you in the beginning, and yeah, I got a little selfish.” He held my hand against his chest. “I feel what you feel. I feel you wanting something but too afraid to take it. I knew Colton would make you happy. And he adds another layer of protection for you. I could sense, and even taste, how you felt tonight. My mind was lost to what I could give you down there. But I promise, I have never, nor will I ever, try to change who you are."

"No more pushing on the public thing?"

He looked like he swallowed a raw egg. "I will wait for you to show me that you want it next time. How about that?"

"That's not going to happen." I smirked.

He leaned forward enough that I could feel his breath on my face. "We'll see." He kissed me softly before leading me up the stairs. "Just out of curiosity, what do you have against it?"

"Some things should just be done in private. They are between you and me… and Colton. I don't want anyone else seeing any part of me. You're lucky I ever agreed to wear this outfit in the first place."

"But I love you in these clothes. I love seeing how perfect my mate is and knowing that no one else can see what treasures lie in there. I see your point though. What if I keep you covered for the whole time? Blocking their view of you?"

"No. It's not happening."

I walked into the bedroom and began to shimmy out of my skirt, letting it lay on my feet. I unwrapped the shirt from my head, then let it fall on top of my skirt. I didn't even have time to turn around before I felt my mate behind me. Every glorious inch of him.

We were lying peacefully in bed, having finished who knows how many rounds, a little later. I swear, his blood was making me nearly as bad as them. Always waiting and ready at a moment's notice. My body was still burning from the inside. I enjoyed lying there in the silence, feeling the liquid parts of him cool. It was one of my favorite parts. Even after he vacated the premises, he was still there. A gentle reminder.

Only something was different this time. One small spark was heating up again. It was almost as if he was still there, still releasing. I moaned and my eyes rolled back.

“Angel?” Deacon started to laugh at me. “What’s going on? I can feel you, it’s like you are still lost in the… why is it building?” He wasn’t laughing now.

I moaned out a scream and rolled to my back. “Your… stuff. It’s moving. Oh, my. I can feel it going… higher. Deacon!”

I was a little scared, but mostly enjoying it. It was like a never-ending tunnel of ecstasy. The torturous part was not being able to go over that wondrous edge.

“What’s going on?” I half pleaded; half moaned.

Deacon’s hands rubbed gently over my stomach, like he was searching for it. I moved his hand to roughly the right spot. His hand being that close made me whimper with need.

“I think my seed is trying to latch onto your eggs. I’ve never heard of anyone feeling it before. But then, most of our stories were lost. We need to help it. I just don’t know what to do.”

“Help, yes, help. I need you, now.” My back arched. I was enjoying this way too much. “Deacon!” I moaned, or maybe it was a whimper.

A moment later he was back where all this started. And it was exactly what I needed. I wouldn’t let him stop, not even when he was nearing the end.

After a half hour of not being able to stop, my body started heating up, like I had a fever. “Blood, I need your blood, and mine, take mine. I need… I don't know..." I lifted my head to talk to him, but dropped it back again, as the need kept building.

My body wasn't strong enough on its own, but his blood had been making me stronger over the last few months. I didn't know how I knew. I just knew that I needed more of it. And I needed it now, or my body would never be able to accept his seed.

Thankfully, I didn't have to explain any of that to him, he could feel it with me. It was just like the moment we sealed our souls together. He tried to pull away after a few minutes, I felt his worry, but I bit down on his wrist and held his head in place. I could feel his desire, his intent to slow down. I both bit his wrist and gripped his hair harder. He growled and picked up speed again.

I finally let him go when I was on the verge of passing out. The blood trade had him emptying out over and over again, he barely had time to take a breath before climaxing again. I tapped his shoulder after he finally began to slow and he literally fell to my side, both of us passing out.

I woke up hours later to a cool cloth on my head. "You're burning up. How do you feel?"

"I don't know. Last night was weird, but also extremely awesome."

"For a moment, I thought I was going to kill you. Why didn't you let me stop?"

I kissed the palm resting on my cheek before picking it up and holding it close to my heart. He sat on the edge of the bed next to me.

"I don't know. I just knew I needed more from you and for you to take more from me."

Deacon laid a hand on my stomach. "You feel different today. I can't place it. Your smell has changed as well. Do you think it worked? Do you think my seed is attached to you?" There was no way to miss the hope lacing his words. Or the fear that was nearly its equal. He had wanted this for so long. And I wanted to give it to him, something that no one else had been able to do.

"It was sure trying its hardest last night. I feel something, something warm. Like there is still a small piece of you in there. This is so weird. Do any of the stories talk about this?"

"No. At least not that I know of. What about your stories?"

I shook my head. "No, the only one we have about vampire children, is the one where your mom died after you were born. I don't know how my ancestors found out so much. Why are you scared? I thought you wanted a child, an heir?"

"I do. I was obsessed with it for a time. But I don't want to lose you. More than half of the humans died during the second trimester. Half of those survivors died during childbirth." I felt the crack as well as heard it in his voice. "I can't lose you. When I bedded females with the purpose of trying for an heir before, I didn't care whether they lived or died. I just wanted to try, for my people. But now, I'd rather we stagnate then lose you."

I sat up and wrapped my arms around his neck. "I love you so much. We will find a way through this. I have a feeling there hasn't been anyone like us in a very long time. We can talk to other vampires, do research. You said, as your fated mate, your blood can heal me. Maybe that was why we needed to do that last night. Deacon, you have been giving me blood every night for two months. How many vampires did that in the past? My cells are stronger than those of a normal human, even than a normal witch. If I get weaker, I will feed off you."

He nodded, but his worry and fear did not fade.

CHAPTER 26

Grace

From the moment I woke up this morning, I stayed in the same position on the floor. My legs crisscrossed under me, the sun shining on my back, the wind coming through the open balcony door, my eyes closed. My friends stayed quiet, trying not to disturb me.

Last night I received a small vision, two paths. One led Todd to Carter's door, and then on to us leaving with him. The other, Todd drove by without stopping, and our path was done. I didn't know what he picked.

If he drove past, I was going to kill him. I did not go to that dang bar every week and let those filthy vampires do all that crap to me for nothing.

My breath caught when two new paths appeared. One where Deacon brought Todd home, and one where we picked Todd up. I knew which one he would choose. I jumped up and grabbed the keys while yelling "Scott!" he came running out of his and Rachel's room a second later.

I threw him the keys and grinned. “Go bring our boy home.” Cheers went up all over the apartment.

Twenty minutes later, Todd strolled through the apartment like a hero. I rolled my eyes as he approached me.

“Honey, I’m home.” He sang off key.

I laughed and threw my arms around his neck hugging him tight. “Welcome home. How did it go? Please tell me you went to Carter’s place this morning.”

Todd chuckled and kissed my head. “Straight to work, huh?” He stopped laughing when he saw my face. “Would it have been that bad had I not?”

“Yes. It would have been over.”

He bopped my nose. “Well, then I didn’t sacrifice my butt and dignity for no reason.”

The others laughed.

“I think you lost your dignity the first time you hurt my butt.” Justin mumbled, a smirk on his face.

“No, he never had any to begin with.” I teased, earning a smack on my butt now. “Come on, sit down and tell us what happened.” I held his hand and pulled him to the couch.

I meant to sit next to him, he had other ideas. I let it slide. If he was needy, then Carter must have really done a number on him.

“First off,” he threw a small box on the coffee table, one I hadn’t noticed in his hand before. “That was a gift from the U.S. government. Captain Hill, the army guy on the other side of the wall gave it to me.”

“What is it?” Rachel asked.

Nobody moved to pick it up, we just stared at it warily.

"It's a burner phone. So, we can contact them whenever we have something. I figure Grace should be the one to carry it, she will know when it is safer to use it." Everyone nodded in agreement.

"Wow. So, this just became a whole new level of real." Justin's eyes were wide.

"What else happened?" I turned the subject off our being recognized as official spies by the government, and the weird, and completely random, flash I had of a large man in an army uniform laughing. And the even weirder warm feeling that came with it.

"Not much really. Deacon is a chatterbox. He was more than happy to give me a little history lesson on vampires. Or rather, Vampire Borns, like him and Colton, and Nightwalkers, the ones we've been dealing with."

"What's the difference? A vampire is a vampire." Scott had started out with an attitude, then stopped and looked at Grace. "Right?"

They were all probably remembering the vision with Curtis.

"Yes, and no. Vampire Borns are just that, they are born that way. Nightwalkers are created. He went into a whole bunch of stuff about his people having half a soul and getting the rest back when they meet their soul mates, which he said Carrie is to him. I guess some witch cursed them a long time ago and killed all their chicks. If they manage to have a human or a witch have their kid, it is always a boy. The mother pretty much always dies though."

Todd continued on telling us everything that Deacon told him, that he could remember anyway. And then about Carter.

"We need to stay on the same play then, Carter has no humans there. We knew this already. We just need to convince him to take us up there with him. That first vision, with Curtis, he was in it. He has access to Curtis." I looked at the rest of them, all a little paler after Todd shared Deacon's warning with us. "I've said it before, and I'll say it again. If any of you want to back out, there will be no hard feelings."

"We appreciate it and all, Grace. But we're in. Are we scared out of our minds? Yes. But that doesn't mean we are going to stop now." Raya answered for the group.

The rest just nodded.

"Alright, well, then tomorrow, we pull out the big guns with Carter. All my visions seem to point to tomorrow. Make sure your clothes are packed up before then. Actually, I'm thinking I might need a shopping trip. Ladies?"

The other three girls cheered. I wanted to find a new outfit for tomorrow night, something that would help with Carter.

I tried to get up, wanting to grab my shoes. Todd wouldn't let me.

"Not yet. I just got back. Stay for a little bit." His hand lowered to my thigh, telling me what he wanted, what he needed.

I nodded and pulled him up with me. "We'll leave in an hour."

I heard a few light giggles as Todd closed the door behind us.

The next night, for the first time, we *all* went to the bar. It was a good thing Carrie and Deacon already knew why we were there, otherwise they may not have let us in. Carrie especially was a stickler about our health.

My first view, upon entering the vamp bar, was of the two of them sitting in a booth. Carrie was leaning against his chest, Deacon's hand resting on her stomach. It was a sweet and private moment.

My stomach dropped.

Carrie turned and looked at me, giving me a slight nod, like she was giving me permission to look at her future. We talked a bit over the last few days, she told me more about my powers, and her own.

I wondered if she felt what I wanted.

I closed my eyes and focused on what I wanted to see. I focused on her. The first flash was of Carrie holding a baby, her cheeks flushed and heated from labor. On one side, I saw Deacon. The other, I saw Colton. They were all extremely happy. And somehow got even happier when a woman with curly blonde hair walked up, holding a baby of her own.

The second flash, Carrie was still healthy and looking at her healthy baby. Almost everything was the same. Just one difference this time, there was only one man standing by her side. I looked harder into her tired eyes and saw the pain there. It was as though someone had taken part of her soul from her.

I blinked my wet eyes as I came back to reality. Carrie's face was grief stricken, she knew it was sad, but not why. I could at least put some of her fears at ease. If we knew the vamp history, I was sure she did too.

"Both you and your baby will be healthy and strong."

"Then, why…" I shook my head, cutting her off.

She knew there were some things I was not supposed to share. She was the one that told me that after all. Her eyes watered, and both her hands dropped on top of Deacon's.

"Thank you. That is the most important thing for now. Is there anything we are supposed to do?"

I shook my head. "No. In both visions, that did not change. Whatever you are doing, or planning, it will work." I gave her a smile. "Congratulations."

Deacon kissed her long and hard. I walked over to the bar, where Carter would be looking for me. Raya and Layla squealed with joy and interrupted the couple's celebration.

Not long after, more donors showed up. Having finally been at the bar on other nights, I could see some of the difference. Sundays were just plain weird in comparison. And there were a lot more vampires, which meant a lot more donors.

A few hours after sundown, the one we were waiting for sauntered in like he was the king of the world.

He greeted a few others with a hug, then his eyes fell on me, then above me to Todd. I was dressed in a lace bra, and short shorts. I learned quickly that he liked to work around the crotch piece. He didn't like the easiness of a skirt. That was the only thing he liked to work for.

With the biggest grin, he came to us at the bar. He was five feet away, when he stopped dead to rights. His head swiveled to Carrie, and his eyes creased. I mentally cursed.

"What's going on, Carter? Everything all right?" Deacon asked carefully, taking a small step in front of Carrie.

"I'm not sure. Why does your mate smell different?" Carter's whole stance was wary.

Deacon chuckled and gave an awkward yet playful shrug. "Well, see, she had this crazy idea, and I went along with it. Happy wife, happy life, right?"

Carter relaxed and started laughing. "And what happened to her personal donor?"

Deacon widened his eyes a bit, trying to pass a not-so-subtle message to Carter. "Not sure, he was just passing through." He barely pushed the words through his teeth.

"What Deacon means to say is that Colton heard about what happened and got ticked. He wasn't happy about a human joining the mix. Haven't heard from Harry in a few days. I kicked Colton out until he had time to cool off. He's lucky I got what I wanted first, or he would be the one missing." Carrie didn't miss a beat while she poured someone a drink and handed it to them with a smile.

Carter bent over laughing. He came up and shook a finger at Deacon but ended up bending over again. I slid up to him, sliding my hands slowly across that broad chest of his.

"Are you done yet? I've missed you. Seven days is far too long. I'm so jealous that Todd got to be with you, and I didn't." I pouted, pushing out my bottom lip.

His laughter stopped real fast. "Well then, guess we need to do something about that, don't we?" He reached behind him, to where he kept his money. I put a hand over his to stop him.

"First ten is on the house."

His eyes sparked up like flashlights. "Missed me that much, huh?" I nodded and bit my finger, looking shy. His chuckle was deeper, darker. "Well, now. Let's go see what I can do to make my little pussy cat feel better."

He pulled us toward the table, then cast a look at Todd, who frowned. Carter laughed and waved for Todd to come too. He jumped up and ran over to us. I had Carter's pants open before we even made it to the table. We already knew what he wanted.

Everything.

Half an hour later, I was still sitting on his lap, the blood dripping down my neck, and laying on his chest. Carter was leaning back in the booth, one hand on my butt, keeping me right where I was, his other hand holding tight to Todd, who also had blood dripping from his neck. Carter liked to see his work. He wouldn't seal it until he was ready to go. Which he seemed in no rush to do tonight.

I felt Carter start to move, showing signs that he needed to head back out. I rocked my hips, making him groan.

“Don’t leave yet. You always leave so soon, and then we have to go back to serving the others.” I whined.

“I have to go, you know that. I only get one day of leave lately, and it takes all of that just to get here and back. I’ve already stayed too long. Trust me, I don’t want you serving others. I want you to save all that deliciousness just for me.”

His hand lifted, and then smacked my butt again, letting me know he wasn’t just talking about my blood.

Todd wrapped his fingers on top of Carter’s, trying to get him to move again. “Then let us come with you. We can serve you every night, just like Carrie does for Deacon and Colton.”

We picked up on his jealousy of their little unit a long time ago.

“Yes.” I purred, dragging a finger down my chest. “We can all be together every day, for hours.” I drew out the last word. “Think of all that time you spend in the car. We can spend it in bed. Or in the shower. Or outside under the stars. You can have us whenever you want.” I was circling my chest and swiped some of the drops of blood and licked it off my finger. His eyes began to glow as he watched my tongue glide over my finger, from the bottom to the top, where I took the whole thing into my mouth, before slowly pulling it out.

“We have lots of friends. They can come with us. Think of how much more efficient your men will be if they fed regularly. They won’t have to leave either. You can show them all your prowess whenever you want. Just say the word and we will be there. However, you want us. Whenever, you want us.”

Todd didn't have to hold onto Carter anymore. Instead, he just laid his head back on the booth, and let Carter have his way.

Carter growled and soon I had blood coming from the middle of my chest. I just held onto him for the ride. My blood was still dripping from the sides of his mouth when he let go with a growl. All three of us released at the same time. His growl pushed us that last bit.

Carter took his time sealing my wounds.

I pouted as I stood up, letting him fall out of me. I sniffled and sat on his other side. He tucked me back into my bra.

"Don't pout, little pussy cat. I will be back." The side of his finger trailed down my cheek, catching the tear I managed to push out.

"But where will we be?"

Carter's hand froze. "What are you talking about? Why would you go anywhere?" His eyes sparked again. This time in anger.

"We heard the rumors this week." Todd started.

"What rumors?"

"That we were all going to be shipped off to the smaller cities. What if that happens while you are gone? What if we don't get to see you again? What if…What if…" I hiccupped and wiped my nose.

Carter was growling consistently now. He didn't deny the rumors though. Todd and I exchanged a quick look when Carter didn't say anything else, his grip on our legs only got tighter. We both moved in slowly, resting our heads on his shoulders like good little pets. He even raised his hands to pet the side of our heads.

"Don't let them take us away from you, Carter. We belong to you. Not them." I begged softly.

“How many friends do you have?”

“Five. Three more girls, and two more boys. They are all here tonight. This is the only way we have to make money and buy food.”

Carter huffed. “You won’t need money anymore. I’ll make sure you have everything you need. Go get your friends, I’ll talk to Deacon.”

I smiled up at him, like he was my hero. “Really? You’re really going to take us with you?”

Carter laughed and kissed my cheek. “Yes, really. I should have done it sooner. You two belong to me, it's ridiculous that I haven’t taken you home to take care of you properly before now.” He swatted my butt again, as I was mostly on my knees. He leaned over and licked Todd’s neck, finally sealing it. “Let’s go, my pets.”

I held onto Carter’s hand as we made our way to the bar. Todd looked around for the others. The twins were still busy, at the same table. Justin looked like a buffet lying on his back. Rachel and Scott were drinking water at the bar.

“What’s up Carter?” Deacon already knew what was up, seeing as his hearing worked better than everyone else’s.

“Looks like I am taking a few of your donors off your hands. You were right, it’ll be better and easier if they are closer.”

“Well, I hate to see them go. They bring in a lot of clientele.” Carter let out a low growl and pulled us both closer to him.

Deacon chuckled and looked over at Carrie. “No judgments, man. I get it.”

He reached over the bar, forcing Carter to release my hand, to shake his. I swapped it for his belt loops, which made Carter laugh.

We weren't completely in the clear yet. Besides, the idea of one vamp instead of dozens was a lovely feeling.

"Do you both want to eat something before we leave? It looks like your friends still have a few minutes." Carter asked, thoughtfully.

I went onto my toes and whispered what I wanted. Carter threw his head back and laughed.

"Yes, little kitty, when we get in the car, you can have all you want."

I bit my lip, which made him growl again and kiss me. I always thought it was funny that he couldn't kiss me without reaching for Todd. Right there next to the bar, he stuck his hand right back inside Todd's pants. Which he had left open. Carter liked to tell him when he could close them. He liked being in charge.

The most important lesson we learned once we started this mission, was to just let go. The vamps could smell whether or not we were really feeling it. Acting wasn't something we could do with them. We had to shut our brains off, and let biology lead the way. That took the longest to practice in the shelter. When it was only the girls, or only the boys, it tended to take longer. Nobody was leaving until everyone had at least one release, with each of the others in the room. Layla was the only one who didn't struggle with it at first. We tried to give the sisters a pass, but they both just shrugged and said it didn't matter. Which was what started the conversation on being weird and them demonstrating for us.

At first, I thought maybe we were over doing it with the practice sessions. Especially with going down on other girls. Turns out, some chick vamps wanted that. Go Layla for pushing for it. Although, she may have had an ulterior motive for that. Either way, everything we practiced had come in handy the last month or so.

By the time Carter released Todd and me, leaving another mess for Carrie to clean up, our whole group was back. Carter rumbled with approval when he looked at each of them. Carrie had boxed up some sandwiches for us while Carter was having his way.

We piled into his car, leaving the stolen one behind, and he took us by our short-term apartment. The three boys went up to grab our things, while we waited in the car. It was a military Humvee, obviously one of the many things the vamps had taken for their own use.

As we left the city, Carter stuck to his word about what I would be eating on the way back. Once I finished, he insisted on making the rounds through the group. He didn't even pull over for us all to change places, we just crawled over each other. Once everyone had had their turn, his words, he had me come back to the front. I laid my head on his lap and let him play with my hair as I fell asleep.

We all woke up when we pulled up to an abandoned house not far from the wall. Carter knew his way around pretty well, meaning he had already been scoping out places for us to stay. Which made me wonder who had been playing who at the bar tonight.

The master suite already had sun blocker blinds and curtains installed. Carter instructed Todd to put our things in there. The three of us would be sharing that room. The others broke off into the two of the other three rooms.

Once Carter fell asleep, not long after sunrise, I laid there staring at the ceiling.

We did it, we finally did it. We were one step closer to Curtis. One step closer to the devil himself.

I felt Todd reaching for my hand, across Carter's wide chest. I held on to him tight, knowing he was feeling just as nervous as I was.

CHAPTER 27

Deacon

I'm going to have a son. That thought had been on repeat in my mind for the last week, ever since the weird episode with Carrie happened. No one said anything about the scent change in her the first couple nights, so I thought we were in the clear. Then Carter walked in. We hadn't discussed what we would tell people, I honestly hadn't even thought about it. My focus and fear was still focused on the odds of my angel's survival.

I was grasping at straws with what I told Carter, he wasn't buying it either. Then my little angel saved the day. She not only explained the pregnancy, but Colton's absence in one. He used to come and go all the time before. But that was before we brought him into our mating. Him leaving now would have been suspicious. She was so serious as she said it, Carter had no reason not to believe her. Grace intervened before he could even try.

"Well, well, well. I had heard a rumor, but I wasn't sure I believed it."

I looked up from the same cup I had been drying for the last five minutes. The sun had barely set, most vampires weren't out yet. This was definitely earlier than Lou usually came out.

"What's going on?" I asked him, cautious in what he was referring to.

He made a dramatic wave toward his nose, like he was smelling the perfect fragrance. Then his eyes fell on Carrie. His eyes were twinkling. I watched my mate, and paid attention to the feelings coming from her. She laughed. A good sign. If she felt bad intent coming from him, she would have been afraid, at least on the inside.

He sat down on a bar stool and leveled me with an intense stare. Carrie walked over and I slid my arm around her bare waist.

"You need something Lou? The donors should be coming in soon."

He sighed and scratched his jaw. "You all didn't get the message?"

"What message?"

"Curtis sent drones out to all the neighborhoods, the places with the highest populations of humans, this morning. I had a feeling you wouldn't have heard."

Now there was fear in my girl, just not because of Lou. "What did he say?" I asked my old friend.

"He said he will be here within the next few days. He is keeping a few cities for Vampires only and shipping the humans off to the smaller ones. Each of them will need to go to their city courthouse and receive a job assignment. He is keeping San Francisco, Los Angeles, and San Diego. The only humans allowed to be here will be donors. Which will be open for volunteers, but also an assigned job. Until then, the humans are under a strict curfew, no one is allowed outside at night. The drones will be patrolling. He is spending a few weeks in the three cities, on a rotating basis, until everything is settled. And then…" Lou took a deep breath. "Then he is making LA his home base. It's time for you to grab your little mate and run, Deac."

Out of everything that he said that last line surprised me the most.

"Why?" I mean, I was going to do that anyway, no way was I going to let Carrie and Curtis be in the same city.

Lou huffed, a little sarcastic, and a little amused. "You know why. I've suspected for some time." he waved at Carrie, "this little surprise just sealed the deal."

"I… I'm not exactly sure what to say to that." I admitted.

Lou chuckled. "I've been around a long time, maybe not as long as you, but long enough. I may or may not have also heard your little friend refer to you as your highness." Lou looked at the roof, trying to remember something. "It had to have been in the 80s, maybe the 70s. I don't know. At first I thought it was some kind of joke, but he never seemed like the joking type. Then I thought maybe you were some type of prince in your old life. I have paid better attention since then. I've noticed a few things. Like when the two of you went to visit the shelters… in the middle of the day. Or the headless corpse that appeared down the street a few weeks ago, then disappeared a few hours later. The timing for you and Colton to become extra protective was too coincidental. Now the pregnancy. It won't be long before the others realize there is no way you would have let a human touch your mate. And with Curtis coming soon, all three of you are a threat. It's time to go, Deacon." Lou stood up and pushed away from the bar.

I held my hand out to him. "Thank you, my friend. I hope to see you soon."

"As do I. Be safe. If I may suggest, leave as soon as the bar closes tonight. And take a different gate." He waved one last time and walked out of the door.

“Do you even know of a different gate?” My angel whispered.

“No. Can we trust what he said?” I turned to her, my hands gripping her waist.

“Yes. His only intent was to warn his friend. He had no hidden agendas. What are we going to do?” Her hands slid over her stomach, and I felt the sharp pains of her worry.

I heard laughter as Nightwalkers came closer. “We will stay open for tonight. We will act normal. And then I will get you and our child out of here.”

I had expected the Nightwalkers to see that there were no donors and leave. That wasn’t the case. They were there to celebrate the old-fashioned way. They drank alcohol and enjoyed each other’s company. And not just by talking.

We even had more female vampires out than normal. I insisted that Carrie stay behind the bar, keeping her distance from their noses. Only a few looked at her funny, thankfully most ignored her.

A little after two I made the last call announcement. Once I had the door locked behind them, I looked at my mate.

“We need to pack what we can and leave. If we go now, we can make it to Carter’s gate around sunrise, they will be hiding from the sun by then.”

“Lou said not to take that gate.”

“I don’t know where else to go. I’ve met the soldiers on the other side, they were nice enough. The shifter Captain will help us.” I picked up my angel and ran up the stairs. Her speed was not going to work for me right now.

“Have you heard from Colton?”

"Not in the last few days. This is normal though. It would raise suspicions if we talked more than we used to. I will send him a message now, letting him know not to come back."

Carrie walked into the room and started shoving clothes into her old backpack. I pulled out my phone and sent the message.

Me: Just got word, Curtis is on way. We are leaving.

While I waited for him to respond, I went into the kitchen and made my pregnant mate a sandwich. She used to skip meals regularly while we worked, not anymore. I was going to do everything I could to keep her body strong. About the time I finished, Colton's reply came in.

C: Head for Vegas.

I cursed. I did not want to take her to my father.

Me: Is it safe? She has a bun in the oven.
C: What??? When did that happen?
Me: The day you left. It's a long story that will have to wait.
C: Vegas. She carries the royal line. That is the ONLY place she will be safe. I will try to meet you along the road. Stay safe. That baby is partly mine too.

I laughed.

Me: Must you share all the good things in my life with me?
C: Yes.

He left it at that. I laughed some more until my, *our,* mate came out.

"What is so funny?" She was trying not to laugh at me.

I held up my phone and shook it back and forth. "Colton. He says to head for Vegas. That's where our clan is right now. I told him about the baby, and he thinks you will be safest there. He is also claiming part ownership of our son."

My angel laughed and walked to me, her backpack on. I hadn't realized she had changed clothes. I was sad to see the skirts go, and the shirts, but those jeans did make her butt look good.

"We do not have time for that, love." She teased, pulling away with a wink. I growled and followed her to the door. "Don't you need to pack anything?"

"No. I will buy everything new. I will buy you everything you want as well, but I didn't want you to leave anything behind that you might want to keep." I paused at the back door. "Please tell me you packed some of my favorite clothes."

She laughed and walked to the truck, not answering me.

She did. Of course, she did.

Didn't she?

If she didn't, I would be buying her a whole lot more. I'd already been fantasizing about her belly, swollen with my son, popping out between those short skirts, and barely there, shirts. Shirts that would be getting even tighter as she carried my son.

I gassed up the truck as soon as I could, then we hit the freeway. As we drove, she laid her head on my lap. I pulled the blanket out of the back, left over from when Todd and I went to the gate, and laid it over her. The drive was quiet and felt like it was taking twice as long as it should have. Despite my pushing the truck to its limits.

We were still a few minutes off from sunrise when the wall came into view.

"Angel. Wake up. We're here."

She mumbled in response, not quite ready to get up. Followed by a big yawn as she rubbed her eyes.

"We forgot to have you feed before we left. Will you be alright?"

I didn't forget, I just knew I wouldn't have the time to feed the way I preferred. "I'll be fine. We will stop at a hotel after we get through the wall. We will *both* feed and sleep for a while." I placed my hand on her stomach, emphasizing why she needed the blood from me.

Carrie was stronger now than when we first met. If she was going to make it through this, it was going to be with what I could personally give her. That had already been my plan before the psychic witch said to stay on the path we were on. So that was what we would do.

"Deacon, are you sure this is the right way? I don't see a gate." Her squinting was adorable.

I looked back in front of me and further down the road. Then I hit the brakes, not too hard, I didn't want to jerk her sensitive body. She was right. There was no gate.

I cursed. "They sealed it. No wonder Lou told me to take a different gate."

"Why did they do that?"

"I don't know. Either one of the teenagers tried to run, which I doubt, or the army on the other side was trying to come through. Hill did say the President was planning an invasion. Maybe Curtis found out somehow."

I studied the wall both up and down. The road was the only place they hadn't built some sort of overhang to provide them with shade. They even had tarps hanging down from them. This was our only way out. Especially now that we had drawn an audience.

“What are we going to do, Deacon?” Carrie scooted over to sit next to me, holding on to my arm.

“We are going through that gate. If they won’t open it. Then I will just have to put you on my back and climb it, after the sun rises.”

“What about the barbed wire running across the top?”

“Not a problem, angel. That was built to keep humans in and out, not the vampires. And certainly not my kind.” I put the truck in drive again and pulled up to the twelve-foot wall.

Carter was the one standing there this time, a curious look on his face.

“What are you doing here, Deac? Didn’t you get the message from Curtis?”

“No, but I heard about it from my customers. Why’d you block the gate?”

“Orders. I don’t ask, I just follow. Why are you here?” He looked up at the sky and shook his head. “Forget it. Come with me to safety, you can explain once we are undercover. This has got to be the stupidest thing I have ever seen you do.”

I nodded to Carrie and we both climbed out of the truck. I met her in front of it and held her tight, whispering in her ear. “Follow my lead.”

“You coming or what?” Carter started backing up, keeping one eye on the sky.

Grace popped out of a tent, with her eyes set on me. She couldn’t say anything without giving herself away. But she did nod at me. I looked down at my mate, who was still staring at the psychic. A message passed between them.

"Deacon! Come on! Your little mate can catch up with Gracey inside. Let's go." Carter ran backward as the sun broke over the mountains.

"Don't think so, Carter. I'm sorry to do this to you. You've been a good friend for many decades. I'm glad you are doing well. But it's time I stop hiding. It's time to take care of my mate and unborn son. It's time to take my place at my father's side."

I turned and bent down so Carrie could climb on my back. I had wanted to just pick her up and toss her on, but she was carrying precious cargo.

"What the hell are you talking about, man? Curtis ain't gonna care about your human mate, or her kid. Just get over here bef… oh… holy…"

The sun hit us, and I closed my eyes, enjoying its warmth. It had been some time since I got to really enjoy it.

Carter cursed softly.

"I guess there are a few things I didn't tell you. And she isn't a human. She's a witch. And I'm not your typical vampire. You need to brush up on your history, Carter." I backed up a few more paces, as the sun coated the road with its rays. "Thanks for the laughs, my friend."

With that last word, I took off running as fast as I could toward the wall. The psychic seemed to think this would work, and I didn't have much of a choice. When I was still a few feet from the wall, I jumped.

I hadn't gauged the distance enough though.

I set one foot down and pushed off the top with the slightest bit of pressure. Just enough momentum to get us over it. My landing was shaky, but it worked.

"I think I'm going to be sick."

I laughed in relief at my angel.

She carefully lowered her feet to the ground but kept her grip on the back of my shirt, steadying herself. I looked up just as a dozen rifles were cocked, all pointing at us.

"Who the hell are you and how did you get over that wall?" A deep voice barked out.

"My name is Deacon. Where is Captain Hill? I need to speak with him."

"Captain Hill was needed elsewhere. I'm his replacement. And I believe you still haven't answered one of my questions."

"I jumped. Now, if you'll excuse me. I need to get my pregnant wife to a hotel. It's been a long night for both of us." I started to walk forward, but a rifle with a silver dagger on the end blocked my path. "I see someone taught you how to deal with vampires. I'll save you the trouble. That won't work on me. Look at the sky gentlemen, the sun is up. I'm obviously not one of them."

"Then what are you? That was some jump." The new Captain pointed out, again.

I sighed, wishing Grace had been able to give us a little more to go on. "I think we need to take this to your office, sir."

The story continues in *Birth of A Queen.*

THE WEIRD WORLD OF TJ LEE

The Cooper Family Chronicles

- Love, Devotion, and Trust...with a side of Brownies (Levi & Callie)
- For Ellie (Emma & Freddie)
- For Emma (Emma & Freddie Cont./Rick & Rachel)
- Forgive & Forget (Tim & Alicia/Zack & Zoey)
- Avenging Angel (Mitch & Charity)

Dark Protectors (frequent crossovers with the Coopers)

- Daughter For Sale (Eli & Vanessa)
- Heartbeats (Alyssa & Ryan)
- Sins of the Mother (Trixie & Ty)

Million Dollar Duet (Crossovers with the Coopers)

- Million Dollar Angel (Elizabeth & Antonio)
- Million Dollar Screw Up (Stacey & Ricky)

Standalone novels (still have crossovers with the others)

- Finding My Sunrise (Samantha/Sarah & Jackson)
- 2 Doors Down (Rose & Ryan)
- Last Christmas (Trish & Noah)

The Yin & Yang Collection (you guessed it, slight crossover here too)

- Oil & Water (Mia & Theo)
- Scalpels & Staples (Sheila & Jeremiah)

The Silver Moon Collection

- Ivory Snow (Snow White - Shifter Style)
- Now Until Forever (Jessica & Jake)
- Fate vs Choice (Cassie & Rick)

The Cursed Ones

- Revolution
- The Birth of a Queen
- The Witch's Curse

ABOUT THE AUTHOR

TJ is an avid reader. Reading was always an escape for her in her crazy messed up world. She's always had a vivid imagination. It wasn't until she was locked in her house for a year and a half, with only her two young kids, and two dogs to talk to, that she finally started writing. She found an even better escape.

TJ is a High School English teacher and a single mom. She holds a Bachelor's degree in Cultural Anthropology and Master's in Cultural Responsive Education. Her life motto, one she says with her students regularly, is to "fly your weird flag high!" She wants everyone to learn to be true to who they are. Accept yourself the way you are. Love yourself the way you are.